# IF I FORGET YOU

# IF I
# FORGET
# YOU

## MICHELLE D. ARGYLE

www.mdabooks.com

If I Forget You

Summary: "When forgetful Avery Hollister heads off to college, it takes her a week to realize the guy she's crushing on is, in fact, three different guys."

*This book is a work of fiction. Any resemblance to actual persons, living or dead, events, or locales, is entirely coincidental.*

ISBN: 978-0989970075

Edited by Diane Dalton

Cover Design by Melissa Williams Design

Visit author Michelle D. Argyle at http://michelledargyle.com/

## To Natalie W.

i forgot what i was going to say here
… but i know you'll understand

# 1

Avery set down her luggage and looked around the cramped hallway of her Aunt Chloe's house. There was old clutter everywhere, but it didn't bother her. What bothered her were her sweaty palms. Moving away from home for the first time should be exciting, but all she felt was an almost paralyzing nervousness. *Don't panic. I can do this.* She wiped her hands on her jeans and faced her aunt, who was grinning like a Cheshire cat.

"I hope you're comfortable here," Chloe chirped. "A new place can be so exciting! College is going to be wonderful for you." She hadn't stopped talking the entire car ride from Spokane to Seattle. Avery just wanted some peace and quiet, but she didn't want to be rude.

"It's great of you to let me stay here," she replied, looking around. "I just hope I'm not going to be in the way."

"In the way of what? I'm thrilled to have you here." Chloe pulled out a thick bunch of papers from her purse. "Now, your mother gave me *this*. She told me you're forgetful and I should make sure you brought everything."

Avery cringed. "She told you? I asked her not to do that."

"Oh, it's nothing to be ashamed of. Everyone forgets things, don't they?" She waved the papers in the air. The fifteen-page list was folded into a neat square. Everything about Avery's mother was neat and clean, the total opposite of Chloe. Even though they were fraternal twins, they were nothing alike. They hardly ever talked to each other.

Avery rushed forward and snatched the papers from Chloe's delicate hand. "Then we don't really need to check anything, do we?" she said quickly. "Mom is overprotective. Sometimes she goes a little overboard."

Like fifteen pages overboard ... even though she had good reason. A nervous laugh escaped Avery's lips as she clutched the papers close.

Chloe narrowed her eyes. "That's an understatement. I have never understood her. How have you survived under her constant control? Living here will be a breath of fresh air, won't it?"

Avery tried to smile, but she couldn't force her lips upward. She had no idea how she was going to get through college without her mom's help, but she would have to do it. She *wanted* to do it. She didn't want to check lists anymore. She could survive without that stuff.

In an effort to calm herself she studied her aunt. Chloe had wild chestnut-brown hair and sparkling green eyes set in an oval face starting to wrinkle. Her skin was olive, making her seem almost tanned. Avery's hair wasn't as dark as Chloe's—more of a limp, mousy brown—and her skin a lot paler, but she had those same green eyes and oval face.

"I think I'll miss Mom a lot," Avery admitted. "But I'm excited for college." This time a genuine smile spread across her face. When she had first set foot on the University of Washington campus, it had felt as if she'd found a missing piece of herself. This was where she was supposed to be. She would make it work.

Chloe beamed. "As you should be. You'll love it here, Avery, I promise." She wrapped an arm around Avery and led her down the hall to her new bedroom, which was connected to a private bathroom, and reminded her that since she would be living here rent-free she was responsible for keeping both clean.

Avery tried not to laugh out loud. *Clean? This house?* Perhaps it was "clean," but it certainly wasn't tidy. Every corner was filled with something—old magazines, baskets full of glass bottles and broken seashells, a pile of fraying string. The walls were cluttered with framed black and white pictures of Chloe and some man she had never told Avery about. The house was fascinating, even if it did put Avery on edge.

Standing in the middle of her new room, she looked around. It was pristine compared to the rest of the house, and although she had stayed in it only two months earlier, it was different now. The dusty filing cabinets had been moved out and a dresser put in. There was a new rug on the hardwood floor, a pair of sunny-yellow curtains over the window that looked out on the street, and the walls were painted a pretty shade of lavender.

"Wow," Avery breathed. "Thanks, Chloe. Mom didn't tell you to do all this, did she?"

"Of course not. I've been meaning to fix up this room for years. Besides, I'm happy you decided to stay here instead of moving into one of those cramped dorms."

Avery laughed. Poor Chloe. "Are you really that lonely?"

"No, I just don't ever get to see my favorite niece— okay, *only* niece." Chloe squeezed Avery's shoulders and then let go. "I don't even know if you have a boyfriend!"

"Oh." Avery's shoulders drooped. *Boyfriend.* What a horrible word. "No, I don't have a boyfriend," she answered, walking around the room and running her finger along the furniture. "I've never ... well, I almost had a boyfriend once, kind of."

"Kind of?" Chloe folded her arms and leaned against the doorframe. "What do you mean?"

*Ryan was my best friend's boyfriend,* she wanted to say. *Or he was until I screwed it all up with my stupid memory.*

"Nothing. It was a mistake."

"I'm sorry to hear that," Chloe said softly. "I do hope you meet someone here at college. Although ..."

Avery looked up, realizing she hadn't thought twice about meeting guys here. Why worry about it when they had always been so far out of her reach? "Although ... what?" she asked.

"It's one of my ground rules. No boys here in your room."

Avery nodded. "I doubt that will ever be a problem," she laughed.

—⁊↑⟍—

Chloe went to bed around nine. Avery wasn't used to sleeping so early, so she sat at her new desk and wrote in her journal for half an hour. Listing what had happened during the day was a long-time habit she wanted to break, but she decided to stay on the safe side for the moment in order to keep everything straight. She wrote down all of Chloe's rules she could remember, like keeping the bathroom clean and washing the dishes after every meal. She didn't want to forget something important and risk irritating her aunt. She wanted to keep up the good relationship they had going with each other.

When she finished writing in her journal, she made a cup of tea from Chloe's stash and pulled on a jacket before slipping out to the front porch swing. The air was crisp for September and smelled rich, like earth and leaves. She looked up at the few stars twinkling between the clouds. She wanted to call her mom even though they'd already talked when she and Chloe had reached Seattle.

Looking down at her phone, she pushed the button to wake it up. She knew she was supposed to be strong and independent now, but it hurt too much to think of her mother alone at home. Ever since Avery's dad had been shot and killed in Afghanistan, nothing had been the same. Her mom seemed to live wrapped in a shroud of sadness. It had been three years, but sometimes the pain of losing him was still so sharp it felt like it had happened three days ago.

Avery chewed on her bottom lip to keep her tears from breaking free. She had left her mother completely alone. All they'd had for the past few years was each other—making sure dinner was ready on time so they didn't have to eat alone and think about how much they missed her dad, long walks downtown, rushed phone calls to check up, and dirt-caked summers in the garden. Then today Avery had left her. That had to hurt her, right? It sure as hell hurt Avery, and she had no idea how to make it go away.

"No, no, that's not what I said!" a male voice called out, ripping Avery from her pity-fest.

Looking across the dark lawn and the fragmented silhouettes of bushes and trees waving in the porch light, she held her breath. From where she sat, she had a good view of the neighbor's house. It was a similar house to Chloe's—an older Victorian model with a peaked roof practically touching both houses to either side of it. The screen door opened as a guy in his early twenties slipped through and started pacing the front porch. He held a cell phone to his ear as he walked. He was tall and slim, and Avery could tell even under his suit that he was in shape. He had a lean sort of build, like a runner. His dark blond hair was carefully styled. So business-like, but young at the same time. Polished. Confident.

"Oh, come *on*," he said after a heavy sigh. "Please listen. I only meant yesterday and today. Tonight was supposed to ... yes, I know ... no ... tonight was—"

He pulled the phone away from his ear and stared at it. Avery followed his movements as he continued to pace the porch and then finally sat down on the front steps and let out a soft groan as he started pushing buttons on his phone. He looked completely dejected. Avery liked the way the porch light shone on the side of him facing her. He had a nice profile, the kind her mother would sketch in squares instead of ovals—as neat and tidy as her lists. For a second, Avery was tempted to put down her tea and go comfort him, but she hadn't even lived in Seattle one day and wasn't sure she felt that brave.

# 2

"Have a good day!" Chloe yelled. "I'll see you at three at the library!"

Avery yelled goodbye and headed down the sidewalk shaded by tall, leafy trees. The sidewalk was uneven, and some of the cracks were filled with damp moss the same bright green as her skirt. The sky was hidden with low-hanging clouds, and Avery was glad she had put her umbrella in her messenger bag before leaving. She had a feeling she should always carry an umbrella in this city.

Chloe lived ten blocks from campus, which was one of the reasons Avery had decided it was a good idea to live with her. She could ride the bus on bad weather days, but she would probably walk most of the time. She liked to look at the plants as she walked by them, recalling the names of a few and wishing she could remember people's names just as well. Biology was the only major that seemed to fit just right. Her bedroom back in Spokane had always been filled with flowers, climbing ivy, and little potted trees. She would have to get some new plants for her bedroom here.

Passing by the neighbor's house, she peeked over to see if she could spot Nameless Phone Guy again. She had lived in Seattle for two weeks now, but had yet to see anyone come or go from his house. The only sign of life was a shiny bullet bike occasionally parked in the driveway.

When she reached campus she had almost broken a sweat. Despite spending a week on campus for orientation and advisor meetings and three days of classes after that, she still had to pull out her map.

It was a good ten minutes before she reached the correct building and made it to the second floor for her English class. The door clicked behind her and a knot formed in her stomach. She couldn't see the professor anywhere. She couldn't even remember what he looked like even though she'd just been in this class on Friday. She was in the correct class. Right? She had English Mondays and Fridays for two and a half hours. School had started on a Wednesday last week, so she'd only been here once. She was too embarrassed to dig in her bag for her schedule.

Her experience with the entire high school student body turning against her last year should have numbed her to other people's opinions, but it hadn't. It had only made her anxiety worse.

She closed her eyes for a moment, focusing on her dad's voice when he'd told her to visualize how she wanted other people to see her when she felt out of her element.

"A fish can't turn itself into a bird," he'd explained, "so think of yourself as a bigger fish, that's all. Still be *you*."

He'd said that when they were out deep-sea fishing on one of his friend's boats. He and Avery tried to go once a month between his deployments. She remembered the salty breeze and the fishy smell of the nets covered in shiny scales. A pang of sadness washed over her as she realized she hadn't been fishing since he'd died.

Why was she thinking about this *now*?

Taking a deep breath, she blinked away what could easily have been a wave of tears and tried to visualize herself as confident and relaxed. She scanned the occupied desks in front of her, finding an empty seat next to a guy who looked vaguely familiar. He had light blue eyes she probably wouldn't remember later. She focused on his hands, curled around a brand-new pen. Hands were always easier for her to remember than faces. His were medium-sized, with all the fingernails chewed but not too far down, stubby pinky fingers, and moderately tanned skin.

"Hi again," he said, grinning. "Saved a seat for you."

"Oh, uh, thanks."

She returned her attention to his face as she sat down. He had a nice symmetrical face with prominent eyebrows and a strong jawline. Something fluttered in the back of her mind. She must have seen him on Friday, but she couldn't remember anything from the encounter. It must have been brief. She hoped he hadn't noticed her memorizing his hands. Awkward.

She pulled her bag off her shoulder and slid it neatly under her chair. Did he want her to say something else? The desks were uncomfortably close. If she moved her arm too far she would probably brush his elbow.

"You look a little nervous," he said, leaning closer.

She tried not to blush, realizing someone actually *was* giving a crap about her nervousness.

"Yeah," she answered in almost a whisper. "For a minute I thought that I was in the wrong classroom, that's all."

A soft smile spread across the guy's face. It may or may not have been expressing pity. She couldn't tell. "This is my second year. I've walked into wrong classes before, so you're not the only one. Besides, you must be pretty smart to take this class as a freshman."

She tried to keep her smile strong, wondering how he knew she was a freshman. She must have told him on Friday. "Not really. I just took concurrent enrollment classes in high school."

He leaned even closer, his elbow brushing hers. A little shiver of excitement rippled through her, but she wasn't about to react to it. For her, relationships with guys were dangerous. But dang, he was hot in a way Ryan had never been. He was wearing a nice pair of chocolate brown corduroy pants and Vans that looked like they'd been tracked through a mud hole. Why all of that was attractive to her, she had no idea. She liked the creases around his eyes and how he kept leaning closer to her, as if he wanted to get to know her right away. This was weird. This was not normal. This was ... nice.

She looked at his face again, wondering if she would remember the soft sweep of his almost-blond hair contrasting heavily with his dark eyelashes, or the way he bit his lip before opening his mouth to say something else.

Before he spoke, a loud, "Good morning, class!" from the professor at the front of the room made her jump. Her elbow slammed into Nail Biter's elbow, but he didn't seem to mind.

"Don't be so nervous," he said with a laugh. "I know we barely met on Friday, but I hope we can keep sitting by each other."

She let out a heavy breath and nodded her agreement.

No big deal. He was right.

She needed to be herself, just like her dad had always told her.

She pulled out a notebook and turned to face the front of the room where the lanky professor she now recognized began his lecture. She started writing, her focus quickly drifting away from Nail Biter. He and his pretty dark eyelashes would have to consume her attention some other time or she'd never remember what was covered in class. Writing everything down was crucial. Nobody else was taking notes, so she tried to write as discreetly as possible.

Halfway through class, she peeked over at Nail Biter's face one last time and then slid her pen over to the margin in her notebook and wrote: *Long eyelashes. Light blue eyes. Angular features. Nail biter.*

⤜⤏❖⤍⤚

When class was over, she rushed out of the room before Nail Biter could talk to her again. She only had a few minutes to make it to her biology class. She found it and made it through without speaking to anyone. When that class finished, she slipped down the hallway and out the main doors. The clouds had cleared and the sky was a bright blue as she walked across campus and came to the quad filled with cherry trees. She had heard the trees were beautiful in the spring when all the blossoms opened into an explosion of pink. A quick search on her phone informed her they were Yoshino cherry trees.

Making a mental note of the name, she kept walking. It was helpful that she could remember *some* things. Getting into college would have been impossible otherwise. It was *people* she forgot most, which was why she had notebooks just for them— usually a new one every month or two. They were notebooks she had never shown a living soul, not even Tam, her ex-best friend who knew the full extent of her forgetfulness and the damage it could cause.

Avery's stomach growled and she pulled out a map to find where she could get some lunch. She hadn't eaten much breakfast, and now she was regretting it. Most everything was off campus, but when she checked her watch she realized she only had fifteen minutes to find food, order it, eat it, and get to class.

Finally remembering the food trucks she saw the week of orientation, she headed in that direction and stopped in front of the one with the shortest line. She stared at the menu, confused.

"Cream cheese?" she asked the guy when she finally got to the window with eight minutes left before her class began.

"Yeah, we got cream cheese," the guy answered as he pulled at the elastic wrist of his clear plastic glove and looked at her like she was crazy.

"No, I mean, does that taste good? I've never heard of that on a hot dog."

"Of course it tastes good—if you like cream cheese."

"You have to try it," a voice behind her said, and she turned sideways to see who it was. A pair of blue eyes met hers. Was this Nail Biter? She looked for his hands, but they were shoved into the pockets of his brown slacks. Great. Maybe it was him. Did he have dull blond hair like this guy? Or darker hair? She remembered the eyes, at least, and something about his features reminded her of squares—her mom's squares she used to sketch angular faces. Yes, it had to be Nail Biter. She had seen someone else in the past week with a face like that, but she couldn't remember who it was, or if it was all the same guy.

She opened her mouth to say she was sorry she had rushed out of class, but he spoke first.

"Everybody around here likes it."

"Thanks," she answered, and turned around to order. She wasn't sure what else to say without launching into a conversation, which she didn't have time for. Punctuality was something her parents had drilled into her since the day of her birth when she had arrived at precisely 12:00 a.m.

The guy at the window handed her the cream cheese and grilled onion hot dog and she moved out of the line.

"Hey," Nail Biter said before she had a chance to rush off. "I'm Owen."

She looked down at his outstretched hand. She could see his thumbnail. It was chewed.

"Avery," she answered, accepting the handshake. Owen's hand was warm and his grip steady. He gave his order to the guy at the window before turning back to her.

"Maybe I'll see you in class," he said with a quick wink. "Or next time you're ordering a hot dog. You'll be hooked. Promise."

She gave him a warm smile and looked down at her watch. The face was cracked diagonally across the middle, but the hands ticked as faithfully as a heartbeat. Her dad had given it to her. As long as it kept working, it felt like a part of him living on. "Thanks. I gotta go. Class in two minutes."

He nodded goodbye and she took off.

*Owen. Owen. Owen. O. O. O. Remember the O.*

"Hi, Avery!"

She looked up to see a girl with dark brown hair waving at her as she hurried by. Forcing a smile, Avery waved back. She had no idea who she was or where they'd met, and part of her was too tired to try to remember. She kept walking.

*Owen. Owen.*

If she hadn't been so busy shoving the hot dog into her mouth, she would have stopped to write his name in her notebook. But he was right. The hot dog was amazing.

Chloe never talked about her job at home, but now that Avery was sitting next to her in the basement of the main library, she wouldn't shut up about it. The smell of old books was heavy in the air. It was almost stifling, mixed with a tangy, glue-like stench and Chinese food. The Chinese was from Chloe's lunch. She slurped a noodle as she grabbed a book out of the huge stack on the wide worktable.

"Attention to detail is everything," Chloe said in between bites as she focused on the book in front of her. "Book repair is an art."

Avery wondered if Chloe should be eating around these fragile books, but she kept her mouth shut. "I'm really glad for the job," she answered, smiling. "Thanks again."

Chloe opened the book, revealing sheaves of loose, yellowed pages and a broken spine. "Heaven should be here any minute. She'll teach you everything you need to know. Might take a few weeks, but you'll learn it all."

"Heaven?"

Chloe took a huge mouthful of rice and mumbled, "Oh, yes, you'll love her. She adores it down here. Favorite place in the world. I've never seen anyone repair books like she does. Hopefully she'll teach you everything she knows so when she graduates next year I'll still have you. I don't have time for this stuff and hardly anyone else wants to do it."

Looking around, Avery wondered what kind of person would find this place better than anywhere else. Upstairs was incredible. The reading room was a grand space with a vaulted ceiling and countless rows of study tables, but down here it was practically a tomb—dank, dark, and musty. Metal shelves spanned the length of the room, filled with books needing repair. Even the walls were yellow, like old paper. Avery would have to put some plants and sun lamps down here or she'd go absolutely bonkers.

Chloe started explaining the basics of book binding repair and Avery tried to keep up. Taking notes was impossible. Chloe was showing her stuff about headbands and natural twine, none of it hair-related, when a thin girl dressed all in black walked into the room.

"Finally got me some help in here, huh, Chloe?" she asked as she set down a big black bag made out of what looked like zippers sewn together. Her skin was a pretty sort of pale, like angel food cake, and her dreadlocks were dyed a deep fire-engine red. They hung all the way to her hips. Avery was sure she wouldn't forget her anytime soon.

"I'm Avery," she said, reaching out a hand. Heaven stared down at it like it was something foreign, and Avery finally lowered it.

"Chloe's told me all about you," she said in a kind voice. A smile spread across her lips as she walked around the table and sat next to Avery ... then scooted several inches away. Avery noticed her long legs were covered in black Victorian lace stockings. "How are you liking classes?"

"They're all right so far," Avery answered as Heaven arranged things on the table in front of them. It was cluttered with everything from cups stuffed with paintbrushes and rulers to stacks of pre-cut waxed paper, balls of twine, scissors, and who knows what else. Avery figured she'd learn what everything was for eventually.

"How many credits are you taking?" Heaven asked.

"She took my advice and is keeping it slow this first quarter," Chloe cut in. "I can't tell you how many freshmen I've seen drop out because they overdo it the first year." She clicked her chopsticks and picked up a piece of lemon chicken. "So don't give her a hard time."

Heaven dropped a ball of twine and rolled her eyes to the ceiling. "Me? Never."

"Thirteen credits," Avery said, answering Heaven's question. "I'm not too overwhelmed ... so far."

"It'll get overwhelming at some point," Heaven replied dryly.

Chloe closed the lid on her Chinese and got up, scooting around the edge of the table toward the door.

"Have fun, you two." She pointed a finger at Avery. "Your shift ends at six, so if you catch the 6:05 on Fifteenth we can eat as soon as you're home."

Avery glanced at Heaven, her face growing hot. "I thought I might walk home, so don't wait for me. I can heat up my dinner in the microwave if I need to."

Chloe's eyes narrowed as she opened the door. "Whatever works for you, Avery. Have fun."

Guilt hit Avery in the gut. Chloe was doing so much for her—letting her live in her house, feeding her, giving her a job. The least she could do was act more grateful.

Heaven leaned down and grabbed her zipper-bag. She dug inside and produced two packages of peanuts, the kind flight attendants hand out on airplanes. She tossed one to Avery, who caught it before it hit her in the forehead.

"You can't work on books without a bag of those," Heaven said seriously as she slipped on a pair of reading glasses. Now she looked even more sophisticated, and Avery smiled. For the first time in years she hadn't immediately looked at someone's hands when she'd first met them.

# ·3·

When Avery got home, the table was set for dinner.

"Smells good," she said as she dropped her bag in the hallway, something her mom would kill her for doing, and sat down at the table.

Chloe turned around from the stove, her hands shoved into a pair of hot pink oven mitts. "You're home on time! I thought you were going to walk."

Avery shrugged. "Decided to take the bus."

She didn't add that she'd almost stepped onto the wrong one.

"Well, great. Everything's ready. Hope you're hungry."

Avery's stomach growled in response, and once Chloe had everything on the table they both dug in.

"So," Chloe said through a mouthful of mashed potatoes, "how'd you like Heaven? Did she overdose you on peanuts yet?"

"Yeah, four packages. Where does she get all those?"

"No idea."

Avery watched Chloe as she ate. Even though she and her sister weren't identical, Chloe's face was similar in some ways, with wide-set eyes, thick eyebrows, and a strong, almost masculine chin. Chloe was a pretty, all-natural woman who didn't bother with makeup or hair products, but she wasn't so extreme as to be labeled "granola." Avery had never thought much about her mom's relationship with Chloe, but now that she was living with her, she kept wondering how close they really were. Could two such completely different people truly get along?

"I miss Mom," Avery said, breaking the silence. "I knew I would miss her, but this is like ... well, it feels like a big hole."

Chloe stopped chewing and raised her eyes to Avery's. "I'm sorry to hear that. Have you called her?"

"Yeah, a few times. She says she's fine."

"And do you tell her you're fine too?"

Avery's fingers tightened around her fork. "Yeah, I guess so."

"Then you're both trying to hide the obvious," Chloe said. "That's something she and I used to do growing up. Oh, wait ... we *still* do that." She rolled her eyes and scooped up a huge forkful of potatoes. "We have old baggage we haven't talked about for years."

A heavy silence took over the room. Avery shifted in her chair as Chloe's words sank in. "I didn't know there was stuff like that in the family."

Chloe smirked. "We hide it pretty well, don't we?"

Avery just stared. When she had stayed here in June, there hadn't been a huge amount of tension between her mom and Chloe, but maybe it had been going on for so long it was like an old bruise nobody reacted to anymore. There was more silence before Avery finally gathered the courage to speak again.

"So ... can you tell me what it is? Does it have to do with that man in all your pictures?"

Chloe gulped down her mouthful of potatoes. It was so loud Avery almost laughed. "Yes, it does. Guess I should have seen that coming, huh?"

Avery smiled and nodded toward the hallway. "He *is* everywhere. Why is he a secret?" She realized she was probably prying way too deep for Chloe's comfort. Then again, why would Chloe display someone all over her walls if she wasn't willing to talk about him?

"He happened before your mom met your dad," she explained as she pushed her plate away and sipped at her lemonade. "His name was William, and he put every other man in our lives to shame. We fought over him and I ended up winning his heart."

She didn't say it with any amount of pride.

33

"Then Mom met Dad?" Avery asked.

"A year later, yes, right about the time William and I became engaged. Susan married your dad before William died, and suddenly I wasn't the bad guy anymore. She felt guilty when it happened." Her eyes grew distant.

"How did he die?"

"He was in a car accident. He was in a coma for six months." Her jaw clenched. "Your mom married your dad right in the middle of all that—before we even knew if Will was going to live or not. He died the month she found out she was pregnant with you."

The unspoken words were pretty clear to Avery. Her mother hadn't been there when Chloe needed her most, and Chloe hadn't forgiven her yet, almost twenty years later. Even worse, Avery was a constant reminder of that pain. It made her wonder why Chloe had ever agreed to let her live here.

Avery wasn't sure what to say, so she picked up her fork and knife and started separating a piece of chicken from the bone. It was greasy and slid back and forth. Her stomach churned.

"I'm sorry, Chloe," she finally managed to say. "I didn't know about any of this. Mom never—"

"No, she wouldn't talk about it, of course. Why should she? At least now she's alone too, just like me." Her eyes went distant. "Be glad you don't have a sister. I think they only bring heartache. Maybe that's why she only had you. Siblings are more of a curse than a blessing. Be grateful."

*Stab. Thanks, Chloe.*

Avery had no idea how to respond. She had always thought her mom didn't have any more kids because she couldn't have them. She had never really pried into anything like that.

Chloe looked up, her eyes filled with tears. She balled up her napkin and set it on the table. "I'll be out back if you need me."

Avery watched her slip out the door to the back yard. She wanted to be angry with Chloe, but mostly she felt sorry for her. She looked down at her plate. Her mother had married right when her own twin sister's fiancé was in a coma. How could she have done that? Maybe they all thought he'd pull through. She'd heard of comas lasting for years, after all. Avery wanted to call her mom and ask about the whole thing, but instead she gathered all the dishes and took them to the sink.

She spent a good half hour cleaning up and then stood in the hallway so she could stare at Chloe's pictures in the fading light. The sun had gone down and she had to squint to see the faces. Walter (or was it William?) was handsome with a short beard and sparkling eyes. Most of the pictures were black and white even though they were taken in the nineties. A camera was strapped around Walter/William's neck in one of the only colored pictures.

So, her mother was once in love with this man ...

That was the oddest thing Avery had envisioned in a long time.

---

It was sunny Friday morning and then pouring rain in the afternoon. Avery had left her umbrella somewhere, and as she walked to her second class for the day she wished she owned two.

Hair plastered to her face, rain dripping off her nose, she tromped up the stairwell in a building that smelled like old tuna sandwiches. Even though she had been to biology every weekday for the past week and a half, she had forgotten yet again where it was. She knew it was on the second floor, but that was as far as her memory went.

Stopping, she leaned against the wall and dug through her bag for her little stack of Post-its. They were right were she expected, and as she continued up the stairs, shuffling through the notes, she cursed Chloe under her breath.

The other night, when Chloe had told her about ... Walter? William? Something starting with W. Anyway, it was as if Avery had given her permission to rant to her about everything else she hated about her sister. Now Avery's head swam with Chloe's constant chatter, stories of how Susan was always the most popular, most outgoing, most organized, most accomplished. Susan had always had to outdo Chloe, so when W came along, Chloe played dirty until she won him—and look where that got her. But seriously ... was *that* the stuff Avery wanted crammed in her head while she was trying to get into the swing of college and her new life? She couldn't focus on her aunt's past family dramas or she would forget something crucial about school and normal day-to-day living.

It was so important to keep everything under control. Calm. Organized. Quiet.

*Bam!*

Something hit Avery's nose, her shoulder, her knee, and she was flying through the air. Landing hard on her tailbone, she slid down two stairs before she could grab the railing to stop herself.

"Oh, shit! I'm sorry!"

It was a familiar voice, and she stared up at none other than Nail Biter ... or at least she thought it was him. O ... his name had an O in it. Did it start with an O or was that the sound in the middle? Come *on*. She had to remember. She hadn't seen him for a few days since English class on Monday. She had either not noticed him in class just a few minutes ago, or he hadn't been there. She guessed he hadn't been there. She was not *that* unobservant.

"It's okay," she answered as he looked down at her with a horrified expression. She must have run right into him, or he ran into her. O, O, O ... *damn it, what was his name?*

He kept swearing under his breath as he leaned over to offer her his hand.

"I wasn't watching where I was going," he said once his cursing ceased. "I was running down the stairs and ... yeah ... there you were."

"It's probably my fault," she answered, laughing. "Really, though, it's okay. I'm not hurt." Then she noticed two of her Post-its stuck to his inner right thigh. She wanted to reach out and grab them, but they were dangerously close to his crotch and she doubted he'd appreciate her reaching in that direction. Nice. That meant her hand had been right there on his thigh. Not on purpose, but still.

One Post-it said *Find out where Ryan is now* and the other said *Bio Room 201 (Fifth door on the left—the map is wrong and you keep forgetting to take the time to mark it).*

She realized it might look like she was staring at something other than his leg, and she tore her attention away from the Post-its as she took his hand and stood up straight.

"Thanks," she answered with a heavy breath, sweeping some stray hair out of her face.

"I take it you're in a hurry?" he asked. He was still holding her hand and it didn't look like he wanted to let go. In his other hand he held a small potted cactus. The plant was thick and round, like a spikey softball. Avery was glad he hadn't dropped *that* when she had run into him.

She looked at her cracked watch. "Yeah, my class starts in a few minutes. Guess I'll see you around? Maybe at the hot dog food truck?"

He looked confused for a minute and then laughed. "Do you like the ones with the cream cheese?"

"Yeah, it was really good. I wanted to grab another one today, but the rain kept me away."

She liked the color of his hair. It was dark blond and bleached by the sun on the top layers. He studied her face for a minute, as if he'd never seen her before. She was about to say, "I'll see you Monday in English," but stopped when she glanced at his hands.

He had filed, perfectly smooth fingernails.

"You busy tonight?" he asked, making her look back up at his face.

"What?" She froze. Was this Nail Biter? She could have sworn it was him. She remembered the mundane details, at least—blondish hair, blue eyes, nice clothes. Today he was wearing a pair of light slacks and black Oxford shoes. It had to be him ... but where were the chewed fingernails?

"I meant, are you free to do something tonight?" he clarified.

Nobody ever asked her out. She let that thought sink in for three seconds before she blurted, "Do you always keep your nails so nice?"

*Stupid, stupid, stupid.*

"My nails?" He looked down at his hands, one of them still curled around the cactus pot. "Um, yeah, I guess I do." His cheeks turned a light pink before he looked Avery in the eyes and leaned forward. "Actually, that's a lie. I bite them *all the time*, but it bugs the hell out of my dad, so I usually file them on the days I'm going to see him. He's meeting me for lunch this afternoon."

So he *was* Nail Biter. He was in her English class and he liked cream cheese hot dogs. Apparently, he liked plants too, and that made her like him even more.

"So," he said, drawing out the word as long as possible. "You free? There's a party over at my house tonight."

"Is it one of those drink-until-you-pass-out kind of parties?" she asked, pulling her bag onto her shoulder.

He smiled. "I won't lie—a lot of people get drunk, but I won't be one of them since it's my house and I have to make sure nobody does anything too destructive. You up for it? We could get to know each other better. Stairwells and food trucks aren't the best places to socialize."

She laughed, and against her better judgment answered, "Yeah, sure."

"Great! You have a pen? Phone? I'll give you my number and the address. It's not too far from campus."

Avery rummaged through her bag again and pulled out a clean stack of Post-its. He still hadn't noticed the ones stuck to his pants. Flustered, she handed him a pen and the Post-its and he scribbled down a few things before handing them back. She was more nervous about him finding her strange notes on his leg and discovering her forgetfulness than she was about where they had stuck.

He had written his name on the note. *Jordan.* Was that the O name?

"Thanks, Jordan," she answered, smiling. "I'll try to come."

"Great." He paused for a second, the smile on his face still as wide as ever. It looked like he was waiting for something, and she realized he might want her number too.

"Um, here you go." She ripped off the Post-it he had written on and scribbled down her name and number on a new one.

He took it. "Thanks, Avery."

"And, uh, can I get my Post-its back?" She pointed at his thigh.

Looking down, he laughed as he pulled the papers off his pants. "Of course! Sorry."

He handed them back without looking at them, and she said goodbye and rushed around him when she realized she was late for class.

"See you around, Avery!" Jordan called after her.

*Jordan. Jordan. Jordan.*

At least she wouldn't forget his name now that she had it in writing. And his address. And phone number. She looked down at his handwriting, wondering how close his house was to Chloe's, when her shoulder banged into another person. Again. She managed to stay upright this time, and looked into a pair of deep brown eyes framed with perfectly curled lashes.

An apology was halfway up Avery's throat, but it lodged there as she took in the rest of the face—a very familiar face.

"Tam," Avery whispered. It came out forced and croaky, making its way past the apology.

Tam's thick lips pulled into a frown when she turned to face Avery head-on, as if they were in some sort of standoff. All Avery needed was a weapon. She wished she had Jordan's cactus. She'd push it right into Tam's face.

# · 4 ·

Even though Tam's hair was the same as Avery remembered—an unruly mess of black curls—everything else about her was different. Her lime green glasses were gone, replaced by contacts, her clothes a different style, her makeup heavier, her eyes rimmed with smoky black eyeliner. She was no longer Miss Innocent Hawaiian Beauty. She was harder, rebellious. Angry.

Tam looked Avery up and down as if inspecting a piece of merchandise, and then everything about her softened: the steeliness in her eyes, the tensed muscles in her jaw. Her lips curved into a smile that almost knocked Avery down the steps again.

"Avery," she said in a tender voice, clearly unsurprised.

Avery wasn't quite as prepared and stumbled over a thousand words on the tip of her tongue. Her flash of anger melted and slid to the floor in a puddle of guilt. What could she say after everything that had happened? *Sorry I stole your chance with the one true love of your life? Sorry you couldn't forgive me and decided to turn me into a pariah? Sorry that I feel guilty and pissed off at the same time?*

"Tam," Avery finally managed to whisper again. She couldn't say any of the stuff floating around her head. "I thought—"

"They offered me a scholarship here," Tam cut in with a bubbly voice. "Isn't that great? I did get offers from a few bigger schools, but this one is giving me a full ride. I couldn't turn it down."

Avery studied her impossibly long eyelashes—much longer than Avery remembered them. Probably extensions. Tam blinked and the smile stayed on her lips. It looked genuine, but Avery wasn't sure if she could trust it. In fact, she was sure she couldn't.

"It's nice to see you, Ave." Tam looked down at her phone and sucked in her breath. "I'm *so* late for my next class, but hey, let's get together. Let's ... do you think we can ... maybe start over? I'm going to a party tonight. You want to come?"

Party. Tonight. Avery's memory whirred for a second and then it finally clicked as she looked down at the Post-it in her hand. Jordan's party. She looked back up. "Did a guy named Jordan invite you?"

Tam's smile widened. "Yeah, he did. You're already going?"

"I was thinking about it."

"Well, great!" Tam leaned forward and gave Avery a loose hug. She smelled like mint. That hadn't changed. Avery stood as still as a statue, too shocked to do anything else. "So glad you're going here too, Ave. I'll see you tonight." She pulled away and looked Avery in the eyes. "And don't worry—I'm not attached to anyone this time." She skipped down the steps and disappeared around the corner.

When Avery finally made it up to her class, she was ten minutes late. The professor didn't say anything and she couldn't remember if tardiness affected her grade in the class or not. It probably did, but she didn't care.

All she could think about was Tam. They had met each other when Tam was sixteen and Avery was seventeen. They may not have known each other their whole lives, but sometimes it felt like they had. Their birthdays were two weeks apart, although Avery was a year older. They used to have sleepovers every weekend, share each other's clothes and shoes, and do each other's hair. They both loved mint-flavored anything. Tam was the first friend of Avery's who'd lasted longer than six months, the one who tirelessly tried to set Avery up with guys and always failed, the one who taught Avery that people are never what they seem, no matter how well you think you know them.

❧

Avery's history with Tam and Ryan was so fresh in her mind because she had written it all down in her journal in great detail. She'd read that journal entry over a hundred times.

It was Homecoming week of their senior year when they met Ryan. Avery was already eighteen and the autumn air was heavy with the promise of football games and Halloween and colder weather.

Whenever she thought back to that day, from beginning to end, it was like a deck of cards in her hand. She flipped through each one in her memory, pausing on the same ones over and over. Some were blacked out, impossible to see, but others, like the pressure and the smell in the air that day as a storm moved in, were unforgettable. Those were the solid memories that ended up in her journal.

There was a party that night at Stacy Edisson's house. She lived with her much older brother and was known to host the best parties in the whole school. The only reason Avery was invited was because she was Tam's best friend. On her own, Avery was nobody. That was how it had always been until she'd met Tam.

Avery couldn't remember anything about school that day until the moment she and Tam walked out the doors and got into Tam's old Volkswagen painted green and gold in the school colors. Tam took her Student Body President title a little too seriously. "Every little bit helps," she'd say, adjusting her signature lime green glasses. "People remembered this car when they voted. They'll continue to remember who owns it, and that gives me a leg up in everything. You have to stand out."

Tam was not a geek, a snob, or an overachiever. Avery had no idea if she was any of these things now, but back then she wanted to be the student body president because she actually cared about the school and her fellow students, from the awkward bookworms in the library to people like Stacy Edisson who dated the captain of the football team. It had nothing to do with wanting popularity or being in charge. She wanted to be involved and make a positive difference, and that was all. That's why Avery had liked Tam so much, because of her genuine desire to help. Avery liked her green-and-gold Volkswagen and the string of shiny brown kukui nuts hanging from the review mirror, a constant reminder to everyone that she was half Hawaiian and proud of it. Avery liked her lime green glasses and the way she never went anywhere without a pack of spearmint gum. Avery especially liked that Tam never got angry or offended with her when she forgot something important.

The Gold Bug wouldn't start that day. Tam turned the key in the ignition twenty times, but the engine refused to turn over. By then, the parking lot was empty, buses gone.

"We're screwed," Tam said, lowering her forehead to the steering wheel. The car was hot from the warm October day. Avery rolled down her window and took a deep breath. The sky was blue, but on the horizon she could see a line of black clouds rolling in.

"Maybe we can call your brother," Avery suggested. "Didn't he bring this thing back from the dead in the first place?"

"Yes, but he's in California this week, remember?" Tam lifted her head from the steering wheel and smirked at Avery. "Never mind. Stupid question."

She was right. Avery couldn't even remember why he was in California. She pulled out her phone and looked at her calendar. "Well, my mom's at her illustrator's conference until five."

"And mine's asleep because she has a shift at the hospital tonight. She'd kill me if I woke her up. My dad's at work, but maybe he could leave." She pulled her phone from her bag and tried to call him, but he didn't answer.

Avery wondered why Tam didn't call one of her dozens of friends with cars, but she didn't say anything.

Of course, they weren't as screwed as Tam let on since the walk home was only two miles, but getting stranded ruined their plans of shopping and hanging out all afternoon. They had a Big Important Party to attend and they needed to look fantastic. Not that Avery expected much out of the party, but she could at least try.

"I really need to get a car," Avery said as they climbed out and locked the doors. "Mom keeps promising, but it just hasn't happened."

"They're more trouble than they're worth," Tam grumbled.

Avery gave her a sideways glance. "And *that* is why Gold Bug will not start for us. Where's the love? The respect?"

They laughed as they started their trek home.

Up until that day, Avery had loved high school. She was comfortable there. She had a best friend who understood her. Her grades were good and she was making plans for college. Most importantly, she was finally accepting her father's death and moving on with her life.

Then Ryan happened.

He pulled up beside them in his car, slowing to a crawl as they kept walking. Tam sucked in her breath as she caught a glimpse of him through the window.

"He's *hot*," she whispered to Avery. "What do you think he wants?"

Avery looked up at the gathering clouds. Sweat rolled down her back, but she knew in a few minutes it would be rain drenching her instead.

"Probably wants to be our knight in shining armor," Avery answered, nodding at the clouds. "I don't have an umbrella. Do you?"

"Nope."

# ⁙5⁙

Heaven handed Avery a bag of peanuts as soon as she walked into the book repair room. Avery was used to the smell of the place, and for a brief moment she wondered if the chemicals in the glue were addictive and got her high every time she was there. Maybe that was why Heaven liked it down here.

Book repair seemed to suit Avery more than any other job she'd ever had, including the one in a downtown flower shop. The flowers were fun, but having to remember so many things with money and discounts and employees' names and positions was too stressful for her. At least with book repair nobody was telling her she'd shortchanged them on purpose.

"You overwhelmed yet?" Heaven asked as she handed her a book with a torn dust jacket. It might have looked like a simple repair, but Avery knew it would probably take her full shift to complete, if not longer. She opened the bag of peanuts and poured some into her hand. They were slightly sticky, and sugar and salt clung to her fingers.

"With my classes?" Avery asked, wiping her hands on her pants and reaching out to touch a plant she'd brought in a few days ago. It was a vine with big, bright green leaves. The color alone cheered up the drab room, but Avery would have to get a sun lamp soon or the poor thing would die. She stroked a leaf as Heaven answered.

"Yeah, your classes." Heaven opened a bag of peanuts and dumped a few into her mouth. Just like every day, her clothes were black. Instead of Victorian lace stockings, she wore a pair of leather lace-up boots that reached clear to her knees. Her red dreadlocks were pulled back into a ponytail, and Avery studied them for a moment, smiling at how they were wild but precise at the same time.

Mulling over her answer to Heaven's question, she thought about all the notes she had taken in her classes and the endless lists of homework—all in the first week! School had never been easy for her. That was one of the reasons she'd agreed with her mom that living with Chloe was a good idea. No stress over dorm mates. No drama to distract her. Then again, drama didn't seem entirely absent in Chloe's house, either. Despite that, Avery had a quiet room where she could study any time she wanted. So far, she had managed to keep up with her classes.

"It's all right," she said as she gently pulled off the dust jacket to lay it out straight. Heaven handed her a piece of mending tissue and Avery set it aside while she inspected the damage to the jacket. "In all honesty, my classes aren't the problem. I mean, high school was hard because ..."

Avery's voice trailed off as she realized Heaven knew nothing about her forgetfulness. Luckily, Avery had no problem remembering Heaven. The steps to mending a book were easy for her to recall, so that hadn't been an issue either. It was like this room was the best place for her brain to work.

"Because ...?" Heaven didn't look at Avery as she asked the question. She was busy creasing a piece of paper with a bone folder. Her mouth always pursed when she did this, creating little pleats above her top lip as tight as the crease in the paper. But Avery knew she was waiting for an answer.

"It's hard for me to remember things, that's all. It makes passing tests almost impossible if I don't cram at the last second—even if I studied hard before."

"That sounds normal," Heaven said, inspecting her piece of paper before she set it aside. "Lots of people have a hard time with tests."

*Not like I do.*

Avery nodded and arranged the mulberry tissue in front of her so she could cut up a strip. She liked Heaven's mellow nature, the way she was passionate about things, like book repair, but in a completely laid-back way, as if she'd absorbed it so completely it was as natural to her as breathing. Realizing this, Avery let out a long stream of air.

"I have a hard time remembering things," she said before she could change her mind.

Heaven positioned another piece of paper for creasing and grabbed another handful of peanuts. "You just told me that. Besides, lots of people have a hard time remembering things."

"Not like me," Avery replied. "I can't remember names or faces most of the time. I have to take notes on everything, not just class stuff. If you ask me what street I live on, I can't tell you without looking it up. I know how to get there, but I can't remember the number. Actually ... the other day, I got a little lost. I think you told me your last name a few times, and I don't remember it. I can't even remember the lectures in my classes yesterday without looking up my notes."

"Meadows," Heaven said with a snort.

"Meadows?"

"That's my last name. My parents must have thought I was a subdivision, right?"

Heaven Meadows. How could Avery have forgotten that? She laughed. "That's ..."

"Unforgettable, right? Yeah, you won't forget it now. Just think of a billboard advertising new lots in beautiful Heaven Meadows. My parents were a pair of lame-ass hippies back when they had me. They aren't even together now."

Avery was tempted to whip out her notebook and write down Heaven's last name, but she didn't. So far she had managed not to take any notes in the book repair room. It was her own private miracle.

"So, is that why you have so many notebooks in your bag?" Heaven asked, glancing at the floor where Avery's bag lay half unzipped. It was stuffed full of notebooks. "I've never seen someone carry that many around. Seems a little overwhelming. Why don't you just use your phone for everything?"

Avery narrowed her eyes. "I use my phone for some stuff, but it's not the same as actually writing something down, and most professors don't let you use your phone in class. Are you determined to make sure I get overwhelmed at some point this quarter?"

A smile flickered across Heaven's lips. "Possibly. Seems only fair since everyone else gets overwhelmed. I think you'd be better off if you ditched the notebooks, though."

Just the thought of losing her notebooks made Avery woozy. "Um, no thanks," she answered.

"Suit yourself, but you can't live life if you're too busy memorizing it."

⏤╱╲⏤

After work, Avery walked home with Chloe. The rain had slowed to a drizzle and Avery didn't bother trying to squeeze under Chloe's umbrella.

"Nothing wrong with a little shower," Chloe laughed, folding up the umbrella and letting it swing from her arm.

Avery smiled. "My hair was already ruined this afternoon, so what does it matter now?"

Although, if she planned on going to the party she'd have to shower and make herself pretty for J ... J ... *what was his name?* She tried to envision his name on the note he'd written for her, but nothing came to mind. As discreetly as she could, she dug the note out of her bag.

*Jordan.* Right.

"You know it rains more in other cities than it does here, right?" Chloe asked as Avery looked up at the clouds.

"I've heard that, but it sure doesn't seem like it."

As they walked along, huge drops of cold water rolled off the trees above and splashed on Chloe's face. She opened her umbrella again and urged Avery underneath. Chloe was warm next to her. It made her think of how she used to snuggle up with her mother on her bed to look at pictures of her dad. Then her mom would pull out her neat bundles of quilt squares, all cut from his fatigues and T-shirts and jeans, and they'd put them together in a pattern. It was those quilts that saved them, Avery realized. Touching them was the only way for her and her mom to connect to him. Memories were too slippery to hold on to.

Avery wanted to go home, make a cup of tea, and wrap herself up in her quilt for the rest of the night, but she couldn't get Tam out of her head. She would be at the party and so would Jordan. Avery wanted to know more about him. She wanted to know why he had looked twice at her when she'd never even uttered his name. Most guys gave up on her after a few encounters. Maybe inviting her to the party was just his way of apologizing for knocking her down the stairs.

"So," Chloe interrupted Avery's thoughts, "have you talked to your mother about how much you miss her? The first few weeks are the hardest."

Avery's shoulders drooped. "Not really," she answered. "She's volunteering at the library for some illustrating classes and that's taking up a lot of her time. I haven't talked to her for a few days. Sorry."

Chloe laughed. "You don't have to apologize to me. She's your mother, not mine. I'm worried you might be having a hard time without her. You two are close."

"Yeah, we are."

Avery did miss her mother, but the ache she felt for her seemed to have merged with the ache she felt for her dad. They were two big, black holes she was trying to patch up a piece at a time. She knew her dad was never coming back and that missing her mom was normal and expected, especially the first few weeks. The difference was her mom was still here, only a phone call away. That ... *that* Avery could handle, no matter how much it hurt and made her feel like a child.

"Being around you has helped," Avery told Chloe after a minute of silence. "You're more like her than you think, and you take care of me like she does." That wasn't entirely the truth, of course. Chloe didn't leave Avery daily notes with happy little drawings on them, reminding her to pick up things at the store or to do her homework or remind her for the twentieth time that the new neighbor's name was Mrs. Song and her poodle's name was Cookie.

Chloe bumped her hip into Avery's and gave her a warm smile. "I'll soak it up as long as you'll let me."

"What do you mean?"

Chloe let out a hearty laugh and the umbrella shook. "You'll want to move out sooner or later."

"What! No I won't. I love it at your place."

Wetting her lips, Chloe shook her head. "You're young, Avery. Eventually you'll get sick of living with

58

your boring old aunt who thinks it's fun to pretend you're her daughter. You'll want more of a social life—more than I'm willing to put up with, I'm sure. I get enough of that from my neighbor."

Avery nearly tripped over a piece of uneven sidewalk. "Your neighbor? Which one?"

"On the north side. Some kid lives there, probably a little older than you."

Avery smirked at Chloe's use of the word "kid." She must think of Avery as practically adolescent. "Is it only him?" she asked, curious.

"Yep, lives alone. I've only spoken to him once. I think his father owns the house, but he's never there." She shook a leaf off the umbrella and pulled out her keys as they neared the house. "Makes it easy for him to throw his obnoxious parties, I suppose. No parents to put a stop to the kegs and pounding bass."

Avery's ridiculously slow brain finally made the connection between Jordan and Nameless Phone Guy. That was why Jordan had seemed so familiar over and over. Angular features. Her mother's square sketches. She finally remembered thinking about that when she'd looked at his profile on the porch. Everything clicked. What were the chances of her running into Jordan, her neighbor, again and again on campus? And he was in her English class.

"Speaking of parties," Avery said slowly as they passed Jordan's house and walked up the drive to their own, "I'm thinking about going to one tonight."

"Oh?"

"Yeah, and I think it's the one next door."

Chloe looked sideways at Avery, her eyebrows furrowed. Avery waited for her to tell her she couldn't go, but instead she continued up the steps and unlocked the front door, holding it wide for Avery to enter. "Well, I hope you have fun," she said as she closed her umbrella and shook it off.

Avery brushed past her aunt, looking over her shoulder as she laughed. "I'm sure I'll have plenty of fun."

She'd just have to get there before Tam. No way was she going to let Tam worm her way between her and Jordan. Deep down, she had a feeling that was what might happen.

"Just don't come home drunk!" Chloe yelled after her. "I know what those parties are like."

"Me too," Avery sighed as she closed her bedroom door. After kicking off her shoes, she changed into a pair of sweatpants and curled up on her bed for a quick nap before dinner. She wrapped her dad's quilt around her and stared at his picture on her nightstand. Unlike most of the pictures she had of him, he was not in uniform. It was just him in jeans and a T-shirt covered in fish guts, both arms held high as he lifted a huge marlin he'd caught that day. His smile was what she loved the most, as if he was saying, "See, Avery! Told you I'd catch something today!"

She smiled. "Hope I catch something too, Dad. Or, I guess I should say, catch some*one*. For the first time ever."

—)ı(—

After dinner and washing dishes, Avery went to her room and called her mom to see how she was doing.

"Hey, Avery!" her mother yelled between huffs. "How are you?"

"Okay, I guess. What are you doing?"

"Oh, nothing much—going for a jog in the park."

Her mom didn't jog. Avery pulled the phone away to look at it in disbelief. "Since when are you a jogger?" she asked, returning the phone to her ear.

"Since last week. Still not sure I'll keep doing it, but it's worth a try."

Avery took a quick inventory of her mom's actions. First, she had started volunteering at the library. Now she had taken up jogging. She was either trying to distract herself because she missed Avery, or she was finally doing random things she didn't think she could do when Avery had been around. Constantly keeping on top of Avery's memory problems had been a full-time job. The really sad thing was that Avery wasn't sure now if she had needed all that help. So far she was doing okay on her own.

Then again, how did she know she wasn't forgetting something important?

That was the problem. She didn't know.

Avery wanted to say, "I miss you, Mom! I miss our dinners together, and weeding the flower garden, and watching old Carey Grant movies ... and I miss you telling me what to do."

"So, what are you up to?" her mom asked before Avery could speak. "Homework? Any dates yet? You remembering everything okay? I've been worrying about that."

"No to the first two questions, and I think so on the last." Avery stood and walked to the closet so she could look through her clothes. Sexy or casually chill? She wasn't sure if she had something that would work for both. She slid hangers across the rack. "I might go to a party tonight. If I can find anything to wear."

Her mom laughed. "Well, that didn't take long! I was wondering when you'd throw yourself into the social scene."

"I wouldn't exactly call this throwing myself into the social scene, Mom. It's one party."

"That's all it takes. It's certainly more than you did your whole senior year after ... you know ..." Her breathing slowed and Avery figured she had stopped jogging. "Maybe wear that yellow dress? I know you packed it because I put it on the list."

*Yeah, that fifteen-page list*, Avery thought with a grimace.

"You know, that short one with the lace hem?" her mom continued. "It shows off your legs."

"Oh!" Avery reached it on the rack just as it was mentioned. "That's perfect, yeah."

"It's casual and sexy. Best of both worlds, right?"

Avery pulled the dress off the hanger and held it up. "You just read my mind."

"Haven't I always?"

There was a long pause as Avery soaked in her words. It was true. Her mom had always read her mind. She probably even knew exactly how much Avery missed her and wasn't saying anything out of respect.

Swallowing a lump in her throat, Avery said, "Well, I gotta go shower. Love you, Mom."

There was an awkward pause. "Love you too."

# ❧ 6 ❧

*Last Year*

When Avery and Tam climbed into Ryan's car that October afternoon, Avery noticed the smell of spearmint heavy in the air. Ryan's strong, unshaven jaw moved up and down as he worked at a piece of gum. "I'm Ryan," he said as he watched Tam slide into the front seat.

"Tam," she said as she buckled her seatbelt and batted her eyelashes at him. "Do you go to Shadle? I don't think I've seen you before."

"Nope, I go to Rogers. You know," he said to Tam with a twinkle in his chocolate brown eyes, "getting into a stranger's car isn't the smartest thing ever." He gunned the engine and the car lurched forward. "I could take you anywhere I want now—do anything I want with you."

Tam, unfazed, laughed at the top of her lungs. "Oh, funny. Since you're bringing that up, I don't think we need to worry."

"Don't we?" Avery asked as she let go of her seatbelt and gripped the strap of her bag. She looked back and forth between Tam and Ryan. Rain started pounding the windshield, big splats so hard they looked like squashed bugs as they broke across the glass.

"Of course not," Ryan laughed. "And look"—he pointed at the windshield—"I saved you two lovely ladies from getting drenched."

"Yes, you did!" Tam laughed, and glanced back at Avery. "Oh, sorry, Ryan, this is Avery."

He turned to the back seat, his eyes widening with recognition. Had he seen her before? She shifted across the seat, hoping he'd give her more of an indication that they knew each other. Instead, he gave her the once-over before catching her eyes and reeling her in like a hooked fish.

She had to admit, he was attractive ... in an odd sort of way. He had dimples in both cheeks when he smiled, nearly hidden by his dark brown, neatly-trimmed scruff. His short wavy hair matched his scruff and his eyes, but he had a crooked, almost flat nose and kind of a thick neck.

"Hi, Avery," he said with a nod.

She gave him a watery smile, unsure how she should respond. Was she supposed to act like she knew him? Because she could have sworn she'd never seen him before in her life. "Thanks for saving us," she said, trying not to stutter.

"No problem. Where do you need to go?"

"Just home," Avery said, her mouth growing dry. "Over by Corbin Park."

"I know right where it is."

Tam was still eating him up with her eyes. Oblivious to Avery's confusion, she bit her lip when he turned to her and smiled again, his dimples even deeper this time. Those things could kill a girl if he wasn't careful.

Ryan pulled away from the curb. "So, Tam, do you and Avery go to the football games?"

Tam shrugged. "We go to some of them."

It wasn't lost on Avery how Tam said "we," as if she never did anything without Avery by her side. Lately, that was exactly how it was.

"Well, I'll have to keep an eye out for both of you next time," Ryan said, glancing at Avery in the rearview mirror. She smiled.

"You can drop us both off at my house," Tam interjected before Avery could give him her street address. "Avery's got to help me pick out my outfit for the party tonight."

"Oh?" He glanced at Avery in the mirror again, confusion plastering his face. "You're both going to a party?"

Tam leaned across the seat and gave him a sticky-sweet smile. "Yeah, you want to come?"

"I'm not invited, and I have something else tonight."

"Cancel whatever you're doing. You can come with us. Nobody'll say anything. You know how this stuff is."

He smirked. "Yeah, I can come after I'm finished, I guess. The party will go late, right?"

"Oh, yeah, it will." Tam leaned closer to him, brushing his elbow with her hand. The connection between them was so intense Avery could feel it all the way in the back seat. She stopped herself from clearing her throat. This was nothing new. Tam was always flirting like crazy.

"See you later. You too, Avery," he said as he pulled into Tam's driveway and they both got out. He followed Tam with his eyes, and Avery gave him a little wave, which he returned half-heartedly. *C'est la vie.* She would probably forget his face and name by that night anyway.

By the time she arrived home, her mother was in her studio, working. Avery poked her head in and said hello.

"Oh, hi," she answered, looking up from her canvas.

"How was the conference?"

"Good." Then her mom's eyes lit up. "Oh! You remember Victor and his wife are coming over tonight, right?"

Victor was one of her dad's Marine buddies from when they had lived in Oceanside. He was one of those big teddy-bear men who looked gruff but had a heart of gold.

"They're coming for dinner, just like last year. Victor's stepson, Ryan, will be coming too. I thought he was pretty cute the one time we met him, remember?"

"I don't remember him," Avery said as her mouth went dry.

Ryan.

It couldn't be the same Ryan she had just met. Was his name Ryan? She pulled out her phone and texted Tam.

*Was that guy's name Ryan?*

Tam answered back. *Yes, why? It's so cute how you forget names.*

*No reason.*

Only, there was a big reason why, and she wasn't sure if she should panic or not.

Her mom cleared her throat after Avery's thirty seconds of silence. "Oh, I'm sure it'll come back to you when you see him again. I've got to finish up on this project then start cooking. Can you help me?"

"I have a party tonight," Avery reminded her, realizing this was probably one of the only times she had reminded her mom of something instead of the other way around. Or maybe Avery had never told her she was going.

"But it's your dad's best friend," her mom said as she stopped moving her brush across the canvas and looked hard into Avery's eyes. "This is good for all of us to get together and talk about your father. It's therapeutic. We need this, especially right now."

She meant because next week would be the third-year anniversary of her husband's death—definitely one of those super glued memories for Avery. It was never an easy time to get through, and Avery was looking forward to the party to get her mind off it.

Standing still, she felt her fingers twitch. She wanted to go to the party so badly her bones ached. Parties had never been her thing since there were so many people and events to remember afterward, but Tam loved them. Anything Tam loved, Avery loved.

Her mom must have seen the battle reflected in Avery's face. She set down her brush and stood. "All right, you can go to your party, but please help me with dinner. How late does the party start? Maybe you'll have time to eat and socialize for a bit before you go."

*In other words, do everything I want you to do, anyway.* Avery could see the desperation in her eyes, the fact that she didn't want to be stuck with Victor's family all by herself. This was a hard time for both of them. Unfortunately, Avery wanted to deal with her loneliness and grief in different ways than her mother did.

In the end, Avery decided to help her, of course. She drove to the store in the pounding rain to pick up groceries for dinner. When she got home, her mom pointed out a few things Avery had missed on the list and Avery had to go back to the store to pick them up. This was a regular occurrence when it came to Avery doing the shopping. By that time, Tam was calling Avery every thirty minutes from her home phone. Apparently, she had left her cell phone in the broken-down Gold Bug.

"You're supposed to be over at *my* place getting ready right now," Tam complained as Avery pushed her shopping cart down the drink aisle looking for club soda. "I've got your outfit all ready to go, and I need those earrings you said you'd bring. Why did your mom spring this on you last-second?"

"I don't know. She probably told me ages ago and I forgot." Avery rummaged around in her bag and pulled out a Post-it. "Yep, she wrote it down for me two days ago. 'Remember the dinner party with the Royals Tuesday night at 7:00.' I wasn't paying attention."

"Of course," Tam said, laughing. "Typical Ave."

"Oh, shut up." Avery crumpled the Post-it and put it back in her purse just as her phone beeped through Tam's babbling. She pulled it away to see a reminder about the dinner. Her mother must have put it into her phone weeks ago. Go figure. How could Avery manage to overlook such an event when it was recorded in two places? She felt like banging her head against the shelves of Coke she was walking past.

"Well, can you get here soon, please?"

Avery let out a heavy sigh as she found the club soda and put it in the cart. She still needed to find two other things, and she cursed herself for overlooking stuff the first time she was here. The clock was ticking and her mom needed her home fast. At last year's dinner, they'd had dessert and coffee and looked at old pictures of her dad. They had all reminisced for hours. Avery hadn't seen her mom smile like that in a long time.

"You know, Tam," Avery said, her voice deflating, "I don't think I can come to the party tonight. This is just ... it's too important to Mom. I need to be there for her, and for Dad. This is as much for him as it is for us."

Silence.

"I understand," Tam said tenderly after the long silence. She knew how much Avery struggled with her father's death. "I'll miss you, though. Like, a lot."

"I know, I'm sorry. You'll have to tell me *everything* tomorrow. Promise?"

"Promise."

"Let's have a sleepover tomorrow night," Avery said in a lame effort to placate Tam as she turned a corner into the bakery. "My place or yours? I'll bring mint brownies."

"Oh, good idea. Um, mine."

Avery grabbed a box of brownie mix and threw it into the cart. "Have fun tonight." Heavy sigh. "Without me."

"I'll try."

That night, Avery answered the door when the bell rang. She blinked twice as she looked at Victor and then at Ryan standing next to his mother. There he was, with his increasingly adorable crooked nose and looking a tad shorter than she'd imagined he would be—closer to her own five-foot four inches. That was when she realized why he had looked so confused in the car when Tam had announced she and Avery were going to a party tonight. Why would she go to a party when she was supposed to be at home entertaining him and his parents?

But the Royals didn't even live in Spokane. Last year they had flown from California. Hadn't they? She put a hand to her forehead as Ryan gave her a soft smile and she opened the door wider for them all to enter.

"So glad you're here!" her mom said loudly from the kitchen. She poked her head into the room as Avery told the Royals to make themselves comfortable.

"Lovely to be here," Mrs. Royal called out as she sat next to Victor. Avery couldn't remember her first name.

"I'm glad you're here," Ryan said in a low voice as he passed Avery on his way to the living room.

"I'll, uh, get you all some drinks," she said softly, giving Ryan a quick glance before leaving the room. She had to get out of there.

"Mom," she said as soon as she was in the kitchen and out of earshot. "Did the Royals move here recently?"

Her mother turned around from whisking some hollandaise in a double boiler, her eyebrows knitted. "No, they haven't moved here." She turned back to the hollandaise, and Avery waited. She knew how important it was to get the sauce right at the perfect time. Finally, her mother lifted the top pan and set it aside. Then her eyes widened. "Oh, you mean Ryan?" she asked, turning back to Avery. "He doesn't live with Victor and Amber, remember? He's staying here with his grandparents until he graduates. We met them at the mall for dinner last Christmas. Ryan goes to Rogers. You still don't remember after seeing him? You two talked all through dinner."

Avery tried not to let her eyes fill with tears. It was times like this that made her feel completely, one hundred percent stupid. She didn't remember even one shred of that dinner. She dug and dug into her memories and came up with nothing. "What restaurant?"

"Olivia's—the steak place. You had the salmon."

Avery shook her head. How could her mother recall so many details? "I don't remember," she whispered so intensely it was almost a hiss. "What am I supposed to say to him?"

Her mom tilted her head and rested a warm hand on Avery's cheek. "Oh, sweetie, it's okay. Just tell him the truth."

But she couldn't. She'd never admitted to anyone except her mother and Tam the extent of her forgetfulness. She knew it would only sound like an excuse. She'd just have to flub her way through it, as usual.

# ⁂ 7 ⁂

After her shower, Avery pulled on the yellow dress and looked at herself in the mirror. Not bad. It was sexy, but comfortable enough she could fall asleep in it if she wanted to. Not that she was planning on falling asleep at the party.

She dried her hair, put on a little makeup, and slipped on a pair of flats. Chloe had gone to bed an hour ago. She had probably stuck earplugs in so she could drown out the noise. It was only ten o'clock and Avery could already hear the bass thumping next door and more than the usual amount of traffic driving up and down the street.

As she looked through the small stash of jewelry she'd brought from home, she realized she should probably double-check Jordan's address against the address next door. Maybe it was only a coincidence

Chloe's neighbor threw parties. When she checked, she was glad to see she was right. It made her wonder if Jordan knew she was his neighbor. If he didn't, he was about to find out.

Avery's stomach turned over when she stepped outside. She'd never been to a party by herself. She'd always gone with Tam, and after the falling out, she had never gone to another one. Nobody would have let her into a party after all of that, anyway. She wouldn't think about it now. Why couldn't all of those memories flit away like most everything else?

There was a little stone path through the trees and bushes between the two houses. Avery followed it through and gripped the strap of her clutch as she surveyed what she was about to walk into. It looked like a typical party. The weather was warm enough for people to hang out on the lawn and the front porch. Everyone had a beer can or bottle or a red plastic cup in their hand. Some girls were dressed skimpier than Avery, but some were in jeans. She walked around a group of guys smoking cigarettes. One of them turned around and winked at her as he looked her up and down, but she didn't stop. Would she recognize Jordan when she saw him? She had looked at her notebook before she'd left, staring at the list she'd compiled of all the Jordan traits from her entries.

*Short, dark blond hair. Highlights—not sure if they're fake. That might be weird ...*

*Light blue eyes.*
*Chews fingernails, but files them for his dad.*
*Dresses nice.*
*Wears black Oxfords.*
*Sharp features like Mom's square sketches.*
*Has a somewhat deep voice.*

Who was she kidding? None of that was going to help her recognize him in a crowd, but how hard could it be? She had seen him a few times now. She could form his face in her mind if she tried hard enough. Maybe. Why couldn't she have inherited her mother's artistic skills so she could draw pictures instead of write lists? She groaned to herself as she walked up the front steps and through the open door. Maybe he would recognize her. She could hope for that, at least.

As she made her way through the entryway and the sitting room, she scanned every face, expecting to run into Tam any second. But there was no sign of her. Avery looked into green eyes, dark blue eyes, brown eyes, hazel eyes. No light blue eyes. Then she realized there was something different about the atmosphere at this party—different from all those high school parties she and Tam had gone to. There was always an air of nervousness at high school parties, no matter how slight, because hardly anyone was old enough to legally drink. There was always drinking, but a lot of times it was more discreet, and adults were rarely around. Avery thought it would be the same here, but as she looked from face to face, she realized everyone here was older than her. It didn't look like any of them were freshmen. She spotted a few men who must be in their late twenties.

"Ave!"

Avery spun around, her clutch whacking a girl next to her. The girl gave her an evil glare and walked away. Tam, in all her glory, stepped through a pair of open French doors and squeezed past a bunch of people to get to Avery, who gritted her teeth. She was irritated that she hadn't found Jordan before Tam found her.

Tam's hair was pulled into a messy bun on the top of her head, curls sticking out every which way. She was in a black camisole and pair of tight jeans. She gave Avery a loose, mint-scented hug.

"Wow, you look great," Tam said, breathless as she stepped back to look at Avery. "Did you drive here? Do you have a car now or are you on campus?"

Avery opened her mouth to tell her she lived next door then decided that was probably not the best idea. "No," she answered vaguely, looking Tam up and down. "You look good too. How'd you get here?"

"Walked from my dorm." She looked off to the side as she put a beer bottle to her lips and took a deep swig. Avery winced. In the past she and Tam had decided together not to drink before they were twenty-one. Apparently, that was out the window now.

"So, have you seen Jordan?" Tam asked.

Avery's heart thumped. "No, I just got here. Where is he?"

"Last I saw him, he was talking to the DJ somewhere over there." Tam pointed to the other side of the room, but Avery couldn't see anything past the sea of people. Before she headed over there, she turned back to Tam, who was watching her with hard green eyes. They softened after a moment.

"How do you know him?" Avery asked. "Is he in one of your classes?"

Tam smiled. "He's my biology professor's son. Funny, huh?" She took another swig of beer. "But that's all I know, really. Guess I caught his eye when he came into class last week to bring her a bunch of papers. He came in again today and waited for me after class to invite me to the party." She blushed.

"Huh." Avery shifted her weight from one foot to the other. "He invited me after we bumped into each other on the stairs."

Tam's nose scrunched. "Just like we bumped into each other. You really haven't changed, have you, Avery?"

Her question was more of a statement. It felt like a slap across the face, especially since it was obvious how much Tam had changed. It was more than just the drinking. Everything about her felt shifted, even further from what she'd been in high school after the fallout. Avery wasn't sure how to react.

"I'm going to get a drink," Avery muttered, and slipped past Tam into the crowd. She thought she could hear Tam calling after her, but the loud music made it easy to ignore her. Avery didn't know what to do around Tam, or what to say to her. All that time together. All that friendship. She had no idea if Tam wanted it back, and if she did, Avery wasn't sure she wanted to give it. Actually, she was pretty sure she didn't.

The kitchen was packed, just like the rest of the house. There was a table filled with drinks and she found a Coke in an ice chest filled with juice and soft drinks for mixers. She opened the can and sipped at it as she headed into the main part of the house again, looking for the DJ. Men bumped up against her, and when one wrapped his hands around her hips to pull her into his arms, she told him to get his hands off her.

"Chill out, bitch," he answered, letting her go. He looked about twenty-five. "Who you lookin' for?"

Was it that obvious she was on the hunt for someone? She gave the guy a faint smile. "Jordan, the guy who lives here."

"Oh, Jordan ... well, yeah, good luck. Everybody's lookin' for him, aren't they?"

He turned away from Avery and she pushed onward, finally making her way to the DJ. He was a heavily tattooed man who looked like he didn't want to be interrupted as he held one hand to his headphones and studied something on his computer at the table in front of him. Avery didn't see Jordan anywhere near him, so she backtracked, catching a glimpse of Tam hanging on some guy's arm, and then spun around to head in the other direction. She spun a little too fast and ran right into someone. Her Coke sloshed up the can and spilled across her hand and onto the gray button-up shirt of the guy in front of her.

"I am *so* sorry," she gasped, looking up into his face. Light blue eyes. Sharp features. She looked down at his shoes. Oxfords.

"I've been looking for you," he said, laughing. He brushed ineffectually at the Coke splattered across his shirt. "Guess we're meant to slam into each other, right?"

Her mouth dropped open at the blatant sexual suggestion. *Slam* in that context only meant one thing at Shadle High. "Um ..."

He laughed, cutting her off at the same time as a particularly loud song tore through the room. Nodding to the beat, he looked down at the Coke in her hands and bent down to her ear. "You're a junior, right?"

"Freshman," she answered as something stirred in the back of her mind. She tried to push it forward, but no luck. She felt like he should already know she was a freshman. "My mom held me back a grade when I was little. I'm nineteen."

He stayed close to her ear. "Then thanks for not drinking. At least, I'm guessing there's nothing but Coke in that can?"

She looked down at the brown liquid fizzing on the lip of the can. She suddenly felt like a five-year-old being scolded. "Yeah, it's just Coke. Why?"

He stood straight. "This party is over twenty-one only. I didn't think about that when I invited you ... I guess I was a little fazed at the moment. You know, knocking you down the stairs and all."

She was about to ask him why he'd invited Tam, but then he grabbed her free hand and led her into a dark room where everybody was sitting on chairs in front of a TV set tuned to a sports channel broadcasting a football game.

"Quieter in here," he said, leading her to an empty spot on a sofa in the corner. "I'm glad you came." He sat close enough that Avery could feel his every movement. He looked her in the eyes, his face mostly in shadow.

"I had to come from so far," she said with a chuckle. "You realize I live next door, right?" She jerked her thumb in the direction of Chloe's house.

There was enough light for her to see his mouth drop open. "What? Some single lady lives over there. She complains about the noise sometimes. I didn't think anyone else—"

"I just moved in for school," Avery interrupted. "From Spokane. She's my aunt."

"Oh, well that's ..."

He kept speaking, but a cheer from everyone in the room drowned him out.

"... perfect, then, isn't it?" he finished up as the commentator on the TV recapped the recent touchdown.

She folded her arms and smirked. "Oh, is it?"

She might look like she was handling this cool and easy on the outside, but her heart was chugging like a freight train.

"C'mon, you know I'm interested, right?"

She set her Coke can on the end table. "Do you always come on to girls this fast?"

"Actually, I never do, but you're different."

*What a line.*

"I had to get you on my turf," he continued, "so here we are." He brushed a finger up her arm and every nerve in her body fluttered to life. She knew she had been attracted to him before, but now that he was touching her it was something completely new. Slowly, she curled her fingers over his. A light touch, but so deliberate she felt the attraction between them sparking like electricity—little points of heat jumping across her skin.

What was going on? Normally, she would hate even the idea of some guy she barely knew touching her.

Normally, she would never get herself into such an intimate situation. Someone was bound to get hurt—and it would be all her fault.

"My friend told me your mom is one of her professors," she said after clearing her throat.

He slid his finger from her arm and she wished he would put it back. "Who's your friend?"

"Tam—you invited her. She's eighteen, you know? I just saw her a minute ago and she was, uh, drinking."

That was right. Rat out Tam. Avery tried to push down the guilt rising in her gut.

Jordan looked away, deep in thought. "Black curly hair?" he asked.

"Yeah."

"I didn't invite her."

So, Tam had lied. Why was she not surprised? She realized she was chewing on her pinkie fingernail and ripped it away from her mouth. "How did she know about the party?" she asked.

"Oh, I told her about the party because she asked what I was doing tonight. But I didn't tell her where it was, and I didn't invite her. She was waiting for me outside her class. We talked for a few minutes and that was it. She's your friend, huh?" He didn't seem impressed.

Avery rolled her eyes and leaned back into the sofa. "No, not really. It's a long story."

He grunted and looked at his shirt. "Hey, do you mind if I go change real quick?"

"No, that's fine. Sorry."

"Not a big deal, honest. I might be a few minutes while I find Tam and kindly invite her to leave. The cops usually show up here at least once during the night—not that I'm breaking any laws. Well, not intentionally, at least." He stood and looked down at Avery. "I'll be pissed if this 'friend' of yours gets my ass busted for serving alcohol to minors. My dad would take this house out from under me in two seconds flat."

"You sure I'm okay here?" Avery asked as her heart began slowing to a normal pace. For the first time in her life, someone she liked preferred her over Tam. It was a strange feeling and it made her lighthearted.

"No, you're fine." He gave her a longing look before he walked away.

She picked up her Coke and took a sip. The football game had absorbed everybody else in the room, so she zoned in on it too. She was afraid if she left she wouldn't be able to find Jordan again.

Then, from outside the room, someone yelled, "Hey, Joel! You gotta see this!" and in a flash of heat, she second-guessed herself. Was his name Jordan? Or was it Joel? Or was his name Owen? Owen *sounded* like Jordan, at least in her head. She vaguely remembered an Owen from somewhere. It was the O she remembered for sure. She clenched her teeth together. *Damn it.* She hadn't brought her notebook. It was nuts how fast she could forget a name, how she thought she had it and then it sank into the nether like a bowling ball thrown into the sea.

# ❖ 8 ❖

Avery's Coke was mostly gone when a figure stepped into view and leaned down. "Remember me?" he asked.

She smiled at him in the semi-darkness. Square features, blond hair. He had changed his shirt into a blue button-down, leaving it untucked. He must have a whole closetful of those button-downs. Avery had to admit they looked great on him.

"Of course I do," she laughed, setting her Coke on the end table. There was no way she was going to tell him she had suddenly forgotten his name. She was pretty sure it was Jordan, but that seed of doubt had been planted and she didn't want to look like an idiot in front of him. Jordan. Joel. What did it matter? She'd look it up in her notebook when she got home. Until then, she could avoid saying his name.

"I was thinking," he said, sitting next to her. "You want to go upstairs for a bit? There are some empty bedrooms up there." He reached out a hand and brushed some hair away from her cheek. "If you're interested, I'm game."

She had to admit the offer was tempting. No guy had ever invited her "upstairs for a bit." She was pretty sure he meant sex. Either that or a lot of kissing and messing around. Her heart pounded and her surprised expression must have been more of an invitation than she thought, because before she could answer one way or another, he grabbed her hand and led her out of the room. She followed him through the crowd and up the stairs, wondering what she was about to get herself into. He tugged on her hand.

"Come on," he laughed. "What's the matter? I've seen the way you look at me."

She frowned, wondering if he meant when their hands had touched or just now or some other time. "The way I look at you? What do you think I want?"

He let go of her hand and folded his arms. The music was loud and the hallway in front of her was dark. There must have been three bedrooms up here. One door was closed and two were open.

"I'm sorry," he said, leaning against the wall as he looked at her. "I thought this might be okay with you. I hardly know you, but I've never had someone look at me the way you do. It's like ... like you're trying to tell me something, or memorize everything about me. It's mind-blowing, all right? I haven't been able to get you out of my head for days. Seeing you here is sending me over the freakin' edge."

She didn't know what to say. Did she look at everyone that way? Was it because she was trying to sear their faces into her memory so she didn't feel like a fool next time she saw them? Probably. Maybe everything with him was a mistake. He must think she was some spectacular girl who wanted to give him the moon. In reality, she would forget he even wanted the moon.

"Are you uncomfortable?" he asked as worry crept into his expression. "Do you want to ...?" He motioned to one of the open bedroom doors. For all she knew, it was his bedroom. He looked so sincere, so hopeful, as if they had made plans to do this a week ago and she was pulling out.

"I'm not sure," she answered truthfully. "I mean, I've never done ... I mean ... gone that far." *Oh, shut up already and get into the bedroom.*

But she couldn't. She had to at least know his name for certain.

"I don't want you to think I'm not interested," she said slowly. "It's only that we hardly know each other, so I—"

"No, I get it," he laughed. "I just assumed, you know, you come to a party like this for a few reasons, and, well ... how about we start slower, then?" He took the one step remaining between them and wrapped his arms around her. She had to admit it felt good.

Pulling her into the shadows of the hallway, he backed her up against a wall and leaned his weight into her. She vaguely remembered the first time she'd seen him on his porch, the hint of strong, lean muscle beneath his suit. He was a runner, she was sure of it. She liked the way he felt against her. He was pushy, but holding back at the same time. As much as she thought she might feel threatened in such a situation, she felt safe. A smile lifted her lips. Her breath caught in her throat.

"One kiss?" he asked tenderly, inching his mouth toward hers. "Then you can decide from there?"

He smelled of alcohol. When his lips touched hers, she was lost in a wave of sensations. She'd only kissed a guy once before—Ryan—and while it had been one of the most amazing experiences of her life so far, how it ended had forever tainted the memory for her. But this kiss was deliciously untainted, his lips soft against hers, parting her mouth ever so gently. And then his tongue brushed against hers and it was different from how Ryan had done it. Not necessarily better, but this was strangely addicting and arousing, especially in a dark hallway with the possibility of more to come. She kept herself steady and in control, kissing Jordan or Joel or whatever his name was, trying to learn what to do as it all unfolded around her in a quiet, slow explosion of pleasure.

"So?" he asked, pulling away all too soon. "What do you say?"

It was obvious he knew how good the kiss had made her feel. Maybe he was a little too cocky, but right now she didn't care. She realized she'd folded her right leg around his left leg. The bedroom was sounding like a great idea.

"You're amazing," she answered, nearly out of breath. All she wanted to do was kiss him again.

He leaned close to her ear as he trailed a finger down her arm to her hip. It tickled and turned her on at the same time. "So are you," he whispered. "What do you want to do?"

What did she *want* to do or what *should* she do? Her head started to spin.

"Nobody's ever told me they like how I look at them," she said, avoiding his question. "You're the first."

His smile faltered. "So you look at everyone that way."

Oh, crap. Backpedal. Back, back, back. "No ... I mean, uh, I want to look at you in the way you think I looked at you. I'm definitely interested, if you couldn't tell already."

He wet his lips and nodded. "Oh, I can tell."

She kissed him again, this time eagerly. There was something about him that felt sincere and real. But she didn't want a one-night fling. She wanted a real relationship. Then again, she should probably get his name right if she wanted a real relationship.

"I want you," he whispered as he pulled away from the kiss. Too soon once again. He brushed his lips across her cheek, up her temple, across her forehead. "You smell so good."

She grabbed a fistful of shirt at the small of his back, fighting the intense need to drag him into a bedroom right that second. "You do too," she sighed, "but is that the only reason you want me?"

He grinned and then turned serious. "Hell no. It's everything about you—everything I know so far, anyway. This dress you're wearing"—he touched the plunging neckline—"your hair"—he moved his hand up to push her bangs a little off her forehead—"the way you're sober, unlike anyone else here. You taste like Coke and vanilla. Everything about you is different," he whispered. "Different, as in genuine ... distinct. You're so quiet and deliberate. I like that." He brushed his lips across hers, but the touch didn't melt into a kiss like she wanted it to.

She watched as his mouth drifted away from her. "Nobody's ever said anything like that to me before," she said, breathless.

"Sounds like I'm the first for telling you a lot of things. It's because nobody has ever looked at you. I mean, people can look at you and never even see you, right?"

That was how she'd felt her entire life, and now here she was in a place she thought she'd never be, kissing a guy who really saw her.

"Are you saying all that because you want something from me," she asked seriously, "or because you really are interested in me? You didn't waste any time pulling me up here."

He backed away a fraction of an inch. "I really am interested," he answered. "I mean, I want you, but ..." He looked into her eyes, his expression softening "You're more than a good time at a party. I want to know everything about you, if you'll let me."

Avery had to catch her breath before speaking. "Tell me everything about you, too?"

He smiled, kissed her, and then pulled away so he could look into her eyes. "I guess a proper introduction might help, right? I'm Kent. I don't think I've caught your name in class."

*Kent ...*

She was in so much trouble.

—᠈᠊—

It didn't take long for Avery to figure out her error, especially when Jordan came up the stairs after she told Kent her name. He didn't look her way, and she realized he was on his phone, listening intently. He entered a bedroom and closed the door.

Kent. Kent. Kent. Where had she heard that name? He was entirely new to her. He had said "in class." What class had she seen him in?

Then she remembered Monday, the guy she'd sat next to. Elbows. Long eyelashes. *That* was Kent. From English. Here she was thinking he was Jordan. Now Jordan was in his bedroom talking to someone. He'd probably gone looking for her and she had disappeared. So who had she seen at the hot dog truck? Had that been Jordan? Or Kent? They both had blond hair and similar body structures. They both had sharp features. She might never know who that had been at the hot dog truck.

"What's the matter?" Kent asked. She was still wrapped in his arms. He smelled good and there was no mistaking she was attracted to him ... but which parts of him were Jordan in her head? She had really screwed up this time.

"You know," she finally answered, "I'm not feeling ... I don't know ..." Her eyes filled with tears and she looked away. "I don't know what I want," she muttered. More like *who* she wanted.

Kent tried to look her in the eyes, but she moved her head farther away. She felt so stupid, like she always did when she made a mistake of this magnitude. She really liked Jordan, and now she really liked Kent.

Jordan was her neighbor and Kent sat next to her in class. There was no avoiding either of them.

"I've gone too far, haven't I?" Kent asked, his arms loosening around her. He swore under his breath. Of course he thought this was his fault. He had no idea what it really was.

"No, no, no," she said quickly. "It's not you, I promise. I like you a lot, and I still want to get to know you—"

"But you want to go slower, I understand." He gave her a little squeeze. "How about we go out sometime soon? We can trade numbers and find a night that works."

She almost let out a loud sigh of relief. If she took this one step at a time, she might be able to figure it out. "That works," she answered. "Thanks."

"So, do you want to, uh ... stay here or go downstairs?"

She let out her breath. "I think I'll head home. The music is starting to give me a headache." She felt like she was going to fall over. What if Jordan came out of the bedroom and saw her with someone else? Which was ridiculous. She wasn't even *with* Jordan. It wasn't like she was cheating on him.

"No problem. Do you need a ride?"

"I live right next door," she laughed. "You can walk me home if you want."

"Oh, cool. Wait, do you know Jordan, then?"

Jordan's name was confirmed. That was good. Apparently, everyone knew Jordan. "A little bit," she answered truthfully. "I haven't known him long."

*I thought he was you.*

"Awesome. He and my dad are friends, so we've known each other for a few years."

Stepping away, he motioned for Avery to walk around him. Once they were outside, he wrapped an arm around her shoulders and steered her through the crowd. She pointed to the path leading to Chloe's house, and they slipped through the brush.

"Convenient," Kent said as he walked her to the porch. "You can hop on over to Jordan's parties anytime you want."

"If he invites me again," she laughed, trying not to sound too off-kilter. She was still shaken up about leaving the party without saying goodbye to Jordan. She would have to text him later.

"You can be my date if he doesn't invite you, how's that?"

"Works for me." But did she really mean that?

"Can I get your number?" Kent asked as he pulled out his phone. "Avery ..."

"Hollister," she answered, and told him her number after pulling out her phone from her clutch. She then pushed the buttons to add a new contact. If he was in her phone, she was much more likely to remember him. *Duh!* Why hadn't she thought about looking

Jordan up on her phone when she couldn't remember his name? She scrolled through her contacts and found him. He hadn't given her a last name.

"Mine's Russell," Kent said, making her cringe inside. She hated last names that sounded like first names. It always messed her up. She entered his full name and number into her phone.

"I'm dead serious," he said. "I want to get together soon. Class doesn't count."

She pulled out her keys, but paused before opening the door. She turned to him, studying his face before glancing down at his hands. Yep, she recognized them. They were a good medium size, and now she knew how incredible they felt when they touched her. All his fingernails were neatly chewed. That meant the hot dog truck guy must have been him. She remembered seeing chewed fingernails.

"Okay, class won't count," she said, smiling. She grabbed her phone again and pulled up her calendar. "How about the same night, though? I have to work until six."

He nodded. "Do you want to get dinner?"

She imagined Chloe slaving away in the kitchen. "No, I'll eat here. It's important to my aunt for us to eat together, even if she won't admit it. Is that okay?"

"No problem." He leaned against the door and put his hands in his pockets, looking as casually confident as she wanted to feel. "I'll plan something fun. Around eight okay?"

"Perfect."

He leaned forward before she unlocked the door, sweeping her into his arms to give her a final kiss goodbye. She savored it, wishing it could last longer until he pulled away and touched her lips with a finger. "See you Monday in class, Avery Hollister."

She watched him disappear through the brush, her breath stuck in her throat. Of course she liked Kent, but she was still reeling from how Jordan's touch had made her feel too. Hurrying inside, she rushed to her room and pulled open her notebook to write down every detail before it all slipped away.

# ❖ 9 ❖

*Last Year*

Avery watched Ryan all through dinner, wondering why he was wearing a Marines shirt when Victor wasn't even his real father. She wondered where his real father was, whether he liked Victor as a stepfather, whether he was planning on going into the military too. She had so many questions about him and she didn't know why. It wasn't as if he was important to her, or connected to her father in any way. She was pretty sure he was far more interested in Tam than he was in her, so what did any of it matter? Unless he might make a good friend. There was always a shortage of those in her life.

After dessert and coffee, they all played a game and then sat around talking as the minutes ticked by. Avery lost track of time, completely forgetting about the party as Ryan sat next to her on a sofa in the corner of the living room. They were far enough away from their parents that they could have their own conversation.

"Yeah, Victor's trying to talk me into enlisting with the Marines," Ryan said with a shrug when Avery asked him about his shirt. So far she had managed to avoid any mention of the last time they had met. "He says it's a great way to get my life started. I can try to take some college courses while I'm serving."

Avery smiled. "I don't think my dad planned on staying in as long as he did, but he kept advancing in rank, and they wanted him there, so he stayed."

Ryan blinked his brown eyes, taunting her with the memory she hadn't forgotten—the way he'd looked at Tam and the connection that had sparked between them. Why did Tam always get the guy before Avery even had a chance?

"I like to take pictures," he said, looking away. "I've never admitted that to anyone. I want to travel so I can photograph everything. Maybe get into photojournalism."

She liked that about him. Honest. Open. At least with her. "Do you think you can do that while you're in the military?" she asked. Her dad had never taken many pictures when he was deployed, so she wasn't sure if it was an option.

"I guess so. I'll have free time." He leaned forward, a sad expression filling his eyes. "There's so many things we can choose to do when we're our age, just starting out, you know?"

At that point, Avery knew she was in trouble. She liked Ryan. A lot. She was starting to like the scruff on his jaw and the way he smelled woodsy and the way his T-shirt fit just tight enough to show off his toned arms. Sure, he was short—maybe only an inch taller than herself, and he had a funny nose, but so what? When she put him all together and looked at him, he was intriguing and different. He really paid attention to people when they talked. How had she forgotten about meeting him the first time? Had she been completely blind?

"I'm not sure what I'll major in yet," she said. "At least I've decided to go to college instead of backpacking across Europe or something. Not that I'd mind that, but I've made a decision. It's one step forward."

He laughed. "Yeah, it's further than me. I envy anyone who knows exactly what they want."

She studied his face. They were in a dark corner of the room and nobody was paying attention to them. He inched a little closer, and Avery's heart felt like it might pound right out of her chest. Was he a player? He didn't seem like a player, but maybe he was. He touched her shoulder and slid his fingers up to her cheek, pausing a moment to play with a few pieces of her hair near her jawline. She held her breath. So maybe he *was* interested ...

Her phone rang and she tore her attention away from Ryan to look at the screen. Unknown number. Against her better judgment, she answered.

"Hello?"

"Ave, it's me."

"Oh, hi, Tam."

Avery tried not to notice the way Ryan's eyes lit up when she said Tam's name. Until that moment neither she nor Ryan had brought Tam up. If she'd known it was Tam calling, she wouldn't have answered. Something about that thought made her feel terrible.

"So, do you think you might come later when your guests are gone? I'm kind of bored. I keep waiting for Ryan to show up. Remember how he said he might?"

"Yeah, I remember." Avery turned away from Ryan, lowering her voice.

"I think I'm going to try to get something going with him, you know? I could tell he was interested in me, don't you think?"

Avery couldn't lie. "Yeah, I think he was."

"So, will you come? Are they gone yet?"

"Not yet, but probably soon. I'll see if I can take the car and drop by."

"Oh, good. There's someone here I want you to hang out with. He's got Avery's Future Boyfriend written all over him."

Avery let out a sigh. Tam was always trying to set her up with different guys. Sometimes it looked like things might work out, and then Avery would do something forgetful or stupid and botch the whole thing. She was pretty sure Ryan would be no exception—and the poor guy Tam had waiting for her at the party was just a dead end waiting to happen.

"Sounds good," Avery finally managed. "I'm not dressing up or anything. I'm pretty tired."

"It's all good. See you later."

Avery ended the call and looked up at Ryan, who was studying her closely. She couldn't get a good read on him. Why had he touched her so intimately if he wasn't interested? He had to be a player. She knew she was right when he opened his mouth and said, "I'm dying to see your friend Tam again. Can I catch a ride with you? I rode here with my mom and Victor."

Avery's shoulders slumped. "Sure."

Ryan didn't talk much on the way to the party. He kept tapping his knee and looking out the window. Annoyed, Avery pushed on the gas and drove way too fast through the neighborhood streets. The GPS in her mom's car told her there was one minute left until their destination was reached.

*So you touch my cheek and play with my hair and act all interested, and now you ignore me because you remembered you want my best friend instead?*

She wanted to say something to him, but she couldn't. She breathed a sigh of relief when she turned the corner and saw a long line of cars parked along both sides of the road. Stacy Edisson's house was easy to spot.

"Guess we're here," she muttered, parking a block away in the only spot available.

He turned to look at her, a smile plastered on his face. "Do you think Tam's interested in me? Should I even try?"

Now was the time to lie and tell him Tam was a player, like him. She could tell him Tam would only break his heart, but the truth was Tam wasn't like that.

"She's totally into you," Avery said with a shrug, and turned to open her door. "Hope you guys hit it off tonight."

She shut the door, waited for Ryan to get out, and pressed the lock button on her mom's keys. Then she took off down the sidewalk, walking so fast her breaths started coming hard and shallow.

"Hey, what's the matter?" Ryan asked, catching up with her. "Are you angry with me?"

"Why would I be angry with you?" She tried really hard not to clench her teeth, but she couldn't help herself.

"Well, you're obviously upset at *something*," Ryan continued, practically jogging beside her. "You weren't like this earlier. I thought we had … an understanding. You know?"

An understanding? She stopped fifteen feet away from Stacy's driveway and turned to face Ryan. "What do you mean?"

He let out a nervous laugh. "The kissing deal. Do you want to call that off? Is it going to make things weird between us if I'm interested in your best friend?"

Kissing deal. Kissing deal. She shut her eyes and held her breath. Why couldn't she remember this? Then she caught the tail end of a memory, slippery as a fish, and held on tight. She was in a restaurant with her mom and the Royals. Ryan was next to her, his dark eyes fastened to hers as she told him something about fishing with her dad and how much better salmon tasted when it was fresh. Then the memory floated away and she had nothing left. Something else had happened that night. Had she written it down in her journal?

"Avery?"

She opened her eyes. "I'm sorry, yeah … it might be weird." She couldn't let on that she'd forgotten something apparently so important.

He narrowed his eyes. "Are you sure? You still haven't kissed anyone, have you?"

She had what Tam called virgin lips, and it was deeply embarrassing. "No."

"Okay, well, I'm still open to our deal if you want to keep it going."

"All right." Her voice was shaky. She couldn't help but look at Ryan's perfect, full lips. Had she agreed to kiss him for some reason? She had to admit it wasn't an entirely terrible prospect ... if it wasn't so obvious it would mean nothing to him.

"Great. After you," he said, smiling as he swept an arm toward the party.

She gave him one last look and followed the sidewalk up to Stacy's front porch and stepped through the open door. Once inside, she immediately regretted coming. There was too much noise, too many people she didn't know, and no sign of Tam anywhere. All she wanted to do was go back home and look through her journal entries for anything about Ryan and the supposed kissing deal.

# ⋅10⋅

As soon as Avery was in bed, she checked her phone and saw that Jordan had already texted her.

*Everything okay? I can't find you.*

Then another one from him. *You want to get together another time?*

She texted back: *I'm sorry, but I had to leave before you got back. Something came up. If you want to get together sometime soon, I'd like that.*

Cringing, she hit send. She could date multiple guys at the same time. She had watched others do it in high school. Non-exclusive dating. No commitments. She wasn't breaking any rules as long as everyone involved knew she didn't want to be exclusive. The question was would she be able to choose one over the other if things did progress?

But who was she kidding? She hardly knew these guys. With her luck, they wouldn't want anything to do with her in two weeks. That was how it usually went. That was why she was so dead-set on following her dad's advice that she stay true to herself. Tam wasn't. She was a nice, shiny goldfish one second and a piranha the next. It was how nearly everyone she'd ever known reacted when she accidentally hurt them. A wall went up and nothing was ever the same again. The only exceptions were her mom and Chloe.

Her phone beeped—a reply from Jordan: *I looked for you everywhere! Sorry you had to leave, but I understand. Busy until Tuesday. I have a dinner meeting that night, but we can do something after that.*

She stared hard at the message. A dinner meeting? It sounded so formal.

*Are you a student?* she typed.

*No, I used to be.*

*Did you graduate already?*

*No.*

Huh. There had to be a story there. If he had an office job it would explain the nice clothes he wore.

She texted: *So you were on campus because your mom works there?*

*Yep.*

It was near midnight now. She could still hear the bass next door. It made her wonder what Jordan was doing besides answering her texts. And what was Kent up to? He'd gone back over after walking her home. He and Jordan were friends. What if one of them mentioned her to the other? This could be very bad.

*Does Tuesday work?* Jordan asked.

*Yes, anytime after 7:00.*

She wanted to tell him about her date with Kent, but decided she could tell him on Tuesday. A text didn't seem appropriate for something like that.

*Great! Goodnight,* he texted. *I'm glad you came tonight.*

*Thanks for inviting me.*

A row of smiley faces were followed by: *It won't be the last time.*

She decided to end the conversation and not text back. After entering her two dates into her calendar, she put her phone away and rolled onto her side to stare out the window just in time to see Tam getting into a cab alone.

Avery had been on exactly two real dates her entire life, and both of them were set up by Tam. The first one was dinner and bowling. She'd thrown up her dinner in the bowling alley restroom and couldn't remember why. She could only remember the embarrassment of having to lie about why she was as white as a sheet when she'd come back out. The second date was a movie. She remembered his name when they went into the movie and forgot it by the time they walked out of the theater.

With all of that inferior experience under her belt, she scarfed down dinner on Monday night and rushed to her room to get dressed. Chloe stopped outside the bathroom as Avery was curling her hair.

"What's his name?" Chloe asked, smiling.

Avery released a curl and breathed a sigh of relief as it bounced into a loose spiral. Seattle's humidity had not played nice with the hairstyles she was used to. Tonight looked like it might work, though. Less frizz, more cooperation.

"Kent," she answered. "Tomorrow is Jordan."

Chloe folded her arms. "Two dates in two days? With different boys? My, my."

Avery released another curl. "Going to that party wasn't a bad idea." Although she had a feeling it would have happened even without the party. "And no, Chloe, I didn't drink. I had one Coke. Oh, and no sex either. I was in my bed—*alone*—before midnight."

"Well, I'm not your mother ..."

"But you care, admit it."

Chloe bit her bottom lip and looked at the hallway carpet. "As long as you don't bring the boys here, all is well. And yes, I do care, especially since I told Susan I'd watch over you."

Skipping over the possibilities of that conversation, Avery added, "One of the dates is with your neighbor."

Avery watched Chloe's reflection in the mirror as her mouth dropped open. "You'll be telling him to move his parties to other locations, correct?"

"Oh, they don't keep you up," Avery laughed. "You don't like them because they make you feel old."

"You nailed that one, but I do go out with friends once in awhile, believe it or not." Chloe watched as Avery finished with the curling iron and then brushed the curls to a soft wave.

"You like the hotter iron?" Chloe asked. "Told you it would work better. Salon grade. Not cheap."

"Yes, thanks. Do you want me to put it back in your bathroom when I'm done?"

"No, you keep it."

Avery noticed the look in Chloe's eyes, a sort of longing, and realized how serious she'd been when she'd said it was fun to pretend Avery was her own daughter. Avery had a feeling it was more than just fun. She also had a feeling Chloe had gone and bought the iron just for her. No way did she use it on her mop of virgin hair.

"Actually," Chloe said gently, "you missed a spot. Let me?"

Avery was pretty sure she hadn't missed a spot, but she handed Chloe the iron anyway and watched as she clamped a random lock of hair inside it. Rolling the hair up, Chloe blinked hard as if to ward off a fresh set of tears. Avery wanted to say something, but she guessed anything would be awkward at this point. She couldn't imagine how much it must hurt Chloe to walk down the hallways of her own house with W's pictures hung up everywhere. The constant reminder must be intense, but she was only doing it to herself. Then there was Avery. She looked more like Chloe than she looked like her mom. She was probably similar to how Chloe might imagine her own daughter would look if she had ever had one.

"Chloe," Avery said in a gentle voice as Chloe released the hair and set the iron in the sink. "I really hate curling my hair. Do you think you could do it for me tomorrow before my date?"

Chloe looked at Avery's reflection in the mirror, her somber expression pushed away by a sudden smile. "I'd love to."

~✦~

Kent arrived in a Jeep covered in two inches of dried mud. The only clean spots on the entire vehicle were the headlights and the windshield. Looking him up and down, Avery noticed his worn-out khaki pants and faded button-down shirt. It wasn't tucked in, and she had to admit it looked good that way. When she had thought he was Jordan, she had lumped this sort of outfit into the same thing Jordan wore—nice, dressy clothes. But now that she had seen Kent's obvious love for the outdoors, she doubted she'd find him in a suit anytime soon.

The sun was setting and it cast a pleasant pinkish glow across his skin. How had she ever thought he looked like Jordan? He had completely different hair, she realized. It was longer on the top, and even a little wavy. Jordan's was short, more spikey and styled.

"Are we going up into the mountains or something? Do I need to change?"

His eyes dropped to her snug sweater dress, leggings, and knee-high boots. He was laughing when he looked back up at her face. "No mountains," he answered between chuckles, "and no, don't go change your clothes. You're perfect, really. Oh, wait, you might want a coat."

She looked up at the clear, darkening sky. It wasn't cold and it didn't feel like it would get chilly anytime soon. Still, she decided not to ask questions and grabbed one of Chloe's heavy jackets hanging near the door.

"Done," she said.

Kent looked back at his Jeep then at her again. "I'll make sure you don't get mud all over you. It's dry, anyway."

"Not to worry," she said with a wink. "I can handle some dirt. I'm studying botany—at least for right now. I like a little mud every now and then."

His face lit up. "Botany? Really? Damn, you're lucky."

"Oh?"

"Yeah, my dad manipulated me into a business degree. I like business, don't get me wrong, but it'll never get me outdoors enough."

"You never know. There are outdoor-related businesses out there."

"Yeah, there are, but I'm not sure they would really be the same." He smiled and swept his arm toward the Jeep. "After you."

"Where are we going?" she asked once she was buckled in.

"You'll see." His lips turned up into a secretive smile, making Avery wonder what kind of date this really was. He merged onto I-5 and drove north. Fifteen minutes later, he pulled into a parking lot for an ice rink.

"The only rink in Seattle," he said as he undid his seatbelt. "My dad's friend runs the place, so I can come whenever I want whether they're open for public sessions or not."

"Well, that's convenient. Do we have the whole place to ourselves, then?"

"Maybe." Kent pulled out a pair of well-worn skates from the back seat and walked to her side to help her down from the Jeep.

Once they were inside, Kent got her a pair of skates and laced up his own. "Do you know how to skate?" he asked, looking up at her from his bench.

Her heart sank a little. "I've never skated on ice in my life. Please don't laugh."

He laughed anyway, but it put her at ease. "You know, I was hoping you didn't know how to skate so you'd have to hang on to me."

"Right." She rolled her eyes at him and sat down to lace up her own skates. They felt wobbly on her feet, and even wobblier when Kent led her to the rink and she eased her way onto the ice. She clawed at Kent's bicep, but it wasn't enough to stop her from going down. She landed hard on her butt. That was going to leave a mark.

Laughing, he helped her up and steered her back to the rubber mats outside the rink. "Let's get your skate guards back on and practice balancing first."

She nodded, feeling ridiculous as he helped her back and forth along the mats. After a while, though, she realized how much fun she was having—how Kent felt so comfortable to her. He wanted to be with her, without someone like Tam nudging him into it. It was the best she'd felt in a long time.

Finally, he helped her onto the ice again, and she managed to stay vertical as long as she held on to him.

"See?" he said as they glided past an instructor coaching a seven-year-old girl who skated a lot better than Avery. "It's fun, isn't it?"

She adjusted her grip on his hand and nodded. "It is ... but, um, how do I stop?"

"Toe pick." He slowed her down and lifted one of his feet to show her the jagged front edge on the blade. "Should we skate over to the middle of the rink?"

"I guess so." She gave the wall a longing look as they moved away from it, and before she knew what was happening, Kent had let go of her hand and she was gliding on her own. She felt smooth and fluid. And then wobbly.

"I'm right here," Kent said next to her. "Move forward with your right foot. Yeah, like that. Now your left. Perfect."

She grinned. "I'm not falling," she laughed. "It's a miracle."

Kent took her hand again, and they skated around the entire rink until he asked her if he could go skate on his own for a minute. She held on to the wall and watched as he took off, leaning his body forward to gain momentum. He reminded her more of a speed skater than a figure skater. When he returned, he was breathing hard and his forehead was damp with sweat.

"I used to run, but I like this better," he said, brushing the sweat away. "What do you like to do?"

She blushed and looked down at her body. "Would you hate me if I said I don't work out, like, ever? I know I probably should, but I've never found anything I really love—not like you love the ice. You're so good at it."

116

He smiled. "Well, maybe ice is your thing, you never know. My mom was a figure skater, so that's where I learned to love it."

"Was she an Olympic figure skater?"

"No, nothing like that. She competed, but not on that level." His eyes grew distant as he looked out across the rink. "She doesn't do that anymore. It's been a long time since she did anything she loved."

"Oh? How come?"

It was the wrong question to ask. Kent looked down at his skates, and the silence between them grew thick and awkward.

"It's my dad," he finally said, taking her hand and leading her away from the wall. "He never wanted her to skate in the first place."

Avery noticed the sadness in his voice, the way he held her hand differently than before, almost desperately, as if he was afraid she would let go and he'd never find her again.

⁓〉〈⁓

When Avery padded into the kitchen the next morning, Chloe turned around from the coffee maker and raised her eyebrows. The smell of biscuits and butter was heavy in the air, making Avery's stomach rumble.

"I'm assuming that was you and Kent out on the porch last night," Chloe said as Avery slid into a chair at the table and fiddled with the placemat. She might forget a lot of things, but her very first good date would never be one of them. Even after a night of sleep, she could remember everything perfectly. The smell of the ice rink, the feel of Kent's warm hand in hers, the creak of the porch swing as they rocked back and forth and kissed and kissed and kissed. She'd never experienced anything like it—like wrapping herself in another person, the smell of him still on her skin. It was cologne and clean laundry and something she couldn't even describe. The smell of Kent.

*Kent ...*

"Earth to Avery!" Chloe said, suddenly five inches away from Avery's face.

Nearly jumping out of her chair, Avery laughed and grabbed the edge of the table. "Oh, sorry. Was that all right? Having Kent over? I know you said you didn't want any guys here, so I didn't invite him in. He told me his dorm was too gross for me to go over there."

Chloe smirked and set a plate in front of Avery, who stared down at the biscuit halves smothered in honey and butter. Chloe went back to the coffee maker to pour Avery a cup. Avery smiled when she pulled out the mini grater. Chloe knew exactly how she liked her coffee with freshly grated nutmeg.

"I don't mind," she said as she fished a whole nutmeg seed out of a jar and then rubbed it across the grater. She'd never owned nutmeg before Avery had moved in, but now she used it every morning. She poured two cups of coffee and sprinkled a pinch of fresh nutmeg into both. "I think it's sweet."

Avery took a big bite of her biscuit. *It was more than sweet. It was amazing.*

"So, does this mean your date with Jordan is off?" Chloe asked as she brought Avery her coffee and sat down next to her. "I mean, you were out there on the porch with Kent for over two hours. That sounds pretty serious to me."

Avery stopped mid-chew. Canceling her date with Jordan had never crossed her mind. "Should I?" she asked with a slight squeak in her voice. "Kent and I hardly know each other. It was one date."

Chloe shrugged and sipped at her coffee. "I have no idea how things are done now," she answered after a long sigh, "but I have a hard time believing you'd want to be with someone else after that much intimacy."

Heat spread up Avery's face. Maybe Chloe was more old-fashioned than she'd thought. Or maybe she was right. Avery didn't have much dating experience, after all, and her memory of social etiquette was not something she could rely on.

"How do you know how intimate we were?" she asked as she peered at Chloe over the rim of her coffee cup. "Were you *watching* us?"

"Of course not!" Chloe set down her cup with a loud clink. "But I'm not stupid, Avery. I know the sounds of that porch swing better than anybody. I know what's going on when I hear rocking back and forth, a laugh and low talking followed by long periods of silence."

Raising the last bite of biscuit to her lips, Avery thought back to last night—Kent and her cuddled together, hands entwined as they talked about how his dad had a degree in outdoor recreation and regretted it. "Hence talking me into a business degree," Kent had explained.

They had also talked about Avery's love for plants, but mostly they'd kissed and had their hands all over each other because they were both tired and warm and comfortable and didn't want to leave the tranquility of another person's attention.

"Am I a bad person for wanting to go out with Jordan now?" Avery asked, surprised she was asking her aunt for dating advice.

"Like I said, Avery, I don't know. If you haven't committed to anything with Kent, I suppose there's no problem. Does he know about Jordan?"

For a split second Avery considered lying, but she couldn't bring herself to do it. "No," she mumbled. "I think they're friends."

Chloe's eyes widened. "Oh, that's not good."

"No, it isn't."

Chloe clucked her tongue and frowned. "I'd tell both of them immediately, if I were you."

# · 11 ·

It was sad how addicted Avery was to the hot dogs with cream cheese and grilled onions. It was her third week of school and she'd already had eight of them. Today would be her ninth, according to her notes—which she still couldn't bring herself to give up. She'd wanted so badly to get past note-taking when she'd moved here, but she was just as reliant on it as ever. Maybe it was pointless to try giving it up.

Her stomach growled. Since it was Tuesday and she only had one class, she had a few hours to eat and study until she had to get to work. As she stood in line, she pulled out her phone and reviewed her reminders list. There were about twenty items, but the top ones were:

*Mom and Chloe's birthday is on Saturday. Get Chloe something TODAY. Mail a card to Mom SOON.*

*Study Chapter 3 of Bio book. Take detailed notes this time because you've already forgotten the first two chapters.*

*Talk to Jordan and Kent SOON. About each other.*

She wondered how she was going to find Chloe a present. What could a woman with a house full of junk possibly want or need? Her mom was a different story. She hated gifts, so mailing her a card and calling her would be fine.

She spun around when someone tapped her on the shoulder.

Kent ... wait, no ... Jordan ... wait, no ...

"You back once again?" he asked, grinning.

Looking down, she noticed he was wearing black canvas Vans. On her way back up, she looked at his hands—only the thumbnails were chewed. This had to be the same guy who had told her to try the cream cheese the first time she'd come—the guy she thought was Jordan/Kent. But he wasn't Jordan or Kent. He was someone completely different.

"I think I'm addicted," she answered as she met his blue eyes. What was with her and blue-eyed guys lately? Three had to be it. She was going to lose it if any more of them stumbled into her life.

A smile lifted the guy's lips as he studied her face and fiddled with the strap of his backpack. "Do you have to run to class after this?" he asked.

Wait, did she have class? Who was this? Why did she keep thinking of the letter O? That had to be him ... the O guy.

Someone cleared their throat behind Avery, and she turned around to see a wide gap between the food truck and her. She was next in line and the girl taking orders was glaring.

"Oh, sorry!" Avery said, and rushed forward to order her meal. When she had her hot dog, potato chips, and drink, she stepped to the side and waited for O to get his hot dog too. He ordered the exact same thing as her.

"Good taste," she laughed as she started walking across the plaza toward the quad, her favorite place on campus.

"So, where are we headed?" O asked, keeping up with her.

"The cherry trees," she answered, slipping her drink into her messenger bag so she could start plucking potato chips out of the flimsy cardboard food tray. "I know they're not in bloom or anything, but I like eating over there as long as the weather's nice."

"I like it over there too."

There was something about this guy that made her smile. He'd talked to her in line. Twice. Then he'd ordered the same food as her, and now he was assuming he could tag along with her to eat lunch. Maybe she liked him because he was so obviously interested in her. High school had been so much the opposite of what college was turning out to be that Avery felt like she was floating half the time. The feel of Kent's mouth on hers flashed through her memory, almost making her trip over her own feet. She caught herself and kept walking.

"I'm guessing you don't have a class right now," O stated as they crossed a road and headed into the quad. "Lucky us, I don't either."

Finally, she stopped to face him. His hair was darker than Kent's or Jordan's. It was still blond, but more brown, like hers, and he kept his sideburns long. A hint of a goatee shadowed his chin. How had she mixed him up with the other two?

"What's your name again?" she asked, feeling confident that she could ask such a question now.

Juggling his food and drink in the crook of his arm, he reached out his free hand and she shook it, amused.

"Owen," he answered. "Sorry if you think I'm stalking you. I take it as a sign we should be friends since we like the same food and keep running into each other."

*Not literally, though, like me and Jordan,* she thought to herself as she popped another chip into her mouth. But Owen seemed nice enough, and eager. Three guys might be interested in her, but she wouldn't let it go to her head. As she looked into Owen's charming blue eyes rimmed with a darker blue, she decided that this was what college was about—meeting new people, taking chances, opening yourself up. High school had been almost the complete opposite for her. Maybe that was why she was meeting so many guys now. Maybe subconsciously she was putting herself out there more than she ever had in her life. So far the results were exciting and horrifying at the same time.

"I'm Avery," she said. "I moved from Spokane. You?"

"Guess we're even more alike," he laughed. "I'm from Spokane too. What high school did you go to?"

"Shadle Park." She wanted to say that she wasn't *from* Spokane, but it didn't matter at this point.

"Ah, that's why I don't know you. I went to Rogers."

Her stomach flipped upside down as she thought of Ryan and his deep brown eyes and the way he'd looked at her on the sidewalk by Stacy's house, as if he was confused about whether he wanted to kiss her or run from her.

"But, hey," Owen continued, "that's not too far apart. We kicked your butt at football." He cleared his throat. "Not that you should take it personally or anything."

They were nearing the tree Avery liked to sit under, and she slowed her pace. "I never paid much attention to football," she answered, taking a seat on the grass. It was damp, as usual. "Not that you should take it

126

personally." She looked up and gave him a wink as he sat down next to her. They both set their food down and Avery fished her drink from her bag and opened it to take a sip. "Wait, crap, you weren't a football player, were you?"

He looked down at his body and shrugged. "Um, no."

She laughed. He was lean, like a runner. No wonder she'd thought he was Kent/Jordan. They were all athletic in some way. Kent was a total outdoor junkie and ice skater, but she had yet to discover why Jordan looked so fit. For all she knew, he could be addicted to the gym.

"Do you play sports at all?" she asked.

"I ride my bike everywhere. Does that count?"

That explained the tennis shoes and a streak of chain grease across the bottom cuff of his jeans.

"Sure, it counts," she said before digging into her hot dog. She loved the tang of the cream cheese meeting the spiciness of the meat and onions. Why couldn't she have met Owen in high school? Every guy in her class she had ever been interested in was either not interested in her, offended by something she'd forgotten, or taken by some other girl. It was a small pool of fish, and just a few miles away there was Owen at Rogers High. And Ryan, but she wouldn't think about him right now. Owen, who could have been a better friend than Tam turned out to be. Avery already felt at ease with him.

"Do you ride?" he asked after swallowing a huge mouthful of food. His hot dog was nearly gone.

"No, I walk or take the bus. I live a few blocks away at my aunt's house."

"Oh, cool. I'm in a house, too, but I rent it with a bunch of guys."

"How do you like that?"

"It's all right, I guess. My roomies are obsessed with drinking. I swear that's why they're here. But hey, screw your classes, right? College is all about the party." He rolled his eyes and dumped the last of his chips into his mouth.

Avery chuckled. "So you don't party with them? What a shame."

"Yeah, a definite shame. Guess they're a lot richer than me. I had to work my ass off to come here. I'm not going to waste it getting plastered my entire first quarter."

She already liked Owen more than she probably should. "I'm with you on that. I get a bunch of financial aid, but it's not enough to make it a free ride."

"I don't believe in free rides," Owen answered. "I've watched people get somewhere with them, but how can they live with that? I don't get it at all."

Avery smiled, happy to find someone with a good, hard work ethic. "I agree."

"Awesome." He suddenly got to his feet.

"Are you leaving already? We're just barely getting to know each other."

He smiled down at her and held out the trash from his lunch. "Just throwing this away. You finished?"

She shook her head. "Still working on it, thanks."

"Be right back."

She leaned against the tree behind her and watched him walk away. What had she gotten herself into? She couldn't be crushing on three different guys. She couldn't.

Before she could argue with herself anymore, she realized Owen wasn't coming right back. Instead, he was talking to a beautiful girl with curly black hair. *Tam.*

Avery almost jumped to her feet. Something was going on with Tam. She had been at the party with Kent and Jordan, and now she was worming her way into Avery's relationship with Owen too—a relationship that had barely begun!

Owen laughed out loud and nodded. He was too far away for Avery to hear their conversation. Was Tam very funny? She was beautiful, that was for sure. She had always been beautiful. Avery picked up her hot dog and took a bite entirely too big for her mouth. Chewing helped alleviate her anger. Her jaw was starting to hurt by the time Owen waved goodbye to Tam and headed back.

*Don't glare at him. It's not his fault.*

As he sat down, Avery swallowed and took a drink. "Do you know her?" she asked, unable to hold in the question.

"Who, that girl?" He nodded toward Tam, who was now walking in the opposite direction.

"Yeah."

"She's in my economics class, but I've never really talked to her before. She just recognized me and said hi." Positioning himself so he was sitting cross-legged and facing Avery, he leaned forward with a smirk. "Why? You jealous already?" He blew on his knuckles. "I've managed to steal your heart in twenty minutes flat?"

Despite her anger over Tam, a grin broke out across her face. His confidence wasn't forged. He really did think highly of himself, but at least for now he was not coming off as conceited or arrogant. More like the opposite. She liked his sideburns, she decided. They made him look intelligent and unruffled.

"Oh, wait," he laughed. "It was the hot dogs, wasn't it? Our three encounters before this must have made an impression and primed you for this charming lunch today."

She paused in the middle of putting a chip in her mouth. *Three* encounters? For the life of her, she couldn't remember the other times she'd seen him. There was the first day of classes and then today. That's all her brain had logged, anyway. Of all things she hated, the worst was this feeling of something missing, like she'd subconsciously chosen to reject certain events and it was somehow her own fault. It *was* her fault. If she'd taken note of the situation or just tried harder to remember, she wouldn't be such a mess.

Forcing herself to smile, she said, "Oh, this whole relationship revolves around the hot dogs. It's fate."

He laughed. "So, do you know her?"

Her forced smile fell at the mention of Tam. She looked down at her food and picked at a piece of grilled onion. "Yeah, we knew each other in high school."

He was silent, and when she looked up he was leaning back on his hands and looking at her with a serious expression. "You really are jealous of me talking to her, aren't you? But does it really have anything to do with me?"

She dropped the piece of onion. "Not really. Don't let your ego get too bruised, though. I do like you."

Surprise lit up his face. "You do?"

"Yeah, of course."

"Really?" He looked shocked, and she was suddenly reminded of how she'd felt when Jordan invited her to his party. Was it possible she was not the only one out there who thought it was unthinkable for someone to honestly like them? The sad thing was that, even though she had three guys interested in her at this very moment, she was pretty sure none of it would amount to anything in the end. She would make some epic mistake—if she hadn't already—and it would all disintegrate around her.

"I really do," she answered him, trying to hold the most serious expression possible.

She was a complete idiot. Why was she encouraging this when she already had her hands full with Jordan and Kent? But looking into Owen's face as his surprised expression slowly faded into hope, she knew she couldn't lie to him or to herself. She *did* like him.

"You want to meet here for lunch tomorrow?" he asked, twisting the dagger she'd stabbed into herself.

She couldn't help but smile. "Wednesdays are crammed for me, but Tuesdays and Thursdays I've got the whole afternoon free."

The hope on his face swelled into joy. "How long do we get to sit here and talk today, then?"

She looked at her watch. "I have to work at three here on campus. I usually study between now and then, but ..." She looked up at the clear blue sky peeking through a tangle of tree branches and leaves. "I think I'd rather sit here with you right now."

He laughed and pulled his backpack into his lap. "Maybe we can study together. Are you a science major?"

A giddy smile crossed her lips. "Biology—botany, specifically."

"Oh, that's perfect. I'm into marine bio. What do you want to do?" He pulled out a biology book, and her heart practically melted.

"Don't laugh, but I'm thinking something along the lines of landscaping or agriculture. I guess I don't really know at this point. I just barely got here."

He looked up from the notebook he was flipping through, his brows furrowed. "You're a freshman? You seem older than that ... in a good way."

Laughing, she took the last bite of hot dog. "I'm nineteen. Maybe that's why?"

"Maybe." He looked at her with a softened expression for a few seconds longer than necessary, and then turned back to his notebook. "So? Bio? Got anything you want to go over?"

"I sure do."

As they pulled out more books and notebooks and lay on the grass on their stomachs, Avery's heart started to pound so hard she could hardly contain it. Maybe this was all a bad idea. She kept telling herself it was okay, but Heaven was right. She *was* overwhelmed. It wasn't by schoolwork or moving away from home—it was by her heart that had somehow split into three parts.

# ❖ 12 ❖

*Last Year*

Stacy Edisson's house was packed. Avery made her way through the crowd, not surprised to see soda pop cans clutched in most people's hands—probably filled with beer or something stronger. She scrunched her nose, irritated that a headache was starting to form behind her eyes. After an evening filled with reminiscing about her dad, and then all her confusion over Ryan, she wasn't sure how long she would last tonight. She had to find Tam.

"Do you know where she is?" Ryan asked, right behind her.

"Are you assuming I'm looking for Tam?" she asked as she glanced over her shoulder. Ryan was right up against her, pushing himself even closer as a group edged past him. His hand brushed against her hip long enough for her to wonder if he'd done it on purpose.

"Well, aren't you?"

"Well, she's the one who asked me to come."

"Do you do everything Tam asks you to do?"

Stopping in her tracks, she turned completely around to face him. His lips were slightly parted, and she couldn't stop looking at them. The kissing deal was driving her nuts. She needed to remember what the hell she had agreed to. "No, I don't do everything Tam asks me to do. What do you think I am? Her slave?"

He shrugged and those perfect lips pinched together to form a smirk that revealed his dimples. After a moment, she lifted her eyes to his and blinked.

"She's a strong personality," he said nonchalantly, "and you're ... well, you remember what you told me before, right? You're the quiet type. Alone."

She had told him that? Gritting her teeth, she straightened her shoulders. "What does that have to do with Tam?"

His smirk fell into a straight line. "Opposites attract, that's all. She seems like the type who thrives off people needing her, and you're the opposite."

"You think I can't fend for myself?"

"That's not what I said."

"Then what are you saying?"

By this point her headache was pounding like a sledgehammer, and she squeezed her eyes shut against the pain. Why did Ryan set her off so much? She didn't normally argue with people like this. Something brushed against her cheek. She opened her eyes to see Ryan leaning close to her face.

"Are you okay?" he asked, studying her as he lowered his hand. "I didn't mean to upset you. I'm interested in Tam, so I want to know more about her, that's all. Since you're such close friends—"

"Oh, stop. I'll find her for you. She's usually with her group. They're not my group, but sometimes I'm allowed to hang with them." She rolled her eyes and turned back around to resume her search. As she cut across the living room and into the kitchen, she wondered if she was so upset because Ryan had a point. Maybe she *did* do everything Tam asked her to do. Did that mean she was a doormat? A friend of convenience? Her headache pounded even harder.

Tam wasn't in the kitchen or the back yard. "Downstairs, maybe," she muttered, and turned to find wherever that was. Like an excited puppy, Ryan stayed on her heels. By the time they got downstairs she wanted to tell him to keep his distance, but it didn't matter. There was Tam, sitting at a table with a bunch of people Avery didn't recognize. They were playing some sort of card game with others standing around, watching. Loud music blared through the room, along with a movie over in the corner.

Tam grabbed a handful of popcorn from a bowl in the middle of the table and dropped a few pieces in her mouth. "I told you that was a stupid move," she laughed. When she caught sight of Avery and Ryan she stopped mid-chew. Her eyes widened.

"I gotta go," she told the group, and put her cards on the table. "Someone want my hand?"

Another girl jumped into her spot and Tam hurried over to Ryan. "I knew you'd come," she said, and then a dark look settled over her face. "I see you found Avery. Did you two meet upstairs or something?"

Avery almost laughed out loud at Tam's obvious jealousy. "I gave Ryan a ride," she explained slowly. It was one of the only times she had ever felt she had the upper hand. Tam was the popular one, the smart one, the one who had taken Avery under her wing like a little lost duckling.

Tam's mouth dropped open. "I don't understand." She kept looking back and forth between Ryan and Avery, as if trying to let it sink in that Avery could even talk to a guy without her help.

"Ryan is my dad's friend's stepson," Avery said quickly before Ryan could jump in or Tam could form a terribly wrong conclusion. Then she realized if she kept explaining, it would become clear to Ryan that she'd forgotten who he was from when she'd met him the first time. She wanted to avoid that, if possible.

"Why didn't you tell me you knew each other?" Tam asked Avery, her eyes turning hard. Not once in their entire friendship had Tam ever been offended— at least openly—by Avery's forgetfulness. But Avery could tell this offense stung. She'd already told Avery how much she liked Ryan, and if Avery used the excuse that she'd forgotten she knew him—even if it was the truth—it would only look like she was trying to cover something up. At least, that was how it seemed it would go over as she looked at the anger in Tam's expression. But she *had* forgotten about him. Tam would have to believe her.

"With everything going on tonight, I just didn't think about it," Avery blurted. That sounded so bad. Tam knew, as well as Avery did, how many chances she'd had to tell her.

"I met Avery last December," Ryan said at the first lapse in the awkward conversation. Avery couldn't tell if he suspected something was wrong or not. "Our families had dinner together." He gave Avery a soft smile, and Tam's eyes hardened even more.

"Oh, well, that's great," she laughed as she looped her arm through Ryan's and turned him away from Avery. "You want to go upstairs?"

Avery didn't miss the way Ryan slid his eyes up and down Tam's low-cut shirt and tight pants. She was as hot as they came, and Avery didn't blame him for falling for her. But seriously, what was he playing at?

As he and Tam walked up the stairs, Tam looked over her shoulder and motioned for Avery to follow them. Avery's heart sank about a mile when Tam mouthed *I found someone for you* and then turned back around.

Of course she would have someone for Avery. Of course she would want to get Avery out of the picture and away from Ryan. Sulking, Avery tromped up the stairs. Stupid Ryan. He had put it in her head that Tam had ulterior motives in their friendship. Maybe they weren't so BFF after all.

━╱╿╲━

The guy Tam had found for Avery was Logan Moore. The only reason Avery remembered his name was because he was her lab partner in chemistry and she'd written it down about thirty-five times so she would remember it and not feel like an idiot every time he said hi to her at the beginning of class.

Logan was cute, and that was a problem.

He was one of those swoon-worthy guys who wore tight T-shirts to show off his muscles and behaved like a gentleman because "girls liked that sort of thing." Avery was convinced he didn't actually want to hold doors open and pick up dropped books and pencils, but it didn't matter. He was just her lab partner. Nothing more.

Until the party.

"He told me he's had a secret crush on you since last year," Tam whispered into Avery's ear once they'd gone upstairs and grabbed some drinks. Avery made sure hers wasn't spiked, and Tam did the same. Ryan didn't check at all.

"I'm not really in the mood to talk to anyone," Avery whined. She sipped her drink and looked over Tam's shoulder at Logan across the room. He was leaning against the wall, hands shoved in his pockets as he coolly watched several girls check him out. A shudder ran down Avery's spine. He brought one emotion to the surface, and the only word she could find to describe it was *blech*.

"There's no way someone like Logan Moore has a crush on me," she growled. "How did you get him to agree to hang out with me tonight? Confess."

Tam rolled her eyes as she sipped her drink with one hand and held on to Ryan's arm with the other. "Believe what you want, my friend, but he's waiting for you. Just go see, all right?"

Avery's heart thudded in her chest, but her resolve to prove Tam wrong finally overruled her fear of talking to someone like Logan. Not that she didn't talk to him in class, but those conversations were always filled with terms like "absolute pressure" and "solubility." Nothing truly social.

As she crossed the room to talk to him, she had no idea what she was going to say. She was sure it would be over in a matter of seconds and then she could go home.

"Hey, Ave." His eyes met hers, and she looked away from the intensity. Okay, so Tam hadn't been bluffing.

"Hi, Logan. Tam said you wanted to see me?"

He nodded and stepped away from the wall. "Thought we could hang out tonight. You want to go out back? Get some fresh air?" *Make out in a dark corner?*

"I guess ... I mean, I really can't stay long, and I didn't bring a jacket or anything, so ..."

He kept his fierce green eyes on hers and held out his arm for her to take, as if such a gallant gesture would win her over. "Not a problem. I'll keep you warm." He flashed her a smile. "Unless you want to stay in here. That's fine too."

"Yeah, that might be better." She forced herself to take hold of his arm, and he led her into the next room where they sat between two couples making out.

"Let's just watch the movie for a while," Logan suggested as she squirmed nervously in her seat. "No worries, Ave. This beats chemistry, right?"

She faked a laugh and glued her eyes to the television, but when two of the characters started making out in the middle of a chase scene and Logan slid his hand farther and farther up her thigh, she knew she had to get out of there. She'd never kissed anyone. She didn't even *like* Logan, and the last thing she wanted was to find herself lip-locked with him.

"I've gotta use the restroom," she stuttered, and scrambled off the couch. "Sorry."

When she'd locked herself in the bathroom, she leaned against the counter and took ten deep breaths. Tam knew Logan would put the moves on her, but Avery supposed that was the whole point. After all, Tam placed a lot of her own happiness in relationships with guys, so she probably figured that was what would make Avery happiest too. But it never worked. She and Tam were two opposite sides of a coin—Tam the shiniest side.

Avery studied herself in the mirror. She looked at the eyebrows Tam had taught her to shape and pluck into perfect arches. She looked at the curls in her hair that Tam had taught her to do. She looked at the plunging neckline on her shirt that showed off a hint of cleavage, something she wouldn't have dared expose before she'd met Tam. All of these things had actually boosted her confidence over the past year. More people knew who she was now, and even if she wasn't as popular as Tam, it didn't matter. The truth was she'd been happier in the past year than she'd been in a long time, and Tam was a huge part of that.

But that didn't mean she had to let Logan put his hands all over her. She didn't want attention from a guy just because Tam had decided to play matchmaker again. She wanted someone to like her just for *her*. Without Tam's influence.

She took a few more deep breaths and opened the bathroom door, determined to find Tam and say goodbye before she left. She was by the kitchen, her expression glowing. Ryan was nowhere in sight.

Tam looked at Avery, confusion sweeping across her face. "Where's Logan?"

"In the living room. He ... I just want to go home, Tam. Sorry."

Her confusion melted into disappointment and maybe a little anger. "Oh, I thought he was a good fit for you. He really does like you, Ave. It wasn't all my doing."

Avery looked away. Was she such an open book? "The problem is I don't really like him, and I'm tired and I need to get home."

"I understand." Taking Avery's arm, Tam led her to a quieter corner of the kitchen. "Before you leave, I have to tell you about Ryan. We totally just made out for fifteen minutes. He's amazing, Ave." Her eyes were dreamy, her cheeks pink, her breaths coming a little faster. "I've never felt like this about anyone. My mom always told me you'll know when you've met someone you can be with for the rest of your life, and I swear ... I really swear that's what this is."

Avery's heart sank and she wasn't sure why. She forced a smile and leaned against the wall. "I'm happy for you, Tam. He's not even like most of the guys you've dated. He seems more down to earth." *And mysterious. And maybe a total player.*

"Yeah, even with his crooked nose." She let out a heavy sigh and rolled her eyes up to the ceiling. "Hell, even *that* looks good on him."

Avery looked around, confused. "Did he leave?"

"What? No, we just needed a little breather. He said he had to call his mom or something. I think he's outside."

Avery nodded. "Well, you'll have to give me all the kissing details when we have our sleepover. Deal?"

"Deal." Tam grinned. "Maybe I'll have even more details before this party's over. Call me tomorrow, 'kay?"

"Sure thing."

Avery said goodbye and pushed her way through the crowds and out the front door. The air was warm and smelled of rain-soaked grass.

Then Ryan was in front of her.

She stopped in her tracks, her attention immediately snapping to his lips—lips that had just spent the last fifteen minutes attached to Tam.

"Hey, Avery." He smiled, as if nothing was wrong, as if she knew exactly what was going on between them. She *wanted* to remember, but all she could dig up was salmon and his face across the restaurant table.

"Hey." She nodded in the direction of her car up the block. "I'm heading home. Will you be able to find a ride?"

"No problem. I'm sure Tam can help me out." He stepped a little closer. "So, uh, I'm not sure when I'm going to see you again, but about our deal ... since you're about to leave, did you want to follow through with that?"

"I ... guess so," she fumbled. "Right now?"

He shoved his hands into his pockets and looked around, finally motioning her to a clump of bushes around the corner. "Over there is fine, you think?"

"Uh, sure ..."

She followed him around the corner, stumbling backward when he backed her up against the side of the house next to the bush. Her shirt snagged a little on the bricks.

"The first thing you have to do is keep breathing, no matter what. If you freeze up, everything will fall apart." He leaned into her, resting a forearm on the side of the house. He looked so casual, so confident. His lips were inches away from hers.

"Keep ... breathing," she whispered. "Right."

So she kept breathing.

She might as well get this over with, whatever it was she had agreed to do. Then she could go on living her normal forgetful life. No harm done.

"This is just about the kissing, right?" she asked quickly as Ryan leaned even closer.

His eyebrows furrowed. "Well, yeah ... right?"

"I-I'm not sure."

*I've forgotten everything. Can I say that?*

That was when he stopped. Even his breaths stopped, and he backed away a quarter of an inch. "Oh," he exclaimed in an almost trembling voice as she squeezed her eyes shut to try to remember even one more tiny detail from that night in the restaurant. "Are you telling me you like me ... like, more than a friend? I'm ... I'm not sure I understand."

She almost bit her tongue. It was too late to sort through anything now, because when she'd opened her eyes to tell him she had no right to crush on her best friend's guy, she'd seen Tam in the semi-darkness a few feet away. Her arms were folded, her expression livid as she looked at Avery.

"I knew it," she hissed. "I knew you were keeping something from me."

Avery stiffened as Ryan backed away and rushed to Tam. "I can expl—"

"I'm not mad at you, Ryan. I heard what you said. This is clearly all Avery's doing." She took a step forward, her anger giving way to something else. Hurt. Regret.

"It's not what you think," Avery said in a weak voice, unsure of how to proceed. How could she explain that *she* didn't even know what this was?

Tam shook her head, her eyes glistening as she turned away. "Don't bother calling me tomorrow, Avery," she said loudly as she stomped away.

Ryan stood still for a moment then hurled a quick, "I'm sorry," at Avery before taking off after Tam.

All Avery could do was lean back against the side of the house and look up at the stars in the sky. With a sick dread in her stomach, she realized nothing would ever be the same again.

# · 13 ·

Jordan was a lot more relaxed about a date scenario than Kent had been. In fact, after Avery said goodbye to Owen and started walking to the library for work, she checked her phone at least eight times to see if Jordan had texted or called. She had no idea what time she was supposed to get together with him, and she wasn't sure if it was because he hadn't told her or she hadn't written it down. She double-checked their last texting conversation. She'd said, *anytime after* 7:00 and he'd said, *Great!* but nothing specific.

As she entered the library, she sent him a quick message asking him what the plans were, if anything. Maybe he would cancel on her. With so many prospects on her horizon, that possibility shouldn't have bothered her. But it did.

"You got a sun lamp," she said as soon as she entered the book repair room and noticed her plant bathed in artificial sunlight.

Heaven looked up from her work and grunted. "I decided I might as well get one before the poor plant died. It was looking rather sordid."

Avery sat down and reached out to run her finger up the base of the lamp. It stretched up and over the plant, which was looking much better than it had the day before. She had meant to go to the store to get a lamp and forgot. Of course.

"I'll pay you for it," she said quickly. "How much?"

Heaven shrugged. "You don't owe me anything. I like the extra light down here."

Avery got to work on repairing a cracked spine, and as she set out her materials and stirred some thick, smelly glue in a paper cup, she reveled in the way the walls almost cradled the silence, as if it was sacred. Something about Heaven's deliberate, careful mood, the taste of peanuts, the smell of the glue, made Avery comfortable but restless at the same time. This job had become something almost surreal, as if the room and everything in it, including the time that ticked away, didn't belong in the real world. As if nothing she said here would slip into any other part of her life. Even Chloe didn't come down here anymore. It was Heaven and Avery, working away in contented silence. Maybe it was a false sense of security, but Avery didn't care.

"So ... I'm kind of falling for three different guys," she blurted as Heaven opened her third package of peanuts and dumped a few in her mouth. "And I thought they were all the same guy ... at first."

Heaven's eyes widened in surprise as she chomped down on the peanuts and swiveled to face Avery. "How is that even possible?"

Avery kept stirring her glue. "Hello, it's me we're talking about. Notebook girl, remember? I forget everything, especially faces. Trust me, it's possible."

"Well, there you go." Heaven turned back to the tub of water in front of her and slowly dipped in a piece of paper. It was then that Avery realized she knew nothing about Heaven except her last name and that her parents had been odd enough to name her Heaven. She knew little things about her, like her peanut fetish and the fact that she loved dressing in black, but outside of that—nothing.

"What's your major?" Avery asked, lifting her brush from the glue so she could watch the thick substance string back into the cup.

"Psychology." Heaven swallowed her mouthful of peanuts. "And before you ask, no, I cannot help you with your poor memory. It was probably triggered by something traumatic in your life, similar to a boulder thrown into your path. You'll trip over it forever until you find a way to remove it ... and, sorry, but I have no interest in helping you remove it."

Avery had to hand it to Heaven for being so blunt and honest. Silence settled between them again as they worked. Maybe Heaven was right, but the problem was she couldn't remember anything particularly tragic happening in her childhood. Her mother had made it clear that she'd been forgetful since the day she was born. It had to be something else.

Maybe she was cursed with a low IQ or general forgetfulness worse than the average person. Whatever it was, she wanted to fix it. College was supposed to be a fresh start, and she was already entangling herself in a worse web than ever before.

When her phone beeped she glanced at it on the table.

*8:00 work for you?*

Swallowing a lump in her throat, she cleaned off her hands and picked up the phone.

*Perfect. Should we meet at your house?*

Heaven looked over and smirked. "Is that one of the guys you're falling for?"

"Yeah, we're getting together tonight. I don't know how to tell him I'm kind of seeing another guy at the same time."

"I thought you said there were three of them."

"I'm not dating the third guy. I'm just really interested in him."

Heaven whistled under breath. "You've got some problems, honey. You can keep them all straight, right?"

Avery clenched her jaw. "Of course I can—now that I've sorted them out in my head. It's fine. I'm fine. It'll be fine."

"That's fine, then. Hope you have fun tonight."

Avery stared at her phone until another message popped up.

*I was thinking we could hang at my place. You cool with that?*

He really was low-key.

*Sounds great. See you then.*

She sent the message and wondered if she should have put an exclamation point after one of the sentences. Maybe not. It was fine. Everything was fine.

*⁓⁓⁓*

It took Avery less than a minute to get to Jordan's front door after getting ready. As casually as she could, she rang the bell and waited. He opened the door a moment later, dressed in a three-piece suit and tie.

*Oh.*

"Come in," he said, grinning as he opened the door and ushered her inside. The house seemed a lot larger now that it wasn't filled with hordes of people. The air smelled of chocolate, and when she looked up at Jordan's face, she noticed something brown smudged across his clean-shaven cheek.

"You've got ... there's something ..." She pointed to her own cheek and then reached out to touch his.

"Oh, whoops," he laughed, and licked his finger to wipe away the smudge before she could reach it. "Ganache."

"Ganache? Are you cooking?" *In a three-piece suit?*

"Um, yeah, I baked a torte this afternoon before my dinner meeting. I thought since we weren't eating dinner together, we could at least have dessert." He glanced down at his suit, which was not only a suit, but a very expensive-looking suit. "I didn't have time to change before you got here."

"You look great," she blurted, trying not to blush. "Seriously. I'm feeling really under-dressed now." She laughed nervously and looked down at her clothes. "And I was about to change into sweats and a T-shirt."

Looking her up and down, he smiled. "You were? Well, honestly, it wouldn't have mattered. You look good in anything." He reached up to loosen the Windsor knot of his slate-colored tie. He shuffled his feet for a moment, and she wondered why he seemed so nervous all of a sudden. It wasn't like she hadn't been in his house before.

"So, chocolate torte?" she asked, rubbing her hands together. "My aunt never makes anything with chocolate. I haven't had a decent dessert in weeks."

His nervousness seemed to melt away, replaced with a beaming smile. "Then you're in for a treat." He turned and motioned for her to follow him into the kitchen. It was clean and sparse except for a few dirtied stainless steel bowls by the sink and a pan on the gas stove. On the counter was an unfrosted chocolate torte next to an empty glass serving dish.

"You ride a bullet bike, wear three-piece suits, and ... bake?"

He grinned. "Why not? My grandmother is a baker. She's taught me a few things over the years. I don't do it that often, but hey, this is a special occasion, so ..."

She tried not to blush as she sat on a bar stool and leaned over to inspect the torte. It looked good enough to eat, even without any ganache. On the counter was a pastry brush, and she tried to picture him using it to swipe crumbs off the torte. The image didn't seem to fit a guy like him. Then again, she hardly knew him at all. She didn't even know what kind of guy he was.

"I don't understand you," she said in a soft voice, straightening to watch him lift the saucepan from the stove. "You bump into me on the stairs, and all of a sudden my being here is a special occasion?"

After a long pause, he set down the pan and shrugged. "Maybe I just want to get lucky tonight."

Her mouth dropped open. He placed his elbows on the counter and leaned forward to meet her eyes. She sat back a little and said, "Get lucky, huh? Do you always come on to your dates this fast?"

"You asked me that the night of the party, remember?" He stood straight and carefully transferred the torte to the serving dish.

No, she didn't remember. She shook her head.

"Well, I told you I'm not like this at all. Still, you must think I'm a little, I don't know, forward?" He lifted his eyebrows, waiting for her answer as his lips twitched at the corners. Teasing.

"Yeah, maybe a little."

*No worse than any other guy I've fallen for in the past week.*

He let out a sigh, almost as if pushing away a part of himself. "Can I be honest with you?"

"You mean you *don't* want to get lucky?" she joked, but it came out sounding much too serious. Could this be any more awkward? She stared at her hands, waiting for his reply.

He blanched. "Oh ... well, uh ... I didn't really mean we had to ..." He trailed off and grabbed the saucepan, suddenly seeming absorbed in the task of positioning it over the torte.

Her stomach sank about a foot and a half into nothingness. She knew him liking her had to be too good to be true. At least she still had Kent, unless she managed to mess that up in the next few days.

But as she looked up at Jordan's perfectly styled hair, the swift movement of his arm as he tipped the pan and expertly poured the ganache over the torte, her heart beat faster at the sight of him than it ever had for Kent. It made her wonder why she had even liked Kent to begin with. Was it because she had thought he was Jordan? It couldn't be that. Making out with Kent had been amazing. Her date with him had been amazing, but maybe that was because she had nothing else to compare it to.

"The truth is," Jordan said slowly, still focused on the torte to avoid looking at her, "my sister challenged me to get a date for next weekend."

He couldn't mean he'd asked her out as part of a challenge. She said nothing, waiting for him to explain further as the ganache spread smoothly over the torte, quickly setting as it dripped down the sides. Her mouth grew so dry she was afraid she might have to rush to the sink for a drink of water.

"We're going out to dinner with my parents," Jordan quickly explained after glancing up at her horrified expression. "It's a tradition every month to try to keep our little family together since the divorce, to keep the peace, I guess. I ran into you on the stairs and thought maybe I could take you, but I promise I was genuinely interested. I still am. I just thought you should know." Cringing, he finished with the ganache and set the pan aside. He glanced at her again, practically shrinking in front of her. "Are you upset?"

She looked at the torte and then up at him, her mouth opening and closing for a few seconds before she could find words. It felt like someone had shoved a handful of cotton into her mouth. "I'm a convenient date, then? A challenge? That's ... it?"

He shook his head and pushed a hand through his hair, messing up the combed style. For the first time since she'd walked through the door, he seemed flustered and nervous. "Shit, I've screwed this up, haven't I?"

"I'm not sure what you want me to say," she finally managed to respond. "I'm not sure what you—"

"I really like you so far, Avery." He gripped the edges of the counter, avoiding her eyes. "But I haven't dated anyone in so long. For reasons I don't want to get into right now, I hardly even *talk* to women these days if I can avoid it. Still, I wouldn't have had the courage to talk to you on the stairs if it wasn't for my sister's challenge." He put a hand to his forehead and groaned. "Actually, I wouldn't have talked to you at all if I hadn't physically run into you. I guess that accident forced me to finally talk to someone as pretty as you." He lifted his eyes to hers, the sincerity in them running so deep she wanted to reach out and touch him. "I'm glad we ran into each other," he said with a soft smile.

"I'm glad it knocked a little sense into me because I think I can really like getting to know you. Maybe it's time for me to get out of my rut." He looked away again. "Anyway, I just want you to know that's how all this started."

Maybe it really was okay. At least he was being up front with her. That meant something.

"I appreciate the honesty," she said slowly, "but you seem pretty popular around here. How is it possible you rarely date or talk to women?"

Letting out a long sigh, he stared down at the counter. "Again, it's not something I want to get into right now."

Avery cringed and bit her tongue. Right. He had just said that and she'd forgotten already.

He looked up at her. "Do you want a drink? Should we go hang out in the living room?"

She shrugged. "I don't drink."

His eyes widened. "You don't?"

"I told you that at your party, didn't I?"

"Oh, right, I forgot." He walked to the sink and started rinsing out the pan. "How the hell could I forget that?"

So she wasn't the only one forgetting things around here.

"It's all right," she laughed. "Really, I'll take whatever you've got that's non-alcoholic."

He left the pan in the sink and turned around. "The police aren't going to come knocking on my door any second, so I think it would be okay for you to drink if you want to. Some wine might loosen us both up, you know?"

"That's true, it might," she said, sliding off the stool and walking around the counter to him. "Is this still about getting lucky?"

He rolled his eyes and brushed a hand across his forehead, leaving a streak of ganache above his left eyebrow. He still had some on his fingers from rinsing out the pan. "Let's forget about the getting lucky confession," he said almost a little too seriously. "That was stupid of me."

Stepping close enough to touch him, she reached up and wiped the ganache from his forehead. He didn't back away. In fact, he moved a little closer, his eyes fastened to hers. He was warm, and as her skin brushed against his, she felt that same spark from before. It sent tingles all the way to her toes. "Thanks, Avery."

"Any time." She smiled and licked the chocolate off her finger, keeping her gaze on his gorgeous blue eyes. What was she doing? This was supposed to be an innocent date. If she started making out with him like she'd done with Kent, what did that mean? She wasn't a player. Or ... well, maybe she was at this point. She should probably tell Jordan the truth now, just like he'd told her the truth.

But it was too late. His mouth met hers, his arms sliding around her, squeezing her close, his lips parting to let her in. He tasted like chocolate, his tongue warm against hers as she kissed him back. His upper lip was a little scratchy, but it felt nice.

What had Ryan taught her? Less was more. In this case, that was absolutely true. Nobody was going to interrupt them in here as he leaned back against the edge of the counter and pulled her as close as he could, kissing her more tenderly than anyone else ever had. Almost as if he was frightened.

She pulled away, her breaths heavier than his.

"I'm sorry," she whispered.

He touched his lips, as if he couldn't believe what had just happened. "Should we, I mean, do you want some dessert?" he said quickly. "We can go watch a movie if you want."

She nodded and stepped away from him. "Dessert sounds good."

A few minutes later, she followed him into the living room where she'd sat the night of the party and watched the football game. Jordan sat on the sofa in front of the television. Balancing her plate on one hand, Avery sat next to him and waited as he pulled up a list of movie options on the screen.

Despite a lamp turned on in the corner, the room was pretty dark. The light from the screen lit up Jordan's face. She looked over at him, studying the square of his jaw, remembering how he'd looked that first night she'd seen him on the porch. She wanted to ask him why he'd been so upset that night, but it felt too weird to say, "Hey, I was kind of spying on you," so she kept her mouth shut.

"I might as well get comfortable," he said as he handed her the remote and set his dessert plate on his knees. "Go ahead and pick what you want."

She took the remote and watched him peel off his double-breasted suit jacket and lay it across the arm of the sofa. Scrolling through the movie options, she hardly saw the words on the screen. Jordan was practically undressing in front of her as he unbuttoned and pulled off the vest then started undoing his tie. When he was finished with that, he undid the first three buttons of his white dress shirt and breathed a sigh of relief as he leaned back and picked up his fork.

"I forget how stifled I feel in these suits," he grumbled, cutting into his slice of torte.

Avery smiled and nodded at his arm. "Want me to help you with your sleeves?"

He grinned. "Sure. Can you handle the cuff links?"

"Uh ..."

"Here, I'll show you." He held out his wrist and turned it sideways for her to see the bottom of a silver

161

cuff link. "Just twist it to the right and slide it up through the hole. Not that I can't do it myself, but hey, if you want to help."

She set down the remote and bent over to peer at the cuff link before grasping it in her fingers and doing as he'd instructed. It slid out freely, and she reached over to unfasten the other one. She dropped the cuff links into his open palm and smiled as he grasped her hand before she could pull away.

"You're more than my sister's challenge," he said softly. "A lot more. I'm not even going to ask you to come to that dinner with me."

"O-okay," she stuttered as he held on to her hand. Part of his chest and collarbone were visible now, showing through the unbuttoned neck of his shirt. She tried not to look, but it was hard. She liked too many guys right now, and a part of her needed to know if that made her a bad person. She had to tell him about Kent. She had to.

They spoke at the same time.

"Jordan, I need—"

"Avery, I want—"

They both stopped and laughed. Jordan squeezed her hand. "You first."

"I ..." But she couldn't say it now that the moment was gone. She groaned inside and slowly pulled her hand away from his. "It's nothing," she finally managed to get out. "I just wanted to say I'm okay with going to that dinner."

"Yeah? You sure? My dad's all business, and my mom's controlling. Then there's my sister. She's just weird."

She remembered the cactus. "Your mom's a biology professor?"

"Yeah, she's crazy with the botany stuff. Her apartment is a freaking greenhouse." He shook his head, laughing as he started rolling up his sleeves.

Avery's eyes widened. "I love plants." She blushed and looked down at her lap. "I'm going into botany."

"I didn't know that. I guess there's a lot I don't know about you."

She looked up to see him beaming. "Same goes for you," she laughed. "Like, why do you wear such fancy suits?"

Fiddling with his fork, Jordan squished a piece of torte on his plate, leaving prong marks in the chocolate. "They're my dad's. He's CEO of an international aircraft manufacturer. He's got a whole walk-in closet full of Armani, and he gives me the stuff he's tired of wearing. I work for the same company. That's why I never finished school. Not that it would have mattered. I hadn't even settled on a major before I dropped out."

"You must be pretty talented to work at a company like that," she said softly. "School isn't the be-all end-all to success, you know."

"Yeah, that's what my dad always says too." He shrugged and she winced. "It's fine. I like my job, but it's nothing like what he does. I get to deal with all the angry people the top guys don't want to deal with. I get yelled at a lot and then I have to sort it all out into nicer words and numbers that make sense, then pass it along to the right people."

"And you like that?" She wondered if that was why he had looked so upset on the phone the night on the porch.

"Yeah, actually, I do." His expression warmed. "I love business. The pay isn't that good, but I know I have to hang out where I am for a while before I can work my way up. Anyway, that's why I wear my dad's suits. Why spend my hard-earned money on something he would just throw out otherwise?" He laughed quietly. "Now you know I'm a college dropout."

"What year would you be if you were still in school?"

"I'd probably be finished with my bachelor's, at least. I'm twenty-three." He took a big bite of torte and looked at her. "I'm pretty bitter about the college thing. My mom's always pushing me to go back, and my dad's always pushing me to stay with him in the working world—or at least go to an Ivy League school instead of 'dinky old UDub.' I feel squeezed in the middle, like I chose my dad over my mom. I know she's hurt by it because it has always been a sort of rivalry between them—doing what you love versus doing what will make you rich. Sometimes you can do both, I guess, but my parents don't see it that way. Mom loves her job at UDub and Dad loves the security of his position, even if the stress is going to kill him early."

Taking a bite of torte, Avery nodded to indicate she understood. She'd never been in such a situation, but that didn't mean she couldn't try to empathize.

"But, hey," Jordan continued, "if he does die early, I wouldn't have to pay him rent anymore."

"This is your dad's house?" she asked. "This torte is amazing, by the way."

"Yeah, he rents it to me." He took another bite and smiled. "And you're right, the torte is pretty good. Glad I could impress you with that, at least."

"What do you mean, 'at least'? The kiss in the kitchen? That was just as good as this torte. Promise."

"You think? Want some more of that action?" He slid his plate off his knees and set it on the floor. He moved closer to her, his thigh brushing against hers. The television bathed him in blue and purple light from the menu screen.

"Maybe."

She swallowed a lump of chocolate and tried to keep the trembling in her hands to a minimum. She wondered what all these guys saw in her. Was her self-esteem really so low that she couldn't see it? Or had she figured it out before and then forgotten? Maybe it was what Chloe had suggested—college was crawling with people wanting sex. Maybe that was all Jordan and Kent wanted. She seemed easy. Vulnerable. Probably because she really was easy and vulnerable, just like her senior year. Nothing had changed. How had she thought things could change between now and then? It took a lot to alter someone for the better. One summer out of school apparently wasn't enough.

"Maybe, huh?" Jordan lifted his hands and shrugged. "Okay."

"Jordan?" she whispered as her mouth turned dry again. "Can I ask you something?"

His eyes twinkled. "You just did, but sure."

She could do this. She balled her hands into fists and then uncurled them to let out the tension.

"Why do you want me here? I know you asked me out initially because of your sister, but I can tell you really do like me, and I'm confused about why. I think if you knew me, if you knew all the things I've done wrong, all the problems I have, you'd move on to someone else."

He stared at her, his excited expression falling into confusion. "Everyone has problems, Avery. Why would that stop me from wanting you here?"

She opened her mouth and then closed it again as the weight of his words settled around her. He had a point—one that hurt. It was ridiculous to expect perfection from herself or anyone else. She looked away as her stomach tightened. Jordan was too good to be true, and here she was making a fool of herself in front of him. She was always making a fool of herself. College wasn't going to be any different. The rest of her life wasn't going to be any different. She had to face it. Get over it. But how?

"Avery, did I say something wrong?"

She shook her head. There was no doubt in her mind that he'd understand her forgetfulness if she told him about it. But would he understand Kent? That was all part of the forgetfulness, and now that she knew the mistake she'd made, it was time to clear it up and come clean.

"How serious are you about being with someone?" she asked as she poked her fork into the ganache. "I mean, you said things are complicated, so how serious are you?"

As he leaned close enough for her to feel his breath on her face, she looked up to meet his eyes. He had a few crumbs clinging to the corners of his mouth, and she couldn't help but smile. He moved in to kiss her once again, this time not as hesitant halfway through. He ran a hand up her arm, making her wish she'd worn short sleeves so she could feel his skin on hers. He reached her neck and stopped the kiss.

"I'm as serious as you are, Avery," he whispered. "I feel a different kind of connection with you than I've felt with anyone else. I want to know you better. I want to spend the whole night asking you questions. First thing I'll ask is your last name."

"Hollister," she answered as she lifted her hand and touched his collar. She inched her fingers to his skin, feeling the bump of his collarbone. She heard his breath catch in his throat as he leaned closer to her ear.

"Hollister—like the clothing company?"

"I have no affiliation," she laughed, parting his shirt with her hand as she gained the courage to explore more of him. She glanced down to see how far she'd gone, and saw a dark line snaking out from under her hand. "A tattoo?" she asked, grinning as he looked down to see her fingers splayed across the top of his chest.

"Yeah, when I was seventeen. Don't laugh."

She withdrew her hand and watched as he undid one more button to pull the shirt open a little more. He had pale skin, and just as she had guessed, he was lean underneath his dressy clothes. Not tightly toned, but not flabby either. So maybe he wasn't necessarily athletic, just a more slender build.

Climbing down from his shoulder to the top of his left pectoral was a vine-like tattoo, almost Celtic looking. She couldn't decide what it was supposed to be as she followed the design with her eyes, studying it, until she realized that was the point. It was fascinating to look at, like an M.C. Escher painting, or staring at the branches of a tree when you're half asleep.

"I love it," she whispered, reaching out to touch it and then pulling back. "Why'd you get it?"

"My mom, believe it or not. It was a birthday present."

"Are you serious? Parents don't let their kids get tattoos."

"Mine did. I chose this one because it reminds me of her—of plants and ... and life. It means more to me now than it did when I got it." He looked down and traced part of the design with his finger. "I'm glad I got it, and I'm glad you like plants too and don't think I'm stupid for getting it."

"Why would I think you're stupid? I love it."

She reached forward to touch the tattoo again, her fingers trembling. As soon as she brushed his skin, something snapped into place between her and Jordan. She blinked, and Jordan looked down at the plate on her lap. "Do you want to—?"

"Yeah." She set the plate on the floor, and in two seconds he was kissing her. She melted into the couch, letting him press her down into the cushions until her head swam with desire, even more than it had when she'd been with Kent. Jordan was intoxicating. If she thought touching him was like electricity, his entire body on top of hers was even better. She had to have more of him.

She found the opening of his shirt again, following the buttons down to where she could undo the next one and the next and the next, until it hung open completely. She ran her hands all the way to his stomach, savoring the feel of him as she went even lower, past his expensive belt buckle and down to the zipper on his pants. She'd never felt a guy there before. He pushed himself against her, making it quite obvious how much he liked her hands there.

*New territory. Too fast. Time to panic.*

With a gasp, she pulled away and wrapped her arms around his middle.

"You want me," he breathed into her ear. "Don't you?"

"Mmm-hmm." It was all she could manage to say.

"You're so beautiful," he whispered, pushing up her sweater until he could trail kisses along the curves of her breasts. He mumbled something about the color of her bra and started tracing his fingers lightly across the yellow pinstripes. His touch tickled, and as if he'd flipped on a light switch, something primal inside her turned on. She breathed faster, harder, and arched her back.

"Don't stop," she whispered, moving her mouth to his neck. He smelled like a chocolate torte, rich and sinful and dark. Nothing could be better than this. Nothing. She couldn't believe she was going so far. She felt so alive. So wicked. After years of wishing for someone like this—for a connection so electric it felt like she was going to short circuit—it was finally happening.

But what kind of connection might she have with Owen? She hadn't kissed him yet.

*Yet?*

What was wrong with her?

"What's the matter?" Jordan asked, removing his hands from her. "Too far? Too fast?"

"No, no, it's not that."

Well, it *was* that. She really needed to tell him what had happened with Kent before he found out some other way. Why couldn't she just come out and say it? Admitting her faults shouldn't be this difficult. She opened her mouth, gathering her courage into a ball of energy in the pit of her stomach.

Then she nearly bit her tongue at the sound of a girl's voice from the back of the house.

"Jordan? Where are you?"

Jordan sat up, his eyes wide. "Oh, no," he sighed. "My sister. I forgot she was stopping by tonight. Shit." He looked down at his open shirt and started fastening the buttons. "Sorry. I'm so, so sorry. She's, uh, she's—"

"Jordan? You in here?"

A figure stepped into the doorway, silhouetted from the kitchen light down the hall. Something about the figure was vaguely familiar, and Avery sat up, smoothing her hands down her sweater to make sure it was where it should be.

"Oh," the girl said, stepping an inch into the room. "You have company."

Jordan turned to look at her, his fingers fumbling with his shirt. "Yes, I have company. Do you mind?"

She put a hand on her hip. "Well, excuse me. Maybe you should do that sort of thing up in your bedroom if you're expecting me to come by. Come to think of it, it's been so long since you've had *this* kind of company ..."

Avery didn't miss the beat of sadness in the girl's voice, as if she couldn't make up her mind whether to keep teasing her brother or sympathize with him.

"Shut up, will you? Get what you need and leave, please. Now."

"Fine, fine, but aren't you going to introduce me?" She flipped a switch on the wall and the room flooded with yellow light. Avery's mouth fell open as she stared at none other than Heaven Meadows, her bright red dreadlocks a fiery halo around her face.

"Avery, what are you doing here?" Heaven's widened eyes went from Jordan to Avery, back and forth like a Ping-Pong ball.

"Heaven is your sister?" Avery asked Jordan, her heart pounding.

"Yeah," he answered, exasperated. "How do you know each other?"

Folding her arms, Heaven leaned her hip against the wall. "Oh, we work together in the library. We have nice, long chats, don't we, Avery? Today's was especially interesting. Guess my brother is one of the three guys you've fallen for, huh?"

As Heaven's eyes narrowed into a full-blown glare, Avery realized once again, like a punch to the stomach, why telling people about her forgetfulness was always a bad, bad idea. You never knew who was going to use it against                                   you.

# ⁖ 14 ⁖

Jordan's confused expression made Avery want to run from the room, but she stayed on the couch, wringing her hands.

"Three guys?" Jordan finally asked, turning to her. "What does she mean, Avery?"

After throwing a glare at Heaven, she leaned forward and looked straight into Jordan's eyes. "I can explain."

He didn't seem upset, but she could tell if she didn't handle things just right everything would look worse than it actually was—unless, of course, everything *was* as bad as it seemed. Maybe she really had screwed this up beyond repair. Then again, it wasn't like she was Jordan's girl or anything. They were only on their first date, for crying out loud. Technically, she didn't owe anyone anything.

"Can we go for a walk?" she asked, wiping a sheen of sweat from her brow. "I'd like to talk about this with you alone." She glanced at Heaven, her heart sinking. She liked Heaven, just as she'd liked Tam at one point.

"Uh, sure. I'll go change my shirt. One sec."

He got up and disappeared around the corner. Heaven, still leaning against the doorway, continued to glare. "I had no idea one of the guys you were talking about was my *brother*," she snapped. "If I'd known that, I would have told you what I'm going to tell you right now."

Avery felt herself freeze up as Heaven crossed the room and leaned over the back of the couch to look her in the face. Her breath smelled of peanuts, and Avery remembered her father worked for a company that had something to do with airplanes. Maybe that was where she got all the little packages of peanuts. Her big, heavily lined eyes blinked twice before she spoke again.

"If you break my brother's heart, I'll eat you alive, understand? He's been through more than you can even imagine. The last thing he needs is someone messing around behind his back—whether you mean to or not. I don't care about your memory problems."

Avery tried to swallow but couldn't. "He asked me out in the first place because of you. I don't want to hurt him, I promise."

"Oh, that." Heaven nodded and stood up straight, folding her arms again. Her nostrils flared. "So, that's all this is, then—my challenge for him to find a date? Is that what you're saying?"

"No ... but that's how it st—"

"You ready, Avery?" Jordan walked into the room, now wearing a T-shirt, brown leather jacket, and a pair of jeans with holes in the knees.

Scrambling off the couch, Avery practically ran across the room and followed him out the front door. She wasn't sure if Heaven was still glaring at her or not.

"I'm really sorry about that," he said as she followed him around the corner to the driveway. "Heaven is really protective of me, even though I'm a guy and she's my little sister. Should be the other way around, but she's not your typical girl, if you haven't noticed."

Avery smiled and nodded. "Are we going somewhere?" She looked down at Jordan's bullet bike and realized he was holding a helmet out for her. She'd never ridden on a street bike before, and swallowed down a rush of fear.

"Yeah, I think it'll be good for both of us. You don't want to?" He looked down at the helmet in his hand.

She could do this. The ride would at least give her some time to think about how she was going to explain herself to him.

"No, it's fine," she answered, and snatched the helmet from him. "I just don't know what I'm doing, that's all."

He grinned as he put on his own helmet and left the visor up. "There's not much to it," he explained. "I'll get on and start the bike. You get on after me, from the left side. Then put your arms around me and hold on. If you need me to stop, just tap my right shoulder."

"Sounds doable." She put on her helmet and thought she must look pretty stupid since it felt so big around her head. Still, she didn't want to die if they crashed.

She watched as he climbed onto the bike and started it up. It was sleek and black and low and the engine rumbled smoothly through the night.

"We're not going far," he said loudly.

"Okay!" she yelled back, and mounted the bike. Her butt slid forward a little, and she wrapped her arms around Jordan's middle. He felt so good against her. She wanted to lean her head on his shoulder, but that was impossible with the helmet on. Bracing her feet against the foot rests, she tensed as Jordan backed out of the driveway and pulled onto the street. When she looked back at his house, she saw Heaven standing on the porch with a piece of torte on a plate, watching them as they took off in a roar of engine noise and Avery's silent gasps.

—⁊⊦⇃—

Riding Jordan's bullet bike was like riding the wind. Avery had never felt anything as liberating as racing down that road, holding tightly to someone who gripped the balance, the speed ... her life in his hands.

Maybe it wasn't as dramatic as all that, but as long as she was on the back of that bike, all her senses were heightened. She felt powerful, which was a feeling she hadn't expected. She'd expected to feel nothing but fear.

When Jordan pulled into an empty parking lot and turned off the bike, he nodded for her to get off. She removed her helmet as soon as she was on solid ground.

"That was really fun," she said, her breathing faster than normal.

"Now you see why I've spent all my money on this baby rather than a car," he laughed, patting the bike. He took her helmet and motioned for her to follow him up a small path. "Come on, I've got something to show you."

She followed him to a park overlooking a body of water. There was so much water in Seattle she had no idea which part this was. The air was cool on her face. The gravel on the paved path crunched under her feet. Jordan looked over his shoulder every now and then to make sure she was still with him. She wondered if he was upset about what Heaven had said. She wondered how much she should confess to him. Was there anything to confess, really? He'd been truthful with her. The least she could do was tell him she'd made out with his friend just last night.

"Jordan, where are we going?" she asked after five minutes of walking.

"A good spot to see the skyline over Lake Union. It's really pretty from here at night."

The trail wound over some grassy hills, each second bringing the skyline more and more into view. Jordan was right. It was pretty all lit up beneath a purplish sky. The lights twinkled on the glassy surface of the lake, all somehow lesser than the yellow-white magnificence of the Space Needle.

"Oh, good, the benches are empty," Jordan said as they neared the top of a hill looking over the lake. "They're usually taken whenever I come."

They sat down on the first bench and Jordan dumped the two helmets on the other one. Avery shifted across the wood planks, unsure of how close she should sit to him.

"Have you been to the top?" he asked as he leaned back.

"Of the Space Needle? Nope."

"Been to the fish market?"

"Nope."

"You said you're from Spokane, right?"

"I've lived there for the past few years." She took a deep breath and held it in for a good thirty seconds. She wasn't sure where Jordan wanted any of this to go.

"Well, I'd be happy to take you around to all the hot spots in Seattle ... if you want."

She didn't know what to say, so she kept her mouth closed. Silence surrounded them, broken only by the sound of talking somewhere behind them in the distance.

"So, about my sister," he said after clearing his throat. "You know, what she said about the other guys? Do you want to talk about it? I'm curious."

"Yeah, that." She swiped a hand across her forehead. She was starting to sweat. Ugh.

*Just get it out, Avery.*

"It shouldn't matter, I guess. I mean, we're not together, you and me. Right? I mean, all I told Heaven was that I'm interested in three different guys. She didn't know one of them was you."

Jordan grunted and leaned forward, resting his elbows on his knees. He looked over at her, his eyes sparkling. "That's it?"

She shrugged. "One of them is someone you know."

"Yeah?"

"Kent."

He sat back again and released a long breath. "I was about to say it's none of my business who else you're interested in. Like you said, we're not together. But, yeah ... Kent kind of changes things."

"I thought it might. I went out with him last night."

His eyes snapped to hers, filled with a question he didn't have to voice with words. Not that it was *any* of his business what she'd done with Kent, but she still felt some sort of obligation to keep talking.

"He took me ice skating. Then we hung out on my front porch. He's nice." *He's also a really good kisser, like you ... minus that electrifying shock that happens when we touch each other.*

"Lots of girls like Kent," he said, shrugging. "So he didn't ... you two ... I mean ..." He looked away and cleared his throat again. "That's none of my business, sorry."

"No, we didn't. Why?"

He practically shrank away from her with embarrassment or something else, she wasn't sure. "No reason. Kent's a bit of a player, that's all. I'm not judging you for liking him, but I'm surprised it didn't go that far. It always goes that far with him and his dates, and I've known him for quite a while."

She wanted to tell him it might have gone that far if they'd had a room to themselves, but she didn't. She kept her eyes on the city lights. Besides, where had things been going on Jordan's couch before Heaven showed up? Not that she'd felt pushed into anything. Far from it. But she was a virgin, and who knew how far she'd actually go? It was one thing to mess around. Quite another to commit.

"So, do you want to keep seeing me, then?" Jordan asked, finally looking at her again. "I'll admit my ego is shattered from knowing I'm not the only bright, shining star in your universe, but I can cope until you decide what you want."

Her lips spread into a smile. He really was too good to be true. "Thanks, Jordan. That means a lot. And yes, I'd like to keep seeing you."

"Can you tell me who the other guy is?"

"Just a guy named Owen."

She cringed, realizing she probably sounded a little too dreamy when she said Owen's name. The good thing was that she'd *remembered* his name. She also remembered his Vans and the streak of chain grease on his jeans. She remembered studying biology with him, spreading out on the grass on their stomachs.

Pushing herself back to the moment, she realized the other good thing was it looked like she wasn't going to have to tell Jordan about her forgetfulness.

"Honestly," she said after another minute's silence, "I've been having a hard time with this. I feel guilty." She lowered her voice and stared at the concrete. "I've never dated anyone before, and now all of a sudden ... look at me."

He looked at her, his lips twitching at the corners. "I think you're being too hard on yourself. It's college. What did you expect to happen? You're pretty and nice and fun to talk to. Stuff's gonna happen. Me, on the other hand—I'm the total opposite. You're the first girl I've been with in three years." He leaned a little closer to her and stretched his arm across the back of the bench. "That's why I said tonight was a special occasion."

She tried not to look at his mouth and think of how good it felt against hers. "Is that why Heaven told me she'll eat me alive if I break your heart? What happened, Jordan?"

He looked out across the lake, slowly lifting his left hand to his mouth. After a few seconds, Avery realized he was biting his fingernails, just like he'd admitted to doing the first time she met him. He chewed on his index fingernail, and then moved to his pinkie, followed by his thumb. Finally, he stopped and lowered his hand.

"Her name was Callie," he said in a fragile voice. "We grew up together. We were best friends; our relationship didn't get romantic until college. We got married the end of our freshman year. I was nineteen. My parents thought we were insane, but they didn't mind because they already loved Callie like a daughter, and Heaven was so happy when she could really call Callie her sister."

He paused for a moment, still staring out at the lake. Avery waited patiently.

"Callie got really sick not long after our wedding," he finally continued, "and nobody knew how things would turn out for her, even her doctors." He took his arm away from the back of the bench and leaned forward. "It's one of those things you see in sappy chick flicks, but it wasn't just a story—it was my life. It was real, and it wasn't fair. It wasn't anything you haven't heard before. People die every day from cancer."

Avery looked down at her hands. "Is that why you dropped out of school?"

"Yeah, I couldn't go back. I had to focus on something completely different. Dad understood and helped me get my job. He paid out my lease on our apartment and moved my mom out of her house so I could have it to myself. Everyone knew I had to be alone with as little to worry about as possible. It was embarrassing, actually, like I was the sick one now, like everyone expected me to die of a broken heart."

Heaven's words made sense now. Too much sense. Avery squeezed her eyes shut. She couldn't do this. She ended up hurting everyone in her life outside of family. It was only a matter of time before she hurt Jordan, and since it was clear he still hadn't completely healed from his loss, she couldn't bear knowing her own recklessness would slice into his already gaping wounds.

"Jordan, I'm so sorry," she whispered. "My dad died three years ago in Afghanistan. It was really hard. It's still really hard."

He nodded. "Nobody's immune to it. I don't even know why you're different for me, Avery ... but you are." He looked at her again. The city lights reflected in his eyes. "You don't even remind me of her. She had bright red hair and freckles. I used to think I'd find someone just like her and I'd be happy again, but then I realized that was stupid. You can't replace people. You just have to fill different gaps and learn to live with the gaps others have left behind."

Her eyes filling with tears, she nodded. That was exactly how she'd felt since her father's death. The gap he'd left had healed over quite a bit, but it was still there. It would always be there. There were other gaps too. The one Tam had left. The one Ryan had left. All those other broken friendships she could only remember if she read back in her journal—all of them broken because of something she'd done, or forgotten to do.

Now, with Jordan right in front of her, she felt he'd already left a mark on her—something deep she wasn't going to be able to erase. He was going to leave a gap, even though she'd only known him a short time. She had to get out of his life before that gap got any wider, for both of them.

# · 15 ·

Thursdays were Avery's easy days, since all she had was her biology class and work. Unsurprisingly, Heaven hadn't shown up for work on Wednesday, and Avery doubted she would show up today either. Avery was grateful, to say the least. She wasn't ready to face Heaven's sisterly wrath yet.

Instead of standing in line for a hot dog, Avery kept on walking to the smaller undergraduate library across the way where she could get a sandwich and coffee on the ground floor.

Maybe she was hiding from Owen. Maybe she wanted a change of scenery. Whatever her reasons, she found herself alone in a dark corner with a turkey sandwich and a latte, wishing she wasn't such a coward. But it was better this way. Simpler. Quieter. If she stayed away from Owen, there was no way she could hurt him—at least, beyond avoiding him, of course. She didn't even know his last name. Or she didn't remember it.

Pulling out her books, she spread everything out on the table in front of her and started organizing her notes. Green Post-its for her architecture class. Blue Post-its for biology. Purple for English. Yellow for people.

*Mom and Chloe's birthday is on Saturday. Get Chloe something TODAY. Mail a card to Mom SOON.*

She squeezed her eyes shut, cursing under her breath. She had forgotten to mail a card to her mother, and she still hadn't bought something for Chloe. She had no idea what to get her.

"Studying hard?"

*Ugh. Not her.*

Opening her eyes, Avery looked up at Tam. Her hair was in a high ponytail today, and she was back to wearing the lime green glasses. Probably just for looks. They did make her look smart.

"Yep," Avery snapped. "Studying very hard. So, if you don't mind ..."

Completely ignoring the affront, Tam pulled out the chair across the table and sat down. "Hmm, is the turkey good here? I haven't tried it yet." She reached over to Avery's plate and snatched a piece of turkey that had fallen out of the sandwich.

Avery glared at her, not sure how far she would let this go. "Listen," she seethed, leaning forward, "if you're upset about getting kicked out of Jordan's party, it's not my fault. You knew it was an over twenty-one party. You're still eighteen."

"And you're nineteen," Tam replied, practically yawning. "Guess you weren't kicked out?"

"No, but how did you even get the address? Jordan told me he didn't invite you or tell you where it was."

Rolling her eyes, Tam popped the piece of turkey into her mouth. "I saw it on your yellow Post-it, you dork. You were holding it when we ran into each other on the stairs."

Avery clenched her teeth. Of course. Not that she remembered much from that moment, but it seemed the only likely explanation. It was time to end this.

"What do you want, Tam? You're obviously after something, so let's get it over with. I guess my senior year of being a social outcast wasn't enough payback for your broken heart?"

Tam studied Avery's face, her big eyes unblinking. "You still think that's what the whole thing was about? Ryan?"

"Well, yeah." Avery leaned back in her chair and folded her arms. "You know it was."

Tam smirked. "It was about a lot more than that, Avery. You broke my trust as a friend. A *best* friend. I took you in, and all you ever did was shove it back in my face over and over and over. Ryan was the last straw. All I did was send you right back to what you were before you met me. It shouldn't have been anything different for you."

Avery blinked. Tam's words stung more than she wanted to admit. Her dad had been stationed on different bases over the years, but she wasn't sure if her lack of social skills and friends had to do with moving around or if it had to do with her personality. She had attended one elementary school, two junior highs, and two high schools, the last being Shadle in Spokane. She hadn't made many friends at any of them. She'd grown up lonely, like Aunt Chloe was lonely now, so maybe Tam was right. She'd gone right back to what she'd always been.

"One thing was different this time around," she said, looking into Tam's eyes. "Everybody knew me as a traitor."

Tam shrugged. "You *were* a traitor, weren't you?"

"I didn't mean to hurt you."

"Didn't you? After that promise you made for things to go back to normal? After all those times I told you about me and Ryan and how good things were? After everything I did for you?"

Tam's nose wrinkled with disgust, and Avery looked away.

"You were broken," Tam said through gritted teeth as she leaned across the table. Her elbow crumpled the edge of a purple Post-it note. "You cried about your dad all the time. I went with you to the cemetery, like, thirty times, just so I could stand there with you as you talked to his grave. I helped you with your clothes, your hair, your makeup, everything. I gave up a lot of time with my other friends just to *be* with you, Avery. I could tell you needed someone, and I stepped in. And what did I get in return?"

Avery looked down at her sandwich and sniffed back a wave of tears. Everything Tam said was true.

"I stole Ryan away from you," she whispered, knowing it was the only thing Tam wanted to hear. Besides, it was true.

"Yeah, and you wonder why I was so upset. It was more than Ryan. A lot more. I gave and gave and gave to you, and I guess you *just forgot* to give back. I always thought it was adorable how you'd forget things, but then when the Ryan stuff happened I realized it was nothing but an excuse." Leaning back, she waved her hand at Avery's Post-its scattered across the table. "Look at you, Ave. Seriously. Just look."

Her eyes glistening, Avery swept her gaze across the table. Her life was organized on paper right down to what page she had to read in her biology book that afternoon. But in reality, her life was turning into a complete and utter wreck. And she had no idea how to fix it, especially without her mother's help.

"You need to change," Tam said softly as she stood and looked down at Avery, who was trying desperately not to cry. "I was dead serious when I told you I want to start over with our friendship, but if you're still the same old Avery, maybe that's a bad idea."

"Go away, Tam," Avery hissed through her teeth. "Just go away."

"Whatever you want."

When Avery looked up, she saw Tam walking out of the building. There was no way Avery was going to be able to study, or even eat, now. She gathered up all of her stuff, dumped her food in the trash, and got out of there as fast as she could.

As soon as she was outside, the rain hit, pelting her as she dug in her bag for her umbrella. Of course. Gone. She couldn't even remember where she'd left it. By the door? In her bedroom? Maybe she'd left it in one of her classes.

"Want to share mine?"

A familiar voice and a familiar pair of Vans. She looked up into Owen's blue eyes. He was nice and dry beneath his black umbrella, and without thinking she slipped underneath it, so close to him that it was only natural for him to slide an arm around her shoulders.

"Thanks," she laughed, looking down at her damp shirt. "You were looking for me, weren't you?"

"Of course I was."

He smiled when she turned in his loose embrace to face him. His goatee was a little fuller today, but still neatly trimmed. His smile broke into a grin.

"This is nice," he whispered, his breathing a little faster. "Glad I decided to walk this way. Want to go inside or walk around?"

"Either is fine with me."

He had assumed, of course, that she wanted to stay with him all afternoon, just as she had on Tuesday. He was correct in his assumption, but she still felt sore from Tam's attack, and even worse, she felt an obligation to tell him she wasn't interested in moving this relationship past friendship. For his own good.

"Have you been to the gardens?" he asked as they headed toward the library where Avery worked.

"No ... what gardens?"

"The medicinal gardens. You'll get to work in them the more you get into your major."

She smiled. "I haven't explored much around here, honestly, but if you want to go there, that's fine."

Owen took a sharp turn and they headed south toward the large fountain in the middle of the main campus. Most students had umbrellas, and those who didn't either pulled up their hoods and scrunched up their shoulders or kept walking as if getting wet didn't bother them in the slightest. The rain didn't seem to bother anyone around here, and Avery had to admit it didn't bother her much either. She was getting used to the smell of it, even the taste of it in the air.

"So," Owen said, his arm still draped around her shoulders to keep her under the umbrella, "any reason you decided against a hot dog today? Worried about the heart attack possibilities?"

She nearly tripped on her own feet. "What? No! I just wanted something different today, that's all."

He gave her a sly look and kept walking. "Heart attack on a bun, yeah. What'd you get instead?"

"A turkey sandwich." *That I didn't eat.*

"Sounds good."

She knew he was waiting for her to explain why she hadn't met him at the food truck. It had been a silent, implied agreement on Tuesday that they'd meet up again, and the hot dog truck was the obvious meeting place.

"I'm sorry, Owen," she said as she kept her eyes on the ground. They rounded the fountain and a small burst of wind blew a spray of fountain water and rain across her cheek. She wiped it away, hoping Owen couldn't tell how uncomfortable she was with his arm around her. "I was thinking maybe we—"

"You didn't have to meet me today," he interrupted, "if that's what you were thinking. I'm not upset."

"Really?"

"Yeah, really ... but I'm glad I ran into you."

193

They walked in silence. They were reaching a part of campus she couldn't remember seeing before. Beyond one of the many tall, ancient red buildings, Owen led her past a garden filled with neatly planted squares labeled with small signs.

"Was that it?" she asked as they kept walking.

"Part of it. If we go a little farther across the road here, there's a covered area by the bus stop."

They reached the other garden and he nudged her inside a little gray sitting area with a roof. Shaking out his umbrella, he sat down and ran a hand across his forehead.

Sitting next to him, Avery looked out at what she could see of the garden. It was lush and green, and a part of her wanted to run in the rain and start looking at all the plants, even if it meant she'd get soaked.

"Owen, I have to tell you something," she said as he folded up his umbrella and snapped it closed.

"Yeah?" He set his backpack on the ground and turned to face her. "What's up?"

"You know how I said I like you?"

"How could I forget?" His expression softened just as it had on Tuesday. Was she about to make a mistake? It didn't matter. She had to get this out.

"I didn't lie—I *do* like you, but I don't think we can let it go any further than it has already. Things are kind of complicated for me right now. I need to focus on school, and I—"

"It's fine," he interjected quickly. "Really, don't worry about it."

She liked the way his hair was curlier today than it had been on Tuesday or any other time she remembered seeing him. It was probably because of the humidity. She had to sit on her hands to keep from pushing one of those curls off his forehead. That made her think about brushing the chocolate off Jordan's brow, and she nearly bit her tongue. Yeah, this had to end. Now. Next up was Kent. She'd see him tomorrow in class.

"Friends is fine with me," he said as he watched her slide her hands underneath her thighs. "Honestly, I wasn't expecting more at this point. We can be study partners. You helped me a lot on Tuesday—way more than my stupid housemates when I ask them to quiz me. They don't care about this stuff like you do." He kicked his backpack and smiled. "Is that okay?"

"Study partners? Yeah, that's great." She exhaled a long, relieved breath, trying not to sound too pleased. Studying she could handle. Maybe ... until Owen realized how much she forgot in a matter of days.

"You're dying to go look at the garden, aren't you?"

Realizing she'd gone back to staring out the open window again, she nodded. "It looks great. So many different plants in one spot."

"They're all labeled too. You'll love it."

She stood up. "You afraid of a little rain?"

"Not at all." He stood and followed her out into the garden, leaving his umbrella tucked in his backpack as he swung it onto his shoulders. "Wait until you see the Hindu monkeys," he laughed. "They supposedly guard this place."

"Sounds ominous."

As they walked through the drizzle, their feet crunching on the gravel below, Avery almost forgot about Tam and the turkey sandwich. She looked at signs that said things like *Oenothara biennis,* which she knew was a biennial primrose plant. Every few minutes she would stop and look at Owen, who would smile at her as he looked up from studying a thistle plant or a pomegranate tree, and the pain would come crashing back.

*"I gave and gave and gave to you, and I guess you just forgot to give back."*

Was she really so selfish, even if it wasn't on purpose? Perhaps it was best for her to keep Jordan, Kent, and Owen at arm's length for that very reason. It was best for her to retreat back into her loneliness.

# ⁙ 16 ⁙

*Last Year*

When Avery showed up on Tam's doorstep with a freshly baked pan of mint brownies, she was hopeful the big misunderstanding could be made right. After all, this was a guy who had come between them, and guys came and went. Friendships were supposed to last through anything.

The problem was Avery really didn't believe that. Too many times she'd inadvertently lost people in her life because of minor, seemingly insignificant things.

"Brownies aren't going to fix this," Tam growled when she opened the door. She was dressed in her favorite pair of purple sweatpants, the waistband rolled down far enough to show a strip of her toned abs and tiny bellybutton. Her tight black T-shirt had PINK stamped across the chest.

"I don't expect the brownies to fix anything," Avery muttered, "but I hoped they'd at least get me in the door so you'll let me explain what happened." She raised her eyebrows. "Pretty please?"

Tam stared down at the pan. Avery could tell her mouth was watering. It was Saturday morning, early enough that she probably hadn't eaten breakfast yet.

"Fine, come in." She let go of the doorknob and turned on her heel.

Following her inside, Avery smiled at Tam's little brothers who were playing video games in the living room. Tam led her into the kitchen where her mother was beating eggs in a bowl. She was as perfectly put-together as Tam, with a tiny waist, big chest, and a headful of gorgeous curly black hair. "Oh, Avery!" she cried out as they walked over to the table. "Good morning. You staying for breakfast?"

"Uh, I don't know," Avery said, looking at Tam. "Maybe?"

Tam snatched the pan of brownies from Avery's hands and marched over to the counter. "We're going upstairs, Mom." Grabbing a spatula, she dug out four brownies, slid them onto a plate, and motioned for Avery to follow her up to her room.

Like everything else about Tam, her room had a lot of green in it. Lime green comforter. Lime green lampshades. Lime green rug on the floor. She and Avery had spent a lot of time sprawled out on that rug, either looking at magazines and listening to music or gossiping about boys or talking about what they wanted to do with the rest of their lives. Avery even remembered crying on that rug at one point—not her finest moment ever. If she remembered correctly, it had something to do with her dad's death. Tam was always willing to give her a shoulder to cry on when it came to that. Now, however, she didn't seem willing to do anything but sit cross-legged on her bed and take huge bites out of the first brownie.

"Close the door," she snapped as soon as Avery walked inside.

"Sure." Avery closed it and turned the lock, then stood in the middle of the room. Her stomach rumbled, and she wished she had taken a brownie too.

"Here." Tam reluctantly handed over a brownie. Avery took it and nibbled on the edge. She'd woken up at 6:30 to make them.

"So, about Ryan," she began. "Please don't hate me. I kind of hate myself because of my stupid brain. I forgot something really, really important."

Tam rolled her eyes and started on her second brownie.

"I went home last night and dug out one of my journals—the one I was writing in last December. That's when I met Ryan for the first time, but I didn't remember it. At all. I know that sounds stupid, but you know me."

Tam rolled her eyes again.

"Well, I found the entry from when I met him. See, last night he was acting all intimate around me when he was at my house. I couldn't figure it out because I knew he liked *you*, not me. Then he said something about a kissing deal ..."

Tam's eyes snapped to Avery's. She stopped chewing.

"Yeah, I know. You'd think I'd remember a kissing deal, right? Well, I didn't. Maybe I didn't take it seriously then, so I just swept it out of my mind. Turns out we had some heartfelt talk about my dad. We talked about a lot of things, I guess, and somewhere in there we talked about my virgin lips. He felt bad for me. He couldn't believe I had never kissed anyone. He said I was too pretty not to have kissed anyone, but he wasn't attracted to me that way. I guess I wasn't attracted to him that way, either. We talked about that. We thought it was funny. So he said we should make a deal. If I hadn't kissed anybody before he saw me again, he'd teach me how to kiss. Totally platonic."

Tam was chewing again, but it was slow and methodic. The wheels in her head were obviously turning. Avery couldn't tell if she believed her story or not, so she continued.

"Last night was the first time he saw me again, and when he had me backed up against the house like that, it's because he was going to kiss me. It didn't mean anything. I promise."

Swallowing, Tam narrowed her eyes. "But I heard him say you liked him as more than a friend."

That was what Tam had *wanted* to hear, and Avery was sure it was what she would believe she had heard until the day she died. Arguing about it seemed pointless.

"He didn't say that, exactly, but yeah, I think he's hot. Still, I would never try to steal him from you, Tam. I'm serious. This was all just a mistake ... because I forgot stuff."

Avery stared down at the green carpet, waiting for a reply. There were so many little things Tam always forgave—like whenever Avery forgot her wallet and Tam bought her lunch and never expected repayment, or all those times Avery forgot to meet Tam somewhere for something they'd planned. Their relationship was filled with countless things like this. Why should Ryan be any different?

But Avery knew why. Ryan was different because Tam saw Avery as competition, even though nothing could be further from the truth.

Tam lifted the last brownie off the plate, studying it before she looked up at Avery. "Ryan told me about how you'd met before, but he told me the deal you had between the two of you wasn't something he felt you would want him to tell anyone, even me."

"That was considerate ... I guess."

"I thought so, which is why I'm happy you've decided to tell me about it so I can stop all my worrying. I had no idea it was a *kissing* deal, but hey, now that we've got it all cleared up, it's over with." She took a bite of the last brownie. "Right?"

Avery nodded. "Sure, I guess so. I'll stay Miss Virgin Lips and everything can go back to normal."

"Yep," Tam mumbled through the brownie. "Normal."

If only it had ended there.

---

It was Halloween before Avery saw Ryan again. Since he'd hooked up with Tam, Avery had thought she would see him constantly. But Tam hoarded him like a trophy she wanted to keep away from everyone, boasting about him almost every second she and Avery managed to get together—which wasn't nearly as much as before he'd come along.

Avery wasn't resentful. She was truly happy for Tam, and listened for hours as Tam told her about their latest date or make-out session or whatever new thing she had learned about him. Avery was pretty sure she knew him better now than he'd appreciate, but that was what best friends were for. She played the part. She was glad things had gone back to normal, so to speak.

When he showed up on her front porch dressed as Indiana Jones, she hardly batted an eye. Tam had told her how much he loved the *Indiana Jones* movies and how she'd had to sit through them twice now.

"Nice fedora," she smirked as she opened the screen door and held out a bowl of candy.

He looked down at the bowl and snatched a fun-size candy bar from the middle. "I think it makes me look classic. What do you think?" He pushed on the brim with his knuckle until the hat sat angled on his head. He did look classic. She still liked his crooked nose, and the scruff on his face went well with the costume.

"You look great, Ryan," she said as he tore open the candy bar and took a bite. She was proud of herself for keeping his name straight in her head, not that she could have possibly forgotten with Tam's constant chatter about him.

"You look great, too," he said, smiling at her ratty pair of sweats and baggy Kermit the Frog T-shirt. "Going for bored housewife, maybe?"

"Should I be offended by that question?" She set down the bowl and leaned against the door to keep it open.

"Nah, I'm kidding, of course." His confident smile faltered for a moment. "So, uh, I'm not here for free candy. I actually stopped by because your mom called me last week and asked me to pick up a pair of earrings my mom left here the night of our dinner. I'm heading out to California this weekend to see her and Victor."

Avery thought for a second, searching her brain. Had her mom told her about that? She was on a short book tour with the author of a book she'd illustrated and wouldn't be home for three days. Or four days, Avery couldn't remember exactly.

She stared stupidly at Ryan. Where would her mother leave a pair of earrings?

"Didn't she tell you?" Ryan asked.

"She might have mentioned it, but I don't know where they are. You want to come in and help me find them?"

Pulling out his phone, he checked the time. "Yeah, I don't have to be anywhere for thirty minutes. I'm meeting Tam at a party down the road."

"Okay, come in."

He followed her inside, stealing another candy bar from the bowl as she led him down the hall into her mom's bedroom.

"Sorry if this is weird to bring you in here," she laughed, "but I don't know my mom's earring collection inside and out, and I have no idea what your mom's earrings look like, so ..."

"They're diamond studs."

"Oh? Valuable, then?"

"Yeah, my stepdad gave them to her last year, but I guess they were bothering her that night and she took them out after dinner and left them on your coffee table."

"I doubt they're still there if my mom found them. They've got to be in here somewhere."

Rummaging through a jewelry box on the dresser, Avery started pulling out all the diamond studs she could find.

"Not those," Ryan said, rifling through them.

His knuckles brushed against her hand, making her breath catch.

"Those don't look familiar either," he said, clearing his throat and moving his hand. "They were teardrop-shaped."

"That's all that's here." Her shoulders drooped as she turned to face him. "I'm sorry. My mom's gone on a business trip. We can keep looking through the house if you want."

"Sure." He shrugged and she caught a glimpse of him in a mirror over on the far wall. He looked ridiculous next to her in his costume ... in the middle of her mother's bedroom.

"Okay, then." Sliding past him, she led him down the hall and into the living room. They looked on shelves and in drawers, in decorative ashtrays Avery hadn't realized they owned, and then headed into the kitchen.

"Can you maybe text her or something?" he asked as she pulled open the junk drawer by the sink. "Or maybe she can mail them if we can't find them?"

"Oh, I'll text her, hold on. My phone ..." She spun around in a circle, trying to remember where she'd left it. Her bedroom, maybe?

"Wait, look." Ryan pulled a small Ziploc bag from a magnet clip on the refrigerator. Her mom's handwriting was scrawled across the plastic: *For Ryan when he comes by.* Inside the bag were two sparkly diamond studs.

She grinned. "Great! Glad you found them." *And glad I didn't have to act like too much of an idiot trying to find my phone.*

"Thanks, Avery." He shoved the bag into the back pocket of his tan slacks and looked at her with an awkward expression. He seemed relieved but anxious at the same time.

"So," she said, leaning against the counter and folding her arms over her embarrassing T-shirt. "How are things with Tam?"

His expression lit up, but it almost didn't seem genuine. "Great, thanks. She doesn't tell you all about it?"

Biting her bottom lip, she nodded slowly. "Yeah, she does, but sometimes it's nice to hear the other side, you know?"

He looked down and traced a square on the linoleum with the toe of his 1930's-style boot.

"It's all good—what she tells me," she explained quickly. "You're a great kisser, apparently. Too bad I missed out on that opportunity."

*Bad thing to say, Avery ...*

Groaning inwardly, she unfolded her arms and looked toward the screen door past the living room, hoping for trick-or-treaters to save her. No such luck.

"About that," he said softly, looking up from the floor.

"About what?" she croaked. It suddenly felt as if someone had shoved a fistful of candy down her throat.

"The kissing thing. I feel really bad. You still haven't ...?"

She attempted a smile, clearing her throat as best she could. "Um, no, but it's fine. Seriously. You're dating my best friend."

"Yeah, I guess so." His expression turned to a pleading stare with wide, imploring brown eyes. "I could still help you out if you want."

She wasn't sure what to think.

"You seem so lonely, Avery," he said. "I've never met anyone as lonely as you. It's what I first noticed about you at that dinner in December. It's why I tried so hard to get you to open up to me. Victor told me you've been quiet the whole time he's known you.

Even with Tam, you seem alone. Then that night at Stacy Edisson's party, when you were hinting that you might have feelings for me, it kind of hit me in the gut how much I might have hurt you."

She looked up at him, finally realizing she'd been focusing on his boots the whole time he had been speaking. He'd taken off his fedora, revealing a serious case of hat hair.

"Then why are you offering to kiss me?" she asked, her chest rising up and down with her quickened breathing. "Don't you understand that it might hurt me if you do? You say you want to help me, but maybe the best way to do that is—"

The doorbell rang, making them both jump, and Avery stalked out of the kitchen. She yanked open the screen and held out the bowl to a group of little kids.

"Trick-or-treat!" they all yelled as they grabbed candy and dumped it into their bags.

She smiled at them and stood in the open doorway, watching as they turned and ran down the driveway to their parents. If only things were still that simple.

"Avery?"

Turning, she watched Ryan approach her. She kept the door open, hoping he'd just leave already. "Say hi to Tam for me," she said softly as he brushed past her and stood on the porch beneath the yellow light. He held his fedora at his side.

"Let me give you the kissing lesson," he said, and her mouth dropped open.

"Why?" she demanded. "I promised Tam I wouldn't do it."

He looked down at the ground and kicked at a candy wrapper some kid had dropped earlier. "Because I can't stop thinking about it," he grumbled as he looked up at her, his eyes desperate. "Please? Can we just get it over with? I can tell it's driving you nuts too."

Her throat closed up for good this time, and she let go of the screen door. It banged shut between them, a loud thud. It reminded her that nobody had ever fixed the broken spring on it. Her dad would have fixed it in a heartbeat, but he was gone now.

"It's not fair to Tam," she said, watching him through the uncovered screen.

He shoved his hands into his pockets and leaned forward. "What's not fair is me not knowing if something might have happened between us if I'd just kissed you that night at the party. I had no idea you were interested in me."

She folded her arms. "So you regret getting together with Tam?"

He didn't flinch. "I regret knowing I've hurt you. I regret maybe passing up something that could have been great. Maybe it's because I keep thinking about kissing you, or because Tam practically ordered me not to, that's bothering me so much."

"So, it's a pride thing?"

He looked her straight in the eyes, as if no screen was between them, as if Tam wasn't between them, as if nothing was between them but a fraction of an inch.

"If you don't want the lesson, tell me right now and I'll leave. I will do everything I can to never see you again. You can forget any of this ever happened."

"Except you're still dating my best friend," she said with a sigh.

"Yeah, there's that."

She looked down at her bare feet and wished she had never met Ryan. It all seemed incredibly unfair.

"I think it's best if you go now." She finally managed to force the words off her tongue as she looked at him. "I'm sorry."

He blinked a few times, standing there in his stupidly adorable costume, and then nodded and turned to head down the steps. When he was halfway across the lawn, Avery thought about the moment at the party when he had asked her if she did everything Tam told her to do. She had denied it then, but as she watched him walk away, she realized it was the absolute truth. Tam ruled her life, whether she wanted to admit it or not.

Before she could stop herself, she yanked open the screen door and ran down the porch steps. He was stepping off the curb to go around to the driver's side of his car, but turned as soon as he heard the screen door slam. The grass was cold on her feet as she ran to him. He stepped back onto the sidewalk to meet her.

"Kiss me," she gasped when she finally reached him.

"What?"

"Oh, shut up."

She pushed his hat off his head, grabbed his shoulders, and kissed him hard on the mouth, not caring if she knew how to do it right or not.

It started out fast, but he slowed her down, teaching her every move without any words at all, easing her into a deeper and deeper connection with him. Less was more, she discovered. He touched her cheek, moved his hand up to her ear, and then buried his fingers in her hair, tilting her head to just the right angle as she slid her hands down his arms, enjoying every dip and curve of him. She almost lost her breath, but reminded herself to breathe and keep going. It was a long kiss. It was her first kiss. It was a spectacular kiss.

Until she opened her eyes to see Tam's car stopped in the middle of the road.

The passenger-side window was rolled down, Tam leaning halfway over the seat as if she was about to say something to Ryan and then froze when she saw him making out with her best friend. Or, from that very moment, her *ex*-best friend.

Avery felt Ryan rip away, and as he left her embrace, something inside her wrenched apart at the seams. The kiss had made it clear that she had allowed a part of herself to fall in love with him, and he might have been falling for her. But she had no doubt Tam would ruin it all.

—⁄∣∖—

Avery knew she was in trouble the second she walked into school the Monday after kissing Ryan. Of course, she'd known she was in trouble long before that. Tam had stumbled out of the Gold Bug, hands on hips, shooting the Glare of Death at her and Ryan. But at that point the whole affair was only between the three of them. Tam was hurt and angry. Ryan was frustrated and regretful. Avery was sick to her stomach. Still, the problem was contained. At least Avery had thought it was contained. Her friendship with Tam was over. She had learned her lesson and would move on.

Tam had other plans. She was probably the worst person to have hurt. Tam was the student body president. She was the most popular girl in school. Everyone liked her. She helped people. She cared about people. She donated blood at every blood drive, for crying out loud. She didn't drink, didn't do drugs, but she was still welcomed into every single group. She'd always been a mystery to Avery, even after they'd become friends. How was it possible to be so charismatic and influential? She supposed people like

Tam became senators' wives, or senators themselves, or presidents of big corporations, or billionaires. As long as it was epic, it didn't matter. Because everything about Tam was epic, especially her payback.

Spinning her locker combination, Avery wasn't lost to the fact that four people had already knocked into her with their backpacks. A group of boys from the crowd Tam had dubbed the Math Geniuses faced her as soon as she closed her locker and turned around. They hissed profanities at her as she walked past them. When she sat down in her history class, nobody sat next to her. People took the front row instead, which was unheard of until then. Nobody sat in the front row unless they were a brownnoser or wanted to punish themselves.

She had been labeled and branded a traitor. A boyfriend stealer. Not that all the other students were innocent of this particular sin, but nobody—*nobody*—would ever do it to Tam.

The news traveled like wildfire. Later, Avery heard that a text had been sent to Stacy Edisson on Halloween night, which she then sent to her boyfriend, Steve, the captain of the football team, who then sent it to all the football players, varsity *and* junior varsity, who then told the cheerleaders, the school band, the yearbook staff, and the school newspaper. By Monday morning, even the lunch ladies and the janitor knew what had happened. Some of them probably didn't care, but Avery was pretty sure most of them did. James, the janitor everybody high-fived in the hallways, gave her the stink eye every time she passed him. It was at that point she knew she was truly doomed. Even her teachers seemed distant with her.

Tam had become the heavenly saint who could do no wrong, and Avery had become the devil. That was her senior year in a nutshell.

Twelve weeks in, she came home from school and buried herself in bed. A knock on her door made her scream, "Go away!"

Her mom opened the door. "I'm not going away."

"I need a lock," Avery grumbled, throwing her blankets over her head. "Please, Mom, leave me alone."

"That's all you *are*, Avery—alone. I think I'm the only person left in your life, honey. Please talk to me. It's still this thing with Tam, isn't it?"

Avery couldn't stop the tears. They stung her eyes, and she let them fall. For weeks now she had kept them inside. She was used to being alone, so what was different about now?

"I hate her," she muttered into her blankets. "I hate her so much. She's turned everyone against me. Everyone knows who I am now. That's something I thought I always wanted, but not like this. This would have died down weeks ago, but she keeps it going."

"Nobody's hitting you, are they?"

"No, Mom. It's completely non-violent, so please don't go to the principal or anything. It'll only make it worse."

"Okay, okay."

Silence. Finally, she pulled off her blankets and looked over at her mother in the doorway. She seemed so sad. Helpless.

"You can't fix this, Mom."

"I know, honey. I think the best thing to do is focus on your classes and graduation. Once you're in college, things will change. It'll be a new start."

Wiping away her tears, Avery nodded. "Do you think I deserve this?" she asked in a trembling voice. She thought about the word TRAITOR scrawled across her locker in black permanent marker. None of the janitors had bothered cleaning it off yet. "I mean, what I did was wrong."

Her mom looked at the floor for a minute. "You hurt your friend, yes, but what she's doing to you is worse." She looked up and shrugged. "At least in my opinion it's worse. She's a vindictive little bitch, isn't she?"

Avery nodded, unable to argue the fact.

"What about Ryan?" her mom asked. "Is Tam making his life miserable too?"

"Not that I've heard. I think she's still in love with him."

He had texted Avery once after the event—two sentences that made her heart ache:

*None of this was your fault. Good luck, Avery.*

She never replied.

# 17

Avery wasn't looking forward to English class on Friday. Kent had already texted her four times during the week to tell her how excited he was to see her again. She had responded to the first two, but not the last two. She let herself drown in a pool of guilt as she slid into her seat next to him.

"Hey, gorgeous." He bumped her elbow with his and then leaned in for a quick kiss, which she expertly dodged by leaning the other way to slide her messenger bag under the desk.

"Hi, Kent."

This was horrible. The guilt. She really did like Kent and she didn't want to hurt him. But what choice was there? Lead him on? He deserved someone who wanted him and nobody else. Her heart was split too many ways to make it fair for anyone.

"What's the matter?" he asked, brushing his nose across her cheek as he squeezed her closest knee. "Do you need to talk through something? Maybe we can go out again tonight. What do you—"

"Turn to page fifteen, please," their professor's voice boomed through the room. Avery looked up to see him glaring at Kent's public display of affection.

"*Kent*," she hissed, kicking his foot under the desk. "Pay attention."

"Oh, right." He smiled and leaned back in his seat, mouthing an apology to the professor.

During class, her mind wandered back to what Jordan had told her about Kent. "*It always goes that far with him and his dates.*"

Well, maybe she was different for Kent, special somehow. Whatever the reason, she was glad she hadn't gone that far with him. She stopped writing in her notebook and stared at her pen hovering over the paper. If she was so relieved she hadn't gone that far with him yet, did she *ever* want to go that far?

Allowing herself a peek at him, she noticed he was chewing on a fingernail as he slouched in his seat and listened to the professor's lecture. He wore his usual button-down shirt and expensive brown corduroy pants. There was something about him that drew her to him, but she guessed it was mostly physical attraction. That, combined with the fact that he liked her, had been enough to catch her for a moment.

But that moment, she realized, was drifting away.

As soon as they were out of class, Kent followed her outside and slipped his hand inside hers. She squeezed it and then pulled away.

"We need to talk," she said. There were fifteen minutes before her next class. Could she get this out in fifteen minutes? Her stomach growled as she and Kent walked past the hot dog food truck. Owen was nowhere in sight.

"Yeah?"

They stopped near the library. Avery's heart was pounding. She wanted to look him in the eyes and tell him everything, but she couldn't even look up at him.

"Avery, what's wrong?" He touched her hand and slid his thumb across the cracked face of her watch. It still surprised her how much he liked her. If he was a player like Jordan had said, how much of his attraction to her was real? Why didn't he just move on to someone else? She shook her head, angry with herself. It didn't matter.

"I don't think we should go out again ... at least anytime soon," she said quickly before her courage faded away. "I feel like I've used you—that night at the party. I thought you were ..."

She finally looked up at him, her breath catching in her throat. How could she tell him she had wanted him because she'd thought he was Jordan? Or had it been the other way around? It had all started with Kent that very first day in English, so maybe it really was him she had liked and her brain had mixed it all up.

His eyebrows rose and he waited for her to continue. She liked that he wasn't making any assumptions yet.

"I thought you were exactly what I wanted," she explained as vaguely as possible "... and I was what you wanted, but I ... it's just too fast for me."

*There. Out. Kind of.*

His lips twitched at the corners and his thumb slid from her watch. "I understand, sure." He nodded vigorously, as if convincing himself this was exactly how everything should happen. At that moment, he didn't seem like the player Jordan had described. He seemed truly heartbroken, and it hurt her to watch it play across his face.

"Kent, I hope you're not—"

"I'm always like this," he interrupted. "I'm always too fast with relationships. It's just how I am, I guess." He shrugged. "Girls figure I'm a player and they leave after a few dates. It's just that I ... I guess I'm afraid to lose people once I have them interested, so I rush everything."

He watched her carefully, probably hoping she'd feel bad and take back what she'd said. Or maybe he wasn't that shallow.

"I don't think you're a player. That's not why I'm doing this." *You have no idea how complicated it really is.*

He stepped back an inch. "I promise I'll slow down. Would that help?"

She chewed on her bottom lip. This was like a quiet tug-of-war. "I just hope you're not upset if I go out with other people, that's all."

He looked relieved. "So, you're saying you don't want to end this completely, right? We can still go out again sometime?"

She knew it was probably best to cut it off, but she'd still see him in English class twice a week. And she'd be lying if she said she didn't enjoy being with him. They had a connection, just not as strong as her and Jordan's connection.

"Sure," she said, nodding. "That's what I'm saying."

"Perfect." He smiled softly, looking as if he wanted to reach out and touch her again. He refrained. "I'll see you Monday?"

"Yeah, Monday." She nodded goodbye as he took off toward his class. She went in the opposite direction. On her way, she pulled out her notebook for keeping track of people and events and stopped for a moment to write about what had just happened.

Halfway through the entry, she paused.

*"Look at you, Ave. Seriously. Just look,"* Tam's voice echoed through her head.

For a long moment, she saw her Post-it notes scattered across the table next to her turkey sandwich. She saw her life in those Post-its. They had been her mom's idea, and they had always worked better than any other reminder system she'd ever tried. The notebooks worked for recording memories. She loved cataloging everything after it had happened, knowing it was forever tucked away on paper. But was it the best way to live? Maybe writing everything down was ruling her life as much as Tam had ruled her life back in high school.

Then a thought occurred to her—one that frightened her to her very core. What if she threw it all away, just as she had planned when she'd first moved here? She was putting a stop to hurting the guys in her life, as backward as it seemed. So why not put a stop to other things? Maybe it was worth a shot. After all, she hadn't had any problems in classes yet. She could still take notes for school, but the Post-its could go. The notebook in her hands could go.

Walking quickly to a trashcan, she almost tossed the notebook into the gaping hole filled with empty cans and food wrappers. Her fingers trembled. No, no she couldn't. It would be like throwing away everything her mother had taught her. She would be throwing away memories. The notebook she held was filled with everything from the past few weeks—details about Kent, Jordan, and Owen. There were entire paragraphs about all the kissing. Details about Kent's Jeep and Jordan's chocolate torte. A description of Lake Union and the city lights reflecting off the water at night. She wouldn't have remembered the name of that lake if she hadn't written about it that night before bed. Would she?

That was the thing. She had no idea. It made her question how well she really knew herself without the notebooks and Post-its and reminders. But there were things she remembered very well. Her father, for one, and he'd been gone for so long. She could remember him like everything had happened yesterday, like her brain knew if it got rid of anything concerning him, she'd shut down. Maybe subconsciously something was going on there. Maybe it was a way for her to fix her forgetfulness for good.

The notebook slipped from her fingers, landing in the trashcan with a thud. Her heart nearly stopped, but before she could change her mind she forced herself to walk away. At every trashcan along the way to her next class, she pulled out another notebook and dropped it in. She threw in her multi-colored stacks of Post-its, including the yellow Post-it that reminded her to mail a birthday card to her mom and to buy Chloe a present.

She would remember.

For the rest of the day, Avery prioritized things in her head the same way she would on paper. There was work, which had become uncomfortably lonely down in that dank room all by herself. Heaven was coming into work before or after Avery's shift, leaving half-finished projects on the table. Avery wanted to confront her and tell her she wasn't going to date Jordan anymore, but the truth was she hadn't seen him since that night. She had no idea where things stood with him.

Next on her list was dinner with Chloe. After that, create an excuse to go out shopping alone so she could find a present for tomorrow. If she kept everything simple, it wasn't difficult to remember the things she had to do.

"You sure you don't want a ride?" Chloe asked as Avery washed the dinner dishes in the sink. "Or you can take my car if you want, I don't mind."

Avery scrubbed at a stubborn spot on a pan and shrugged. "No, the bus is fine. I don't know the roads that well, anyway, and parking can be a pain."

"There's always GPS on your phone for directions."

"I know, but it's fine, I promise. I'll just take the bus. I want to get out and see the city a little and not have to worry about driving."

"Okay." Chloe leaned against the counter, watching Avery. "I'll probably be in bed by the time you get back."

Avery nodded. "I'll give you a call if I need anything."

Later, after she'd finished up a few homework assignments, Avery slipped on a pair of walking shoes and a jacket and walked to the bus stop a block away. The sun had gone down, leaving the sky a light gray clouded over with some nonthreatening rainclouds.

Nobody was at the bus stop, and as she waited she almost pulled out her phone to check her reminder list for anything she might have missed. No. She wouldn't check it. She could remember things. She could.

Before the bus arrived, the familiar rumble of a bullet bike grew closer. Avery's heart thumped a few times as she looked up to see Jordan approaching, probably coming home from work. He drove by, doing a double take as he passed, and then slowed down. Making a U-turn, he drove back to the bus stop and pulled up to the curb right in front of her. She couldn't help but smile. He looked so good on that bike in a suit and tie, even with a helmet over his head.

"Ave," he said, lifting his visor. "Where you going?"

She looked up to see the bus approaching a few blocks down. "Heading into town for some shopping. I need to get my aunt a birthday present."

He nodded and looked over his shoulder at the bus. "Do you want a ride? The bus isn't fun at all."

Laughing, she shifted her feet and remembered the thrill she'd felt riding on the back of Jordan's bike.

"So, you're saying you want to shop with me?" she asked, raising an eyebrow. "Or are you just going to drop me off somewhere?"

He pulled off his helmet and ran a hand through his flattened hair. "No, I'll keep you company. Where do you want to go?"

"Downtown to Westlake."

"No problem. Maybe we can get a coffee or something—or, if you want, I can take you down to the Market. It's right there. Lots of shops there too, but a lot of them might be closed this late. Maybe another night, earlier?"

"Um, sure, I guess."

"So, the mall tonight, then?"

He looked so hopeful. What was she doing? This was not the way to end things with him. She'd managed to straighten things out with Kent and Owen, so why not Jordan?

"Yeah, a ride would be great."

A grin spread across his face. "Good. Hop on and we'll stop by my house for another helmet."

Before she knew what was happening, they were on I-5 heading into downtown. The cool night air whipped her hair against her back, and she held on to Jordan as tightly as she could. The freeway flew beneath them, the bike an extension of Jordan's movements. When he tilted his body, the bike tilted with him. Changing lanes, he zipped through traffic, and they were soon pulling into a parking garage at the shopping center.

Avery pulled off her helmet and breathed a sigh of relief as she stepped onto firm ground.

"I think I could get used to that," she laughed, trying to pull her fingers through her hair, "but my hair, not so much. It'll take three hours to brush out all these tangles."

Jordan laughed and took her helmet, locking both helmets to the bike before they walked into the shopping center and Avery led him into a candy store.

"Does your aunt have a sweet tooth?" Jordan asked as she browsed the bins filled with odd assortments of gummy candies and jellybeans.

"I honestly have no idea," she mumbled, stopping in front of a little display of rock candy suckers. Each stick was at least six inches long, covered in square crystals all stuck together. She pulled a green one off the display and twirled it in her fingers, reliving a day with her father when she was little. He'd bought her one of these. It was really the only thing she remembered about that day, besides her dad's smile and the way he'd lifted her onto his shoulders so she could see everything as they walked and she ate the sucker.

"Do you want that?" Jordan asked, inching closer.

"What? Oh, maybe." She held on to the sucker and kept walking through the store, taking in the smell of sugar, the echoes of the mall just outside the glass walls, the feel of the sucker leaving her hand as Jordan gave it to the cashier so he could pay for it. Not that she'd asked him to pay for it, but he seemed pretty intent, so she let him.

Pulling him into store after store, she licked the sucker as he plucked sour jellybeans from a bag he'd bought for himself. For an hour, she let her mind wander through a million things, none of them having to do with the hot guy in a suit at her side. She liked the way he stuck right by her, acting interested, but she couldn't bring herself all the way into the moment. For some reason, trying to find Chloe a present made her distant. She kept thinking about W and what Chloe had lost, and about her mom and how every phone call now got shorter and shorter. Granted, it was only a few weeks into the quarter, but at this rate Avery feared she and her mother wouldn't even be calling each other by the end.

What had happened to clinging to each other so her dad's death didn't hurt so much? It was as if she'd not only dumped her notebooks into the trashcan yesterday, but something else too. Something she couldn't ever get back.

"How's your coffee?" Jordan asked after they'd settled themselves at a table in a nearby coffee shop.

"It's good, thanks." She sipped her coffee and looked out the window at buses driving by, their taillights leaving streaks of red in her vision.

"Avery?"

She looked up at Jordan. He'd taken off his tie earlier and rolled it up in his suit coat pocket. Looking at his shirt collar, she remembered trailing her hand down his chest and the weight of him on top of her. It had only been a few days ago, but it felt like forever. She was already hurting him, she could tell. Her distance was confusing him. It was confusing her too, but not in the way she'd expected.

"I'm fine," she said softly.

He watched her for a moment, as if trying to figure out a puzzle. "I know we're not together," he finally said, "but I'm here for you anyway. I can tell something's wrong. Do you want to talk about it?"

"I miss my dad," she whispered down at her coffee, afraid to look Jordan in the eyes. "I miss my mom, too, even though she's still alive and only a few hours away. I know I sound childish, but it hurts, and I—" She looked up at him, meeting his eyes as red and yellow lights from the traffic slid across his face. "I'm afraid I'm going to hurt you, Jordan. I like you a lot and I don't want to hurt you. I already told you about Kent and Owen, but there's something I haven't told you."

Could she tell him? She wanted to, so badly. She thought about her journal falling into the trashcan, about Tam telling her she hadn't changed one bit, and she knew that if anything was going to change, it had to start here.

"What didn't you tell me?" He leaned forward, pushing aside his coffee.

"I didn't tell you that I mixed you up with them."

His brow furrowed. "Huh?"

Panicking for a moment, she glanced out the window and counted to twenty. Would she sound completely ridiculous?

"I forget things really easily," she explained in a breathless voice, meeting his eyes again. "It's not something I tell many people. I forget faces and names, and for a little while, I thought you and Kent and Owen were one person. When I realized my mistake, it was too late, and that's how ... how I ended up liking all three of you. I'm sorry. I know it sounds stupid, but I—"

"Avery, slow down. It's okay."

A smile lifted his lips, and she was pretty sure it wasn't an amused smile, but one of relief.

"No, listen," she said before her courage drained completely dry. "I don't want to end up hurting you. You've been hurt enough with your wife's death." She put a hand to her forehead. "I can't remember her name."

His smile fell. "Callie."

"Yes, Callie. See, I've hurt a lot of people on accident. If you're looking for someone solid you can count on ... I'm ... I'm not that person. I know how long you've been alone now, and you say I'm different, but I—"

"Avery, I said it's okay." He reached out and touched her wrist, brushing his fingers over her watch, just as Kent had done. "I'm not expecting anything, okay? Giving you a ride here isn't something you have to repay me for, and I've already told you dinner this Friday isn't something you have to do if you don't want to."

She'd forgotten about the dinner on Friday. She blinked.

"Have you told Kent and Owen what you just told me?" he asked.

She shook her head.

"Oh, okay." Sitting back in his chair, he wet his lips and looked out the window. Now it was his turn to be distant.

"You don't think I'm crazy?" she asked, confused. It was as if she'd thrown a great weight off her shoulders. She felt relieved but anxious.

"Crazy?" He looked away from the window and gave her an understanding smile. "No, not at all. I kind of figured you had a problem remembering things already."

*Oh, no.* "You did?"

"Yeah. I've noticed you repeat things a lot, but it's no big deal." He flashed her a smile. "I think it's endearing."

Tam had thought her forgetfulness was endearing, too, and that hadn't carried over when jealousy entered the equation.

"Well, you've been warned," she said. "So don't forget it."

His eyes twinkled over his coffee cup. "Even I forget things sometimes, but I don't think I'll ever forget that you mixed me up with Kent. How that's even possible, I have no idea."

She sighed. "I think I'm attracted to blondish hair and blue eyes. You all have that going on."

"Kent's eyes are more gray, aren't they?"

She squinted, trying to remember Kent's eyes. His eyes or Owen's eyes had dark blue rims around a lighter blue iris, but she couldn't remember whose was whose. She had probably written it down in her notebook, but it was too late to look that up now.

"I honestly don't know," she mumbled.

"And Kent's hair isn't really that light, is it? It's more like a dark blond, I guess. I just can't see how we look even remotely alike."

He was teasing her now, and she set down her cup and rolled her eyes. "It happened, okay? If you want me to go out with you on Friday, you can't tease me about this. And don't tell anyone, please. Especially Kent. Heaven knows, but don't talk to her about it."

"Oh, Heaven," he laughed. "She was still at my house when I got home on Tuesday. She told me I won't win the challenge if it's you I bring on Friday. She said it won't count unless we're dating exclusively. She's just being a brat so don't worry about her. I'd still like you to come."

Avery folded her arms. "And if we were dating exclusively, what then? Would you get some sort of prize or something?"

"I would get the satisfaction of knowing I met her challenge, but I'll feel like I've met it either way, so don't worry. We don't have to be dating."

She wondered if hanging out with him was the same as dating. Probably not. As they rode back home, she tried not to love the way it felt to hold on to him. He was confident and in control about everything in his life, even the hard things he'd gone through. It was impossible not to love the way it felt to be wrapped around someone like that. She had told him about her forgetfulness—about one of the most embarrassing mistakes she'd ever made—and he'd shrugged it off. She supposed that compared to losing a spouse from cancer, her little weaknesses were insignificant to him. He probably saw the world on a much larger scale. It was something she wanted in her own life, but she wasn't sure she wanted to cross the bridges it might take to get there.

# ❖ 18 ❖

The hardest thing about Avery's mother's birthday was how empty it felt now that her dad was gone. It didn't matter that her mom had told Avery not to worry about celebrating it, or even remembering it anymore. It didn't matter that her dad had been deployed during several of her birthdays in the past. It came no matter what. Just like her dad's birthday. Just like the anniversary of his death.

When Avery rolled over in bed Saturday morning her heart felt heavy with grief. She slid her eyes past the picture of her dad and the marlin to the neatly wrapped present she'd bought for Chloe last night. She had picked out a picture frame—probably the most boring, thoughtless gift she'd ever chosen. But inside the card taped to the front she'd written that she was going to hire a photographer to take a picture of her and Chloe together, aunt and niece, because there were no photos of her and Chloe on the already cluttered walls. It had literally been the only thing Avery could think of to buy her last night. Jordan said it was a thoughtful gift.

Padding into the kitchen, Avery wasn't surprised to see Chloe busy making breakfast, just like any other Saturday.

"I should make you breakfast today," Avery said, yawning as she sat down at the table and poured herself a glass of orange juice.

Chloe shrugged and slid a muffin from the tin she'd just pulled from the oven. "You know I love cooking for you."

Avery smiled. Her mother liked to cook too, but not with as much enthusiasm as Chloe. She wondered if they even called each other on their birthday.

"Honey butter or peach jam?" Chloe asked as she split the muffin with a butter knife.

"The butter sounds good."

A moment later, Chloe set the plate in front of Avery and sat down with a cup of coffee. "What are your plans today? School work or more dates?"

Avery realized those were pretty much the only things she ever did lately. She took a big bite of muffin, wondering when the right time would be to give Chloe her present. She swallowed. "I thought we could spend the day together after I call Mom. Maybe we could go into town and you can show me some of your favorite places?"

Chloe's eyebrows went up. "No dates, then?"

"Nope. It's your day today."

"My day?" She took a long sip from her coffee, looking confused. "What do you mean? It's just another Saturday."

Another birthday ignorer. So be it.

Finishing her muffin, Avery wiped her mouth with a napkin and stood up to make herself a cup of coffee. "So? We can still spend the day together, right?"

"I'd like that ... if you're really sure about it. I mean, the only places you've wanted to be seen with me are the supermarket and campus."

Avery paused in the middle of grating her nutmeg. She hadn't thought of it that way, but Chloe was right. She'd been living here for a month now and she hadn't once asked Chloe to take her anywhere.

"School's been busy, that's all," Avery explained, finishing with the nutmeg.

"Not to mention the boys," Chloe laughed.

"I've only been on two dates. It's not that big of a deal."

Actually, it was a huge deal, but she was sure Chloe already knew that.

"I suppose not, but I'm happy you want to spend time with your boring old aunt."

"Then what should we do today? You pick." She almost added, "since it's your birthday," but decided to keep it low-key. They'd get to that later.

"Maybe lunch downtown? Some shopping?" Chloe's eyes looked brighter and brighter every second. Avery sat down and sipped at her coffee, her heart warming up at the sight. Chloe was so easy to please. Unlike her mom, who was picky about too many things.

Chloe clapped her hands together. "Maybe after that we'll head over to Bainbridge Island for dinner. There's a new art museum there, and some great bookstores. We could see a movie. You in the mood for that?"

Avery smiled. "Anything you want, Chloe. Let me go call Mom and then we can get going."

In her bedroom, she changed her clothes and sat in front of her closet to look for a pair of shoes as she waited for her mom to answer the phone.

"Hey, Avery!"

"Hi, Mom. So, I, uh ... I forgot to send you something for today." Avery pushed aside a pair of boots and looked for her favorite striped flats.

"For today?" her mom laughed. "What do you mean?"

Her heart sinking, she grabbed the flats and set them in her lap. "Your birthday. I was going to send you a card, but I forgot to do it in time. I know you hate your birthday and everything, but I—"

"Honey, my birthday is next Saturday."

There was a long pause as Avery let the information seep in.

"Oh, honey, you're so cute when you mix up your dates," her mom said.

More silence. Avery didn't know what to say. How could she have been so stupid? All that worrying over nothing when she'd had a whole extra week to get a card sent off and buy something for Chloe. Why hadn't she checked it on her phone calendar? She had only written "Saturday" on the Post-it reminder, which had been thrown out with the others. Of course she'd mixed it all up.

"I'm sorry, Mom."

"Don't worry about it. Did you do something for Chloe too?"

"I bought her a present, but I haven't given it to her yet."

"Then she'll never know you got it wrong, right?"

Her mother was taking on the tone Avery had loved growing up—the tone that said it was okay for her to make mistakes and feel stupid because it would all work out in the end. Now, however, she resented it with every fiber of her being. She didn't want it to be okay. Getting stuff wrong like this—over and over and over—wasn't okay.

She quickly changed the subject, and after fifteen minutes of talking about school and her mom's new illustration project, she said goodbye and slipped on her favorite pair of flats. At least, she'd thought they were her favorite. Halfway through Bainbridge Island she had blisters on her heels.

***

For the next week, Avery concentrated on school and nothing else. It was difficult to hold everything together without her notebooks and Post-its. She had her class notebooks, of course—she couldn't survive school without those—but when it came to social things, she'd completely given up writing anything down.

Kent sat next to her in class on Monday and they had some sort of conversation she had forgotten by Friday. She studied with Owen on Tuesday and Thursday, taking advantage of the nice weather to eat hot dogs beneath the cherry trees. She couldn't remember much of those conversations either—only that Owen was trying really hard not to give her the impression that he wanted more than friendship. She knew he wanted more, but keeping him at a distance was for his own good. Deep down she knew she'd already chosen Jordan. Her relationship with him was like riding on the back of his bike. It was new and exciting and scared the hell out of her at the same time.

The most frightening thing of all was how badly she wanted more.

But then she would remember Callie and it would all slip away.

She couldn't hurt him, and she knew without a doubt that her forgetfulness would hurt him somewhere down the line, no matter how much he said he understood. It was as inevitable as rain in Seattle. Her only hope was to fix her forgetfulness, something she'd at least taken the first step toward by throwing away all those notebooks. Her brain was a muscle. She'd train it to remember, and then maybe, just maybe, things could work with Jordan.

She smiled to herself as she walked up the stairs to her biology class on Friday. This was where she had run into him two weeks ago, where she'd been mortified that her Post-its had stuck to his leg. It made her laugh now, and she was thrilled by how much she remembered from that encounter. She remembered the cactus, his filed fingernails, how nervous he'd seemed when he asked her to his party.

Reaching the top of the stairs, she looked down the hall and paused. Her smile fell as she saw Tam leaning against the wall, right next to Avery's classroom door.

"Tam." Avery gritted her teeth. *Acknowledge her and walk into class. Easy.*

"Hey, wait." Tam grabbed Avery's arm.

Avery stopped in her tracks. Class would start in three minutes and she didn't want to be late. "I don't want to talk to you," she growled, ripping free from Tam's hold. "You made it clear you don't want anything to do with me since I'm 'still the same old Avery.'"

She should have gone into class, but curiosity got the best of her and she waited for a response. Tam looked like she always looked. Long eyelashes. Dark eyeliner. It was maddening how good she looked. Put together and confident, as usual.

"I'm sorry I said that," Tam said, glancing at the floor. "I'm sorry about everything our senior year. I feel bad about all of it, even if you made mistakes too."

Avery adjusted the strap on her shoulder and shifted her weight. It was true that she'd made mistakes. She'd kissed Ryan—right in front of Tam, no less. It was a cold, hard fact. "What are you saying?"

Tam shrugged. "I just wanted to say I'm sorry."

"That's it?" Avery tilted her head and folded her arms. It was something she thought she'd never hear from Tam. "Apology accepted. I'm sorry too, for what it's worth. Ryan liked both of us. It was a bad situation."

"Yeah, it was." Tam let out a heavy sigh. "I know you have to get to class, but I had to let you know. I'm sorry—about everything. It seems so juvenile now, you know?"

Avery wasn't sure if she completely agreed on that point, but she nodded anyway. "I'll see you around," she said, and grabbed the door handle. Something about the whole situation felt too fast, too forced.

"Oh, wait. This is for you." Tam held out a Post-it note. "There's no official invitation, but I thought I'd write it down for you. It's a Halloween party next Friday night—*not* over twenty-one. Wear a costume if you want." She smiled weakly, and Avery took the Post-it. Was this a setup of some sort? She wanted to believe Tam's apology was sincere, but warning flags were shooting up everywhere.

"Where's this at?" she asked, looking at Tam's pretty cursive writing.

"Over in Ballard. My dorm mate's sister has a house there. I thought it would be good for us to go together, just like old times. I promise I won't try to set you up with anyone."

Avery almost laughed, but she couldn't quite manage it. "How are you getting there?"

"Dorm mate has a car. Do you want us to pick you up?"

"I ... guess so."

"Okay, text me your address."

Maybe it was a bad idea, but she figured she could pull out later if she didn't feel up to it. All she wanted to do right now was get rid of Tam so she could think about what had just happened. She looked down at her watch. "Gotta get to class," she said, forcing a smile. "See you around."

"Yeah, see you." Tam's eyes softened, her entire expression almost pleading. "I really am sorry," she said, her voice cracking. "I'm trying to change."

Avery twisted the knob on the door, her mind reeling. "Are you saying I should change too? Since you're being so noble about all of this now?" *Completely out of the blue.*

Tam stepped back. "That's not it at all."

"Well, like I said, see you around."

Avery walked into class, her heart pounding. The world felt upside down.

# ❧ 19 ❧

Avery was halfway through dinner when she remembered it was Friday. *The* Friday she was supposed to go on a date with Jordan and his parents.

"Oh, no," she gasped as she stared down at her plate. "I forgot."

"Oh?" Chloe twirled her fork through her pasta. "What did you forget?"

"A date."

"With who?"

"Jordan, and it's supposed to be a dinner date."

Chloe set down her fork. "Oh ... well, you don't have to finish if you don't want to. I won't be offended."

"He hasn't even called me or texted. Maybe it isn't happening." She pulled out her phone, only to find that he had texted her three hours ago. Go figure.

She'd been so caught up in worrying about Tam and the stupid Halloween party next weekend that she hadn't even bothered checking her phone.

*I'll pick you up at 7:30 or you can walk over to my place. We'll be riding in my sister's car. Hope that's okay. And thanks again for doing this. I owe you.*

Lovely. She checked the time. 7:00.

"I've got half an hour to get ready," she said, pushing away her plate and standing. "Sorry, Chloe."

Chloe waved her hand. "Go!"

Avery changed into the yellow dress that showed off her legs. She pulled on a cardigan and swung her purse over her shoulder. She yelled goodbye to Chloe and promised she'd do the dishes when she got home.

"Don't worry about it!" Chloe yelled from the kitchen. "Have fun!"

Avery headed out the door and spotted Jordan on his front porch steps, dressed in his usual three-piece suit. He looked so good she wanted to kiss him right then and there. Then she remembered they weren't on those terms anymore. In fact, she had no idea what terms they were on. He probably didn't either.

"Hi," she said, giving him a little wave as she cleared the bushes dividing the two properties.

He looked up from his phone and grinned. "You look fantastic. Is that the dress you wore to my party?"

"Yeah. I can't believe you remembered that."

He cleared his throat and stood. "Heaven should be here in a minute. Are you two ... have you ..."

"I haven't seen her since that night in your living room. I have no idea."

"Oh, this should be fun." He sat back down on the steps. "Have a seat while we wait."

"Sure." Sitting next to him, she put her purse in her lap and arranged her dress so she wasn't flashing the street. She glanced at Jordan's clean-shaven jaw and then at his fingernails. They were filed and smooth. He shifted across the step, running a finger along a gray pinstripe on his slacks. She looked away, blushing as she remembered him tracing the pinstripes on her bra.

"H-how've you been?" she asked as she twisted a piece of hair around her index finger.

"All right, I guess. My job isn't that exciting."

"I thought you said you like it."

She finally lifted her eyes to his. They were so blue—bluer than Kent or Owen's.

"I do, but work is work. Sometimes I just want a week off, that's all. Sometimes I like to spend more time with my friends."

Those blue eyes gleamed, and she blushed again. Why the hell was she blushing? "You want to throw another party, is that it?"

He smirked. "Heh, yeah. Those parties are fun. They were kind of what helped me get over Cal—"

He stopped short and looked away.

"Callie?" she asked, proud of herself for remembering the name.

"Yeah. After she died I didn't want to be around anyone. I hid away for a long time, but then I started making some new friends and they all liked to drink, and the parties just kind of evolved. It's not that I'm that likeable. I just happen to have a house and enough money to pay for the booze."

She laughed, but it died quickly. "Did being around people help?"

"It did. I like to see people happy." He started tracing the pinstripes on his pants again. She wanted to take his hand and hold it. She wanted to tell him it was an admirable trait to like seeing people happy. Sometimes it seemed like that's all anyone wanted until they weren't happy themselves, and then they wanted the world to be miserable with them. Jordan, however, seemed to have thrived on the opposite.

"Here comes Heaven. You ready for this?"

A dark green BMW pulled up to the curb. Heaven's bright red dreadlocks were visible even through the tinted windows.

"I thought she'd be more the Seventies Volkswagen bus type," Avery whispered as they walked across the lawn.

"The BMW was a leftover from the divorce," he said. "It was in both my parents' names, and instead of fighting over it they just gave it to Heaven."

247

"Nice."

"There was a lot of that kind of fallout," he mumbled. "Now I get to remind myself of the whole ordeal every time I use the china Mom gave me or ride in this stupid BMW."

"That sucks."

"Yeah."

He opened the passenger side door and motioned for her to get inside. Right next to Heaven. Great. Jordan got in the backseat and Heaven pulled away from the curb, her jaw tight.

"Okay, you two," Jordan grumbled as he leaned forward between the two front seats. "No hating each other from here on out. Heaven, you know how these dinners work."

She tightened her grip on the steering wheel and then relaxed. "I've been avoiding Avery at the library for almost two weeks. I think I've got the anger out of my system."

Avery looked questioningly at Jordan, who smiled and leaned back in his seat. "Just like my little sis—step away for a bit and you're fine."

"I was worried she was going to hurt you, Jordan."

"She told me what happened. It's fine."

Heaven grunted. "Avery, if you're going to hang around me and Jordan, get used to this. All we ever do is argue."

Jordan kept his eyes on his sister, and Avery suddenly understood why he'd wanted to fulfill her challenge to bring a date tonight. The juvenile rivalry between them was so palpable it could be cut with a knife.

"So, Heaven," Jordan said with a smirk of his own. "Where's *your* date."

The car slowed a little. "I couldn't get one," she snapped. "You win."

*✶*

Avery quickly discovered why Heaven was the way she was. Her mother, who introduced herself as Karma, was just like her. No dreadlocks or black clothes, but in personality they were the spitting image of each other— unexpected mood swings, bluntness, easygoing and uptight at the same time. Avery had a feeling Jordan was just like his dad, but since he hadn't shown up yet, she had to wait to find out.

"He's not usually late," Karma said, checking her watch. She was across the table from Avery, and kept giving her an apologetic smile as she fiddled with her freshwater pearl necklace. "He can be such an ass about these dinners."

"Maybe his flight was late," Heaven said. "Don't be so hard on him, Mom."

249

Avery looked at all three of them one by one. "So, uh, does he not live here in Seattle?" She had assumed he did.

Karma shook her head. She had platinum blonde hair and dark, thin eyebrows. Avery had expected someone earthier, since she was a biology professor. "He lives in Chicago, but he flies here a few times a month. It's not a big deal." She leaned forward and rested her dainty chin on her knuckles. "Jordan tells me you want to go into botany. You're a freshman, right? Are you taking biology?"

"Oh, yeah, my advisor put me in with Professor Bell."

Karma let out a long sigh. "He's all right. Let me see if I can get you transferred to my class. Would you mind? What hour would you need?"

"The 11:45 block," she said, hoping that was correct without having to look at the schedule on her phone. "Monday through Friday." At least that wouldn't put her in Tam's class. She glanced at Jordan, who forced a smile. There was a lot behind his expression, as if he was apologizing and begging her forgiveness. She smiled back, trying to make it clear she was okay with this. He'd warned her his mom was controlling.

"Oh, that's perfect. I've got a class at that time." Karma pulled out a small notebook and jotted something down.

Avery cringed, thinking of her own notebooks probably sitting in a landfill by now. This whole night was either going to stick in her memory like glue or fade away into nothing.

Jordan nodded toward the front of the restaurant. "Dad's here."

"Oh, good, we can order," Karma said without even looking behind her shoulder for her ex-husband.

"Just call him Tim," Jordan said to Avery as a tall, thin man in his early fifties approached the table. He wore a sharp three-piece suit, charcoal gray. Not surprising. His hair was the same color as Jordan's, but combed in a more retro style. Avery thought he looked familiar, probably because she'd seen his picture somewhere before. If he was as rich as Jordan had implied, he was most likely a leader in the economic world.

"Hello," he said, smiling at Avery before acknowledging anyone else. "Are we lucky enough to have a guest this evening?" He turned to Jordan, expectant.

"Dad, this is Avery. She's my date tonight."

"A ... date?" Tim looked truly shocked but pleased, and Avery didn't miss the triumph on Heaven's face. "Well, that's lovely. Welcome, Avery." He reached a hand across the table, and she took it, impressed with his firm grip and the way he met her eyes.

*Tim.* She had to remember his name was Tim. So far she was doing all right.

A waiter pulled out Tim's chair for him. He ordered a bottle of champagne and then turned to his family, nodding a quick hello to his ex-wife.

"So, how did this happen?" he asked, looking bemused. "You must have stolen his heart, Avery. We've been trying to get Jordan to date for months now."

"More like years," Jordan interjected. "Please don't embarrass Avery. Can we just order?"

Tim leaned back, exchanging a polite smile with Karma. "Of course, but I have a bit of news first. Avery, I apologize for jumping right into family business."

"Oh, it's fine." She sat up straight and looked at Jordan, all of a sudden nervous. Why had he brought her here? She felt completely out of place.

Jordan, who must have sensed how uncomfortable she was, grabbed her hand underneath the table and squeezed. His touch reminded her yet again how much she wanted to be near him.

"I talked to some of your superiors," Tim said, looking at Jordan. "I got you the promotion you've been waiting for."

Jordan's hand stiffened, his expression wavering between shock, fear, and excitement. "Oh."

Tim guffawed. "Oh? That's all you can say?" Then he looked at Avery and his expression changed. "You're a student, aren't you, Avery?"

"I'm a freshman, sir."

He nodded and scratched a spot on his jaw. "I see."

Jordan slipped his hand from Avery's and leaned forward. "When would the position start?"

"As soon as you're ready. They need someone by the end of the month."

"That's less than two weeks."

Tim shrugged. Karma exchanged glances with Heaven. Avery stared at her cutlery. She had a feeling the family was getting entirely the wrong idea about her. Jordan had brought her to meet his parents, after all. But now something had turned the entire situation upside down, and she didn't even know what it was.

"I'll think about it," Jordan said, nodding as if to convince himself everything was under control. "Give me a few days?"

"Take your time. Some things are more important than a promotion." Tim looked at Avery again, hope filling his eyes.

Halfway through dinner, while Karma and Tim and Heaven were talking, Avery leaned over to Jordan and asked him what had happened, exactly.

"I asked for a promotion," he explained, turning to face her. He had a smudge of butter sauce on his bottom lip, and it was all she could do not to reach out and wipe it away. "Dad pulled some strings and it went through." He paused for a moment, studying her face. "It means I'd have to move to Chicago right away."

She stared at his lips, her skin clammy. "I thought I had all this time to figure things out," she said, "but I guess I was wrong."

Jordan kept looking at her. It was obvious he didn't know what to say. He finally let out a long breath. "We've only known each other a couple weeks," he said in a voice so quiet she hardly heard him. "I mean, I'd be willing to see how things go, but you said you don't want to rush things, so ..."

"Yeah, I did say that," she observed with a sigh as her eyes drifted to her plate. The stuffed flounder was beautiful, but it wasn't appetizing. Her stomach was still full of Chloe's pasta. "I mean, I keep thinking what it might be like if we just go for it, you know?"

"Go for ...?" Jordan's eyes widened, and Avery winced.

She picked up her fork to poke at the bed of asparagus beneath the flounder. "Not that. I meant ...Would I sound too much like my aunt Chloe if I said 'go steady'? I don't know how else to put it." She rolled her eyes at herself. "Gosh, I sound lame."

"No you don't," he laughed. "It sounds perfect to me. *Sayonara* to Kent and Owen?"

She looked straight into Jordan's eyes. "Yeah. *Sayonara*. I mean, they'll still be my friends, but ... yeah ... *sayonara* to dating."

And she meant it. When she looked over at Tim, he was eyeing the both of them with a smirk on his face. Avery blushed and turned back to Jordan.

"So, are these dinners a way to keep your dad in the picture?" she half-whispered.

"Yes, mostly Heaven's idea. She always wants to fix everything. This is the only way she knows how."

He touched her bare knee, right below the hem of her dress. His skin was warm, and heat ran all the way from her head to her toes. She smiled as he rubbed his thumb back and forth, looking into her eyes.

"She thinks if I get together with you, it will fix me," he said.

She touched his hand on her knee, feeling his wrist bones, running her fingers through the dips between his knuckles. "Are you still broken?"

"A little, yeah. I'm not sure I'll ever get over what happened, but I'm trying. I wanted a promotion so I could get out of Seattle and start over ... but then I met you."

"And you'd give up a promotion for some girl you've known less than a month?" she asked in a teasing tone. But they both knew she was serious.

He caught her fingers between his, inching closer. "I'm thinking about it. My dad can always help me get another promotion if I work hard enough for it."

"What if I hurt you? It might be in a different way than what happened with Callie, but still, my memory can't be trusted. I'm serious, Jordan."

Leaning forward, he brushed his lips across her cheek. He smelled like butter and wine, and she held tightly to his hand. "Sometimes getting hurt is worth it," he whispered.

❧

Avery should have been nervous on the way back home, but all she could think about was how good it felt when Jordan looked at her. He was serious about giving up a promotion. *For her.*

Sitting in the front seat of Heaven's car, Avery shook her head in disbelief. She hadn't even known him a month yet, but she'd seen enough in her life to know some things didn't require a lot of time. Broken hearts didn't take long. Mending them took a lot longer. But falling in love? That seemed to be different for every couple. No rules applied.

"Hope you two have a good night," Heaven chuckled as she pulled up to the curb in front of Jordan's house.

When Avery looked over at her, Heaven give her a wink. What did she think was going to happen?

"Good*night*, Heaven," Jordan said through his teeth as he got out of the car. Avery followed him.

"Like I said, I hope you two have a good night. Together." Heaven waved goodbye, a grin on her face as Jordan and Avery watched her drive away.

"Well, maybe she has a point," Jordan said, turning to Avery and pulling her into his arms. "You think?"

Looking from Chloe's house to his, Avery swallowed a lump in her throat. "I'm a virgin, Jordan," she whispered as her mouth went dry. "You know that, right?"

He squeezed her tighter. "I figured as much."

"You've figured a lot of things about me, haven't you? Did you figure you're only the third guy I've ever kissed?"

"Was Kent the second?" he asked, not looking hurt at all.

She shifted her eyes to the sidewalk. "Yeah."

"Avery," he said, forcefully enough for her to look back up into his eyes. He lifted a hand and touched her cheek. Soft. Understanding. "I'm not going to force you to do anything. If this is too fast for you, it's okay. But I need to know if you want to give us a try. This promotion isn't something I want to give up if you're having doubts, if you like Kent more than me, or if you want to keep dating other people."

She shook her head quickly. "I don't like Kent more than you. Not even close."

A smile melted his expression into relief. "Should we try this out for tonight? See how you feel after that?"

She wet her lips, her head spinning as her heart pounded in her chest. She wanted him more than she'd ever wanted anyone. She could overcome her anxiety. Nothing was standing in her way. He knew about her forgetfulness and he accepted it for what it was. He knew she'd kissed his friend and he didn't mind.

"I think I'm falling hard for you," she said softly. "I didn't even feel this way about Ryan."

"Who's Ryan?"

"A guy I'll have to tell you about sometime. It happened in high school."

"Oy," he laughed as he pulled his keys from his pocket and headed for the house. She followed him. "I have some of my own stories from back then."

"Mine are a lot more recent," she sighed as he opened the front door and they stepped inside. She slipped off her heels, as if it was the most natural thing in the world to make herself at home in his house. He flipped on the hallway light and then stood a few feet away from her, fiddling with his cufflinks. He looked as tense as she felt.

"You want to watch a movie?" he asked as he reached up to loosen his tie. "Would you mind if I go change first?"

She swallowed another lump that had formed in her throat. "How about if I help you change?"

*That's right—get right down to it.*

His face brightened, and it was then that she noticed a picture out of the corner of her eye. It was a wedding picture of Jordan and Callie. He had a past. It wasn't that she had forgotten, but in the midst of falling for him, it had been shoved to the back of her mind. He'd been married, and it felt as if she might seem immature to him—so naïve and inexperienced.

He noticed the direction of her gaze. "That's Callie," he said, lifting his hand toward the picture. When he turned back to her, his expression was solemn. "I'm sorry, Avery. I didn't think about how that might bother you. It's one of the reasons I've avoided relationships. It's some pretty heavy baggage, you know?"

"It doesn't bother me," she replied, stepping closer to him. "Like you told me before, everyone has problems."

He brushed his fingers across her hand. "You remembered something I said."

"I did, didn't I?"

He kissed her, and within two seconds flat she was lost to anything but him. He led her upstairs to his room where she slipped off her dress and helped him out of his suit, which took a lot longer than the dress.

"Don't worry about anything," he sighed into her ear as she fell back onto his bed, still in her underwear. His blankets smelled faintly of his cologne and the soap he used. He brushed some hair away from her face. "Pink bra today?" he asked, tracing his finger up one of the bra straps.

"Are you obsessed with bra colors?" she giggled.

"Maybe. Are you nervous?"

She nodded. "A little."

"Well, like I said, don't worry about anything, okay?"

She looked at his eyes sparkling in the dim light then moved her gaze around his room, noticing a fish tank on the far wall. It glowed blue as little fish zipped back and forth through the plants.

"You have fish?" she asked as he settled on top of her and started kissing her neck. The thin material of his boxer shorts brushed against her naked thighs, and she wrapped her trembling arms around him. She doubted her underwear would stay on long. Or his.

*Stay calm, Avery. Stay calm.*

"Yeah, I'll show them to you later," he mumbled against her neck.

"And there's the cactus you had the day I ran into you," she said, stretching a little to get a full view of the softball cactus sitting on a shelf above his bed. "Did your mom give it to you?"

He chuckled as he leaned on his arm and brushed the back of his hand across her cheek. "Yeah, she gave it to me."

"Why were you on campus that day?" she asked, truly curious, but also stalling because she couldn't believe she was practically naked on his bed with him on top of her. Her heart was going a billion miles an hour and she didn't know how to make it slow down. She was sure Jordan could feel it.

"I was dropping off some stuff she left here last time she came to dinner."

Avery nodded, appreciating the fact that he wasn't pushing her away from the conversation. "I like that you stay close to your parents. That's pretty cool."

Continuing to stroke her cheek as he gazed into her eyes, he nodded. "They've always been there for me. It's weird, but it's like their divorce brought us all closer together. The fighting stopped and we could all just be ourselves."

"Must be nice to know it doesn't have to be a huge mess."

"We still have our moments." He leaned down and started kissing her again, sliding his fingers underneath the hem of her panties to tug them down. She sucked in a breath and he stopped and looked her in the eyes again. "I haven't pressured you into this, have I?"

"Not at all," she answered firmly. "I'm just ridiculously nervous."

He held her gaze. He seemed so sure of himself, so understanding. "It's normal to be nervous the first time, but it's just me ... just plain old Jordan."

She exhaled and realized he was absolutely right. After that, his kisses melted her into a puddle of tranquility. This was it. It was happening. She'd feared it for so long it seemed silly now. It wasn't awkward or scary at all, probably because Jordan knew what he was doing. She tried not to think too much about that.

Halfway through, he cradled her close to him, his eyes filled with something deeper than she'd ever seen in anyone's eyes when they looked at her. He loved her, at least in that moment, and she finally knew what it was like to love someone the same way. She knew she'd never forget it no matter what happened.

# ·20·

For the next two days Avery lost track of time. She didn't check her phone. She forgot about Kent and Owen and Ryan. There was only Jordan. She wore a pair of his sweats and a T-shirt when he cooked her hot cereal and biscuits for breakfast. She brushed her hair with his comb. He pulled out a new toothbrush for her from a stash underneath his bathroom sink.

"I get a few every time I go to the dentist," he laughed. "I think I have thirty-five of them now. If an apocalypse happens, I'm covered in the toothbrush arena."

"Or the girlfriend-staying-for-the-weekend arena. You know I could just go get my own next door, right?"

"But then you'd have to leave." He pulled her into his arms and nuzzled her hair. "I don't want you to leave. I haven't been this happy in so long, Avery. I didn't think it was possible."

She trailed a finger up his bare back. "I didn't either."

"So, the promotion ... should I take it?" Pulling away to look her in the eyes, he waited for her answer.

"I can't decide that for you, Jordan."

He nodded. It was Sunday and he hadn't shaved at all.

"I'll tell my dad no to this one," he finally said, mostly to himself. "I don't want you to feel like any of this has to mess with your school schedule—and I can't do a long-distance relationship. That's what broke up my parents."

"Oh?"

"Yeah, Dad moved to Chicago and Mom didn't want to follow him. They tried to make it work for a while, but things got worse and worse until they separated for good. Sometimes I think it was just an excuse, but who knows." His shoulders slumped. "It hurt Heaven the most. She hates to see people she loves unhappy. She's been trying to get me together with someone for a solid year now."

"And look at you now." Avery twisted her fingers around the hair at the nape of his neck.

"Yeah." He leaned down to kiss her, but a moment later the doorbell rang.

"I'll bet that's Heaven," he mumbled against her mouth. "I texted her yesterday and told her not to walk in anymore."

"Do you want to answer it?" She rubbed her hips against his, trying to coax him to ignore everything but her.

"No way. She can come back later." With that, he scooped her into his arms and carried her to his bedroom.

A few hours later Avery realized that she'd missed her mom and Chloe's real birthday. So much for remembering things.

⁓⁓⁓

"Chloe?" Avery called out as she entered the house Sunday night. Her head was stuffed with memories of Jordan and his bed, his fish and the cactus, the food he'd made for her, how she hadn't spent two seconds away from him for two solid days. She had planned to spend another night there, but his boss had called and asked him to head out on a flight for Chicago ridiculously early the next morning— not for the promotion, but for some important meeting that would probably last all week. He said it was a regular occurrence for his job and joked about quitting. She kissed him goodbye and he promised to let her know when he'd be back. She nearly jumped out of her skin when Chloe appeared around the corner, her hair messier than usual.

"Where have you been?" Chloe gasped, her face full of worry. "I've tried to call you, text you, but you didn't answer. I called your mother, but she hasn't heard from you either."

Avery blinked a few times. Hadn't she told Chloe where she'd be? Apparently not.

"I was next door at Jordan's." She blushed and looked at the floor. "It was an amazing weekend. I'm sorry I didn't tell you I'd be gone. I ... forgot."

Which was the absolute truth.

Chloe's shoulders fell. "I knew you might run off for a day or two to spend time with friends once in a while, but I thought you'd tell me beforehand." Her expression relaxed as she rushed forward and gave Avery a quick hug. "I went over to Jordan's this afternoon. Rang the bell twice. I was starting to wonder if I should call the police." She laughed nervously.

Avery felt even guiltier than before, remembering how she and Jordan had ignored the bell. She'd forgotten Chloe's birthday yesterday *and* sent her into a panic for two days. "I'm so sorry, Chloe," she said, deflated. "For the first time in my life I have a real boyfriend. It made me forget about everything else, including your birthday."

Chloe's face brightened and she clapped her hands together. "You two are together? Exclusive? That's wonderful!"

"Yeah," Avery beamed. "It's really amazing."

"He can come over for dinner," Chloe said. "I'd like to get to know him if you're serious about him. Only ... please remember my rule about the bedroom." She cleared her throat and gestured down the hall.

*Don't forget that, Avery. Don't forget it. Don't forget it.*

"Won't be a problem," she said sternly, mostly to herself. "He lives next door anyway. I can go over there if we want to ... you know."

Chloe laughed. "Are you being safe?"

Avery's face turned hot as she remembered Jordan making sure they were safe every single time. Not that it was any of Chloe's business.

"Yes, we're being safe. Don't worry, Chloe. I'm going to go call Mom to tell her I'm sorry for missing her birthday yesterday. And if you'll wait a second, I have a present for you."

Chloe's eyebrows shot up. "You do?"

"Yep. I'm really sorry I missed it. I hope last weekend makes up for it?"

Chloe wrapped an arm around Avery's shoulder and led her into the kitchen. "You never have to make things up to me. Especially things you forget."

⚊⟩⟨⚊

The week dragged by without Jordan. Avery still sat next to Kent on Monday and Friday in English, and on Thursday she studied with Owen. Halfway through lunch, he asked her why she was so distant. She took a huge bite of hot dog and looked up at the Yoshino cherry trees which were now a mixture of bright yellow and gold. The ground was slowly becoming more and more covered with the leaves, but that didn't stop her and Owen from sitting outside if the weather was nice enough. Today was warm even though some light clouds diffused the sun.

"I'm dating someone," she finally said as she watched a leaf twirl down between them.

When she looked at him she found a huge grin on his face. "That's great. You seem a little sad, though."

Her shoulders relaxed. No wonder she liked him. It said a lot about him that he was truly happy for her. "He's gone for the week. I miss him."

"What's his name?"

"Jordan."

"Well, Jordan is a lucky guy." He dropped a few chips into his mouth. "I've been on a few dates, but nothing's really clicked yet."

"Oh?" She leaned forward, excited for him. "A biology major like me?"

"Not even close," he laughed. "One's a dance major, the other is engineering."

"Wow, *two* girls. Go, Owen." She grinned, not only because she was happy for him but because his dating experience made her feel better about liking multiple guys at once. It was normal. It didn't make her an awful person.

"Yeah, they're both pretty great." He caught her gaze and she realized he was silently saying, *"But not as great as you."* That wiped the grin off her face.

"So, you ready for your test tomorrow?" she asked, patting his book sitting between them on the grass.

"Getting there. Help me out a bit?"

"Sure thing."

The rest of the day slipped by, and before she was ready for it, Friday night stared her in the face. The week had been unbearably slow and fast at the same time. Halloween was next Wednesday, but it seemed everyone was holding parties the weekend before. Kent had invited her to one, but she'd turned him down. Tam texted her three times, reminding her to send her address so she and her friend could pick her up at nine.

"Fine," Avery mumbled to her phone as she finally responded to the third text during work. "I'll go."

"Go where?" Heaven asked. "Jordan's still gone, isn't he?"

"Yeah, this is some party my friend Tam wants me to go to."

*My friend Tam.* So that was what Tam was now? A friend again?

Avery hit send on the text and gritted her teeth. She didn't want to go to the party, but she knew Tam would take it as a slap in the face if she didn't go. She decided not to test the limits of Tam's supposedly heartfelt apology. The party was a surefire way to see if Tam was serious about renewing their friendship. If the party was some sort of trap to hurt Avery even more, she'd know it was time cut the strings for good. If it was a harmless party and a way for Tam to mend broken bonds, then maybe Avery could finally move on from all that pain and let things heal. It was a comforting thought—comforting enough to make her even a little excited.

"Is it a costume party?" Heaven asked. "It's probably a good thing Jordan isn't here if it is. He hates costume parties."

"Yeah, I'm not planning on staying long. I'm getting a ride with my friend, but if I get bored I'll catch the bus home."

"Good plan." She leaned back in her chair. "Are you going to give me any more details about you and Jordan?"

So far, Avery had only told her that she and Jordan had spent the weekend together, nothing more. Apparently, that was enough to ignite Heaven's hopes.

"I told you," Avery said, her cheeks warm, "we've decided to be together, so things should stay the same for a while, I hope. It's not like we're getting married or anything. We haven't even known each other a month yet. Besides, you know how careful he is with commitment."

"More than you'll ever know," Heaven said in a dark tone. "I'm glad you've decided on one guy, at least. That's a huge step forward, and I've noticed you got rid of some baggage." She nodded toward Avery's messenger bag on the floor, now much less bulky than before.

"Yeah, I decided to try relying on my memory instead of writing everything down. Not for class stuff, but everything else. So far it's been ... shaky. I forgot my mom and Chloe's birthday." She rolled her eyes at herself. "And I'm pretty sure there's other crap I'm forgetting too, but I'm happier not knowing what it is, I guess."

Avery glanced up from the strip of leather she was wrapping around a spine to find Heaven looking at her with a surprised expression.

"What?"

Heaven's lips turned up just a bit at the corners. "You're different than I thought," she said almost reverently. "I'm sorry for thinking otherwise."

"I didn't even know how you felt before, so it's fine." Avery turned back to the leather. "I guess."

"I mean, I'll still eat you alive if you hurt Jordan, but I'm thinking that's less likely to happen now."

Avery paused in her work. "I don't want to hurt him," she said gently. "I promise."

Heaven nodded. "I believe you."

—⟩|⟨—

The party was just as Avery had imagined: filled with people she didn't know, loud music, and a super-excited Tam dressed up as a belly dancer. She truly looked the part, Avery thought as she followed her up the porch and into the house. She hadn't bothered dressing up in a costume because she couldn't care less about impressing anyone at the party.

"You interested in meeting anyone?" Tam asked as soon as they were at the bar—a real in-home bar, Avery noticed, not just a cooler filled with ice and bottles of beer. At least the party seemed somewhat sophisticated. "I mean, I told you I wouldn't set you up with anyone, but if you're interested ..."

Tam leaned across the bar and asked the burly bartender, who looked about thirty-two, to make her a bourbon and beer mixture. He eyed her carefully. "I'll need to see some ID," he said, glancing at Avery. "Did Alex let you two in?"

Straightening her bare shoulders, Tam huffed. "Nobody was checking ID at the door."

He sniffed. "They should've been checking, but it ain't my party. Still, I can't serve you alcohol unless you can prove you're legal. If you want, I can make you a non-alcoholic drink."

"That'll be fine," Tam relented. "You want something, Ave?"

Avery nodded and turned to the bartender. "Can you do a Reno cocktail?" It was a non-alcoholic drink her mom ordered sometimes, and she'd always wanted to try it.

"Sure."

As Tam ordered her drink, Avery swept her gaze across the people in the room. Aside from the costumes, it looked a lot like the same sorts of people at Jordan's party. "So much for under twenty-one, huh?" she said. "You knew, didn't you?"

Tam made a *pshaw* sound and folded her arms. "Nobody told me there was an age limit," she said, shrugging. "My dorm mate said it would be fine since it's her sister's party. You know how these things go.

There's a rule, and then as the night goes on it all gets thrown out the window. It doesn't matter."

"So you're not planning on getting drunk tonight?"

"I guess not ... unless I can find someone to get real drinks for me."

Tam paid the bartender for both drinks and Avery followed her through a few rooms. The longer Avery walked around, sipping her overly tart drink, the more she felt out of place.

"You sure you don't want me to introduce you to someone?" Tam asked again, turning away from the guy she'd been talking to.

Avery tightened her grip on the stem of her cocktail glass and nodded. "I've been dating, Tam. It's okay. I don't need help in that department right now."

Tam's hopeful expression crumbled. "You're dating people? Really?"

Avery blinked. "Is that so hard to believe?"

"I don't know." Tam continued leading Avery through the house. "You really don't believe me about being sorry, do you?"

Avery stopped in her tracks and stared at the red liquid in her glass. "Not really," she said loudly enough to be heard over the music. "What did you expect? That I'd just welcome you back into my life? I feel bad about what happened too, you know, but what you did to me was ruthless. Even when it seemed to die down, people remembered. Nobody ever treated me the same."

"I know, and that's why I feel bad about it, all right? Things are different now," she said, looking at the people bustling around them.

"Why? Because you're not the queen anymore?"

Avery knew she'd hit her mark as soon as Tam's eyes hardened. "Yes, actually," she admitted, focusing on Avery with a hurt expression. "I'm so used to being important, you know? I feel like I'm nothing here. My dorm mates couldn't care less that I was the student body president. My professors don't care about my high school GPA. They don't care how many guys I kissed or how many times I organized blood drives. They just don't care."

And it was then that Avery realized her ex-best friend was opening up in front of her, right in the middle of a house full of people dressed as sexy bunnies, vampires, and zombies. Tam didn't want to hurt her; all she wanted was to hold on to the last shred of those glory days in high school—and Avery was that last shred.

"All that shit I cared about in high school means *nothing* here," Tam continued, her eyes glassy now. "I thought hurting you would make me feel better, and it never did. All it did was make me angrier because you just kept going." She lifted her eyes to Avery. "You just kept being *you*."

Avery screwed up her nose, confused. "What else could I have done?"

"I don't know. I expected you to break. I expected you to transfer to another school or something drastic like that. I didn't want to see you anymore, but I couldn't get away from you. The more I turned people against you, the more I couldn't get you out of my life."

"But you completely ignored me."

"I tried to, but it didn't work. I thought about you every single day."

Avery let out a heavy sigh. "I'm not sure what you want from me. I'm sorry you don't feel important now, but guess what? *Most people feel that way.* Maybe it's time you joined reality."

Tam's jaw went slack. "Is that what you think of me? That I'm some spoiled bitch?"

Avery kept her mouth closed, unable to think of anything that wouldn't sound completely heartless. It was true. Her opinion of Tam was pretty low, and she didn't know how to change it. She wasn't even sure if it was worth the effort now. The longer she looked at Tam's cheap costume, the way her bottom lip jutted out in a little pout, the way she looked as if someone had just slapped her, the more Avery wanted to walk away and never see her again. It would certainly be easier.

"I see," Tam finally said. "You still hate me."

"I don't *hate* you, Tam. It's just that you want to fix our friendship for completely selfish reasons. Can't you see that?"

"And your reasons for refusing to forgive me aren't selfish?"

Avery opened her mouth to say that of course she forgave her, but then she realized it would be a complete lie. She felt heat rising to her face. "I'll find my own way home," she said, giving Tam a death glare and walking away.

So much for repairing anything, but at least there hadn't been any fighting over her forgetfulness. That was an improvement. Sort of.

When she turned a corner she nearly ran into a guy. The last of her drink sloshed precariously close to the rim of her glass. "Sorry," she muttered, and turned to edge around him.

"Hey, you said you didn't want to come!"

Looking up, she saw Kent's gray eyes. Jordan was right. They weren't very blue, at least not in dim lighting. In English class they looked different.

"I didn't know this was the party you were inviting me to," she said. "Besides, we're under-aged, so we shouldn't even be here."

"Speak for yourself," he laughed. "I'm twenty-two, remember? I don't think they're being very strict, anyway." He nodded toward the bar. "How'd you get one?"

"It's non-alcoholic." She lifted her glass and gave him a weak smile. "I'm such a rebel."

He laughed. "Looks like it's almost gone. Want another one?"

"I guess so." She narrowed her eyes, wondering if she was forgetting something important. "I don't remember you telling me you're twenty-two. I thought you were a sophomore."

"Not everyone's as gung-ho as you," he chuckled as he took her glass. "I played around for a bit before I started school. I'll be right back."

She watched him head off to the bar, her drink in hand. Then she remembered that he'd been at Jordan's over twenty-one party. How had she not made that connection before? She felt so stupid.

When Kent returned, he handed her a fresh cocktail and sipped at his own drink. "Did you come with someone?" he asked, looking around.

"No, so if you can give me a ride home, I'd appreciate it."

He grinned. "Absolutely. I'll try not to drink too much."

"Perfect." She took a sip of her drink, wincing at how tart it was. This time it tasted a little stronger, but it was good. She smiled at Kent, happy that he was here so she didn't feel so alone. Still, she missed Jordan.

"Let's head over there," Kent said, nodding toward the room where the music originated.

"Sure, just a sec."

She reached into her back pocket to text Jordan, only to see that he'd already texted her earlier.

*I miss you so much. I'm at a stupid poker party my dad dragged me to. I'll be home Monday morning. Want to talk tonight around eleven?*

Grinning, she texted back that she was at a party too, and made a mental note to tell Kent she'd like to leave by ten thirty. Jordan answered right away.

*Don't mistake anyone for me and start making out with them.*

Chuckling, she took a few sips of her drink and texted back: *Oh, stop teasing me. You know I wouldn't do that.*

*Did you dress up?*

*I'm wearing a black T-shirt. Do not be impressed.*

The drink in her hand felt lighter, and she realized she'd already drunk most of it. Her head felt fuzzy. She spun around to find somewhere to put the glass.

"There you are," Kent said, approaching her. "I thought you said you'd follow me into the other room."

"Oh, I meant to." She looked around, confused. "I was texting Jordan."

Kent's smile fell. "Jordan? You mean Jordan Meadows? Your neighbor?"

"Yeah." She squinted. "He's your friend, right?"

"Yes, he is." He looked down at her drink. "You want some more?"

"Yeah, sure." She handed him the glass and turned back to her phone to check for a reply to her last text.

*I hope you have fun! Miss you lots. Talk to you tonight.*

*Looking forward to it.*

And what the heck? She might as well type it: *I love you.*

She slipped her phone into her back pocket and let out a long, happy sigh. Maybe he would think it was too much for a text. She hadn't told him she loved him yet, not in person. But it was the truth and she wanted him to know it ... unless he didn't reply to the text. Then what? She pulled her phone back out.

*I love you too, Avery.*

The music sounded louder in her head, but she didn't mind. At that moment, she didn't mind much of anything.

# · 21 ·

When Avery opened her eyes, the sun was streaming through her blinds. It was warm across her bed, and she pushed back her covers to find she was wearing her T-shirt and panties instead of pajamas. That was odd.

Rolling onto her side, she looked at her dad's picture and took a deep breath. Her head was pounding like a sledgehammer on an anvil and she couldn't string together more than two thoughts at a time. She groaned and wrapped an arm around her middle. She was going to puke.

Stumbling out of bed, she raced to the bathroom and retched into the toilet. Random scenes from the party flashed through her mind. The Reno cocktail. The tart flavor. Laughing with Kent in the middle of a strange crowd. She'd been happy for some reason, but everything was a blur. How had she gotten home?

Tam? No. They'd argued. Kent must have brought her home.

Dropping to her knees, she bent over the toilet again, her stomach roiling. More came up. Her head felt like it was going to split. Tears rolled down her face. She remembered sitting in Kent's Jeep. She'd asked him point-blank if he'd put alcohol in her drink and he told her he had. It was a clear memory, but only a snippet. He'd helped her inside the house, but there was nothing after that, just an empty space inside her head, like so many other memories fizzling out to nothing. This one, however, seemed darker than normal, as if it had never existed at all.

Wiping away some fresh tears, she stumbled to her feet and back to bed. When she woke again a few hours later, she checked her phone to find a message from Jordan.

*Have fun last night? I'm assuming you did since you didn't answer my call. I won the pot in a poker game, so I'm thinking maybe we should go to a fancy restaurant when I get back. What do you say?*

She stared at the words, her mind whirling. Poker game? She scrolled through previous texts and bits and pieces of last night came back to her. She'd told him that she loved him ... and then what?

She put down her phone and rubbed her forehead. Something bad had happened, but she didn't want to go there in her head. She couldn't. When she opened her eyes again, she noticed something on the floor near the foot of her bed—a small square package. Her stomach plummeted. That couldn't be what she thought it was. Scrambling off the bed, she scooped up the package. It was red with white lettering and ripped down the center. Empty.

Disgusted, she tossed it back onto the floor. A condom wrapper. In her room. How could she possibly forget about something like this? Had she slept with Kent? Why would she do that? Kent was only a friend now. She couldn't possibly have slept with him and forgotten about it. Or maybe she had ...

Her knees went weak, and she nearly collapsed to the floor before grabbing hold of the edge of her bed. What had she done? This was something she could never erase, even if she couldn't remember what had happened. It was an odd sensation, one that made her skin crawl. She stared down at her arms, dread clutching her insides as she imagined Kent touching her. Everywhere.

Feeling the sudden need for a shower, she ran into the bathroom and stepped under the stream of hot water. She tried to dig into the black memory again, but with no luck. When she ran a bar of soap over her body, she winced as something stung—a scratch on her left thigh. Jagged, as if she'd scraped a zipper across her skin. It was bright pink and raw.

Grabbing her hair in her hands, she squeezed the sides of her head and gritted her teeth. *Remember. Remember. Remember.*

She could remember everything about her father. She could remember plant names. She could remember all the details of being with Jordan. Why not this? Memories didn't just drift away into nothing. They were there, she was sure of it. She just had to find them. She thought about the journals she'd thrown away.

"He'll think I'm a total skank," she told the tiled wall. "I can't tell Jordan about this ..."

Could she?

Once she was out of the shower, she wrapped a towel around herself and picked up the condom wrapper again. A shudder ran down her spine as the possibilities of what could have happened ran circles around her. If it had been opened, wouldn't the actual used condom be lying around somewhere? She looked through the trashcan, which was mostly empty. It wasn't in there. She searched her floor by the bed then ripped off all her blankets and sheets, shaking them out one by one. Nothing. Maybe the wrapper had stuck to her shoe at the party and she'd tracked it inside. Maybe it didn't belong to anyone she knew at all.

Relief flooded her, but it didn't last long. She knew she wouldn't rest again until she figured this out.

◆—)◆(—◆

"Are you all right?" Chloe asked from the dining table when Avery made her way into the kitchen for a cup of coffee. Her stomach still didn't feel up to much more than that.

"Yeah, I've got a killer headache. I need coffee."

Chloe adjusted the reading glasses on her face and folded up the newspaper she'd been reading. "Don't take this the wrong way, honey, but you look like you have a hangover."

It was far more than a hangover. Avery clenched her teeth and opened the bag of coffee beans by the coffee maker. After taking a deep breath of the rich, warm aroma of the beans, she said, "Yeah, I thought I was drinking virgin cocktails last night, but some of them must've been the real thing. I've never ... well, I've never gotten drunk before, so I'm not used to this."

"The coffee should help," Chloe answered. "Anything you want to talk about?"

"No, it's fine. I won't be drinking again anytime soon." Avery let out a weak laugh and rolled her eyes at herself. She had to keep acting like nothing was wrong or Chloe would get suspicious.

Avery measured some coffee beans into the grinder and snapped on the lid. She pressed the lever, letting the chunky whir of blades against beans drown out everything else even though the noise made her headache fifteen times worse.

She stopped grinding and lifted the lid. The smell was even richer now—dark, like the black memory in her head. She grabbed a filter and put it into the coffee maker.

"Are you sure?" Chloe pressed. "You seem ... oh, never mind." She waved her hand in the air and turned back to her newspaper.

Her hand trembling, Avery cringed as she measured the coffee grinds into the filter. Chloe was far too observant. How was she going to get around this? Then she remembered Tam. "Just a fight with an old school friend I ran into," she said as dramatically as she could. "She's really a piece of work."

It was then that she saw a glass container out of the corner of her eye. It was a dry mix of ginger tea. Avery knew the taste of it on her tongue even though she didn't remember ever making a cup of it. It tasted a lot like lemons and the ginger was pleasantly sharp going down.

*"You're so beautiful."*

The words echoed in her mind, drifting up from the black memory, taunting her. Jordan had called her beautiful, but the voice she was remembering now wasn't his.

"That sounds daunting," Chloe laughed. "What happened?"

"Oh, it's over now," she answered, hoping to stop Chloe from pumping her for more information. "Seriously, I think my headache will get worse if I talk about it." She squeezed her eyes shut.

"It's not anything to do with Jordan?" Chloe persisted.

Avery's voice cracked as she replied, "This has nothing to do with Jordan."

"Oh?"

"It's ancient history." Her head pounded as she turned around to face Chloe. "Can we talk about this later? Please? I want coffee. That's all I can handle right now."

Chloe gave her a sympathetic smile over the top of her paper. "All right."

As Avery filled up the carafe with water, she wondered how she could face Jordan now, even if he did understand her memory problem. Who in their right mind would let something like this slide? Maybe if she called Kent and simply asked him what had happened, she'd have more to work with.

Once her coffee was ready, she skipped the nutmeg and carried her mug to her room. Her hands shook as she pulled out her phone and scrolled down to Kent in her contacts list. He might laugh at her. Or he might understand.

His phone rang and rang and rang, finally clicking over to his voicemail. She left a brief message asking him what had happened last night and saying she'd found something of his in her room, then hung up and sent him a text.

*I really need to talk to you. Call me?*

Next, she sent Jordan a text, telling him she was excited to see him on Monday, even though she was sick to her stomach over it. She had to get through the rest of today and Sunday. Both loomed ahead of her like a stormy sea. She knew Chloe's suspicions would only worsen.

Looking up at her dad's picture, Avery took in a deep breath. She needed a safe place and someone who wouldn't judge her or pry. She needed somewhere she could sort things out in her head. She thought of the hot dog food truck, of golden leaves falling to the ground, a pair of caring blue eyes.

# 22

"You really don't mind me staying here?" Avery asked as she walked down the hall of Owen's rented house. The air smelled like burnt toast and the carpet was in desperate need of a vacuum.

"Are you kidding? Girls stay here all the time," he laughed. "The guys won't mind, I promise. They can behave themselves, and if they don't, I'll kill them for you."

She smirked as he held open a bedroom door. "This is my space. I can sleep on the couch in the living room for as long as you're here."

"I can't take your whole room."

"Sure you can. You won't have any privacy otherwise, trust me. It's only until Jordan gets back, right?"

"Yeah, Monday."

"Then I'll be fine." He leaned against the doorframe and folded his arms. He seemed quite pleased to be helping her out.

"How's the dating coming along?" she asked as she set her bag on the floor next to his dresser. She'd packed quickly, knowing if Chloe found out she was leaving she'd try to get her to stay and talk about what was bothering her. She had waited until Chloe left for the store, and then she'd stuck a note on the front door saying she'd be back Monday night. The bus ride to Owen's street only took five minutes, so she wasn't even far away.

"I've got one tonight," Owen answered, smiling as he looked around his room. She could tell he was looking at it through a different pair of eyes now, wondering what she was going to think.

"Oh? What are you going to do?"

"Dinner and a movie. Are you sure you'll be okay here by yourself?"

"I'll be fine, I promise."

"There's a Greek place down the road if you get hungry. I can't guarantee there's anything in the fridge." He groaned to himself and glanced down the hallway. "Actually, don't even go into the kitchen if you know what's good for you. It's pretty bad."

"I can only imagine." A house full of college guys was an adventure in and of itself, she realized. But it was better than Chloe's nagging. It was incredibly nice of Owen to have answered her phone call and invite her over the second she said she was feeling lonely, stranded, and desperate to stay somewhere other than home.

"I should be back by eleven. If you need anything, I've got this." He lifted his phone and smiled. "I've got to get going. My cab should be here any minute. Can't really take my date out on the back of my bike."

"You're really sweet, Owen. Thanks." She rushed forward and hugged him, her heart pounding in her chest. It wasn't that she had romantic feelings for him. In fact, in the past few weeks as they'd studied together she'd become less attracted to him and more enamored of his friendship than anything else. The fact that he actually cared about her and respected her space and decisions was mind-blowing.

He wrapped his arms around her and squeezed once. "You're welcome. You sure you'll be fine?"

"Absolutely. I'll get some homework done."

He pulled away and nudged her shoulder. "Don't study too hard. It's Saturday. See you later."

When he was gone, Avery shut his bedroom door and poked around some of the stuff in his room. He was certainly into marine biology, just as he'd said. Posters covered his walls: pictures of the ocean, the periodic table, diagrammed fish. His little bookshelf was filled with school textbooks and no fiction. She didn't see a fish tank, which made her laugh. She turned to his bed. It was really the only comfortable place to sit. Settling there made her nervous for a moment, but it passed. She checked her phone and listened to a message from Chloe.

"Hi, Avery. I got your note on the door. Thanks for telling me where you'll be this time. Please let me know if there's anything I can do for you. Be safe, okay?"

Avery looked at her phone, her heart sinking. Why did she feel like she was always hurting people no matter what she did? She set her phone on Owen's brown quilt and started tracing the squares with her finger. There was something about that ginger tea jar that wouldn't stop nagging at her. She'd had a cup of it last night, she was sure of it now. She couldn't remember making it, but maybe Kent had?

She kept tracing the squares on the quilt, digging deeper into the black void of her memory. Like feathers floating in the air, fragments of images bounced up and down, taunting her. She reached for them, grabbing and catching nothing. Then one came into full focus and she gasped. She was riding in Kent's Jeep. He'd put the heater on, and she felt so tired. Good, but tired, as if someone had taken twenty pounds off her body and set her on a light, fluffy pillow to go to sleep. If she turned too fast she felt queasy, but other than that nothing felt bad. If anything, she felt happy.

The porch light was on when Kent pulled into the driveway. Then she was on the front steps and Kent was pulling a note off the door. Avery snatched it from his fingers and focused hard on the words.

*I went out with some friends. I'll be back around one.* XOXO

"Went out with friends?" she asked nobody in particular. "Chloe doesn't have friends."

"I'm sure she has friends," Kent chuckled, slipping the key from her hand and putting it into the lock. "She's a grown woman, isn't she?"

Then she was in the kitchen watching Kent from the kitchen table, thinking about him on the ice rink, sweat dripping down his brow. Mostly, she thought about how sad he had looked when he'd talked about his mom.

"Here, drink this. You'll feel better," he said, setting a cup of tea in front of her. The sharp scent of ginger and lemon surrounded her.

"Thanks, Kent. This is nice of you."

"No problem."

She sipped the hot drink, savoring the spiciness and warmth as it went down her throat. It felt soothing. Kent started talking about English class and then he laughed. She laughed too, even though she had no idea what was so funny.

"You're so beautiful," he said, reaching out to touch her cheek. She didn't try to stop him. His hand felt good there. It felt comforting, even though she wasn't sure why she needed to be comforted. Then out of nowhere she felt her pillow beneath her head. Kent was somewhere close by, his breath on her face, his hands tugging at something on her hips.

"What ... what's happening?" she mumbled, squeezing her eyes shut as the dizziness kept coming in waves.

"Shhh, relax."

She felt cold all of a sudden. More tugging. Something sharp scratched her thigh, but then Kent's lips were close to her ear. Hands pushed on her legs, forcing them apart. Pain. She tried to twist on her side, but couldn't move.

"Kent, I ..."

"Shhhh ..."

His voice floated around her like dandelion tufts in the wind. She reached out to touch one, but the room spun again. Something heavy pinned down her shoulders. Pain once more, deep in her abdomen, between her legs, then a low, deep groan in her ear. Tears slid down her cheeks. Something was terribly wrong. She knew what was happening, but it didn't make any sense. Kent wouldn't hurt her like this. He was her friend. The bed seemed to tilt on its side and she grabbed her blankets, afraid of rolling onto the floor. Crying out, she felt damp skin. A wrist. Fingers. Kent squeezed her hand.

"Go to sleep, Avery. You won't even remember this by morning."

—ᛣᛚᛤ—

The worst thing about memories was time. Some of Avery's fondest memories were so warped and tainted she often wasn't sure how truly accurate they were. They were worn-out boxes inside her head, opened over and over and over, while others remained closed. Locked.

When it came to the memory of what had happened last night, Avery wanted to lock it up and forget about it, but she knew it was impossible. It was becoming a box she opened up repeatedly in a desperate attempt to make sense of it. She wished Kent had been right about her forgetting it, but he'd underestimated her crazy brain and the way it stored information.

By 10:30 she was a wreck, bursting into tears then calming herself down only to remember what had happened all over again. How could she have been so stupid? So naïve? Or had Kent just been especially good at fooling her?

She stood in the middle of Owen's room, her arms wrapped tightly around herself as the sounds of his housemates reverberated outside the bedroom. She rushed forward and locked the door, her hands damp with sweat. There was laughing and a football game on TV. Somebody walked down the hall, passing the door. Each time she heard a noise, she took another step backward, finally ending up at the far wall, her body trembling as she sank to the floor and pressed her face to her knees. She kept her crying as quiet as possible, but the tears wouldn't stop. It had all been her fault. She'd been stupid to go to that party in the first place.

Hours seemed to pass as she cowered against the wall until somewhere past her muffled sobs she heard a soft rap on the door.

"Ave? You okay in there? I'm home."

Owen. She couldn't face him now. She couldn't face anyone. Her face turned hot as she stumbled to her feet and glanced out the window, wishing she could leave. Her crying must have been louder than she'd thought.

"I-I'm fine," she called out as steadily as she could. "I hope you had a good time."

There was a long pause. "You don't sound fine. Can you open the door? I won't come inside if you don't want."

She tensed as the memory of Kent pinning her down on the bed slammed into her like a freight train. "I ... I ..."

"Avery, please."

Slowly, each step heavy, she walked across the room and put her hand on the door lock. She clicked it to the right then twisted the knob, inching the door open until a thin sliver of space was between her and Owen. She could make out his nose and chin.

"Can I get you anything?" he asked. "The guys said they heard you crying in here. They said it's been going on for hours."

Great. The walls were probably as thin as paper. "I can't talk about it," she whispered as she ran a finger along the edge of the door.

"Do you have your phone? Do you need to call Jordan?"

Jordan. She hadn't even thought about calling him. She imagined telling him her disjointed memory. If she did tell him, she knew it couldn't be over the phone. But he wouldn't want to hear about it. Who would?

Taking a deep breath, she let go of the door and stepped backward. "Owen, I ..."

He opened the door, his face ashen as he looked at her. "You don't have to explain anything," he said gently, not making any move toward her. "I'll be here, okay? If you need anything, I'll be right here."

With that, he backed away until the door clicked shut. She rushed forward to lock it again. For a long moment she felt the same as when she'd sipped that ginger tea—as if the world was spinning out of control. Her mind was fuzzy and blank. When she turned to look out the window, reflections of the streetlights glistened on the road as rain drizzled from the sky. She shut her eyes and felt nothing.

━✦━

Avery had no idea what time it was when she woke up on Sunday. A blanket of dark clouds hid the sun. Rain pattered against Owen's window, sliding down the panes in crooked, transparent lines. Owen's bed smelled like bacon for some reason, or maybe that was coming from the kitchen. Her stomach growled, probably because she hadn't eaten since Friday evening. Groaning, she rolled over and tried to push away the memories of the party and Kent. She would get past this and move on. It was possible. It wasn't any worse than her father dying, and she'd finally learned how to deal with that.

When she made it to her feet, she rushed for the door so she could find the bathroom. She'd had to pee since last night, but she had been too frightened to leave the bedroom.

She unlocked the door and pulled it open, only to trip over something as soon as she stepped forward. She caught herself on the doorframe and looked down, confused. A grunt, and then the heavy thing on the floor moved.

"Owen?" she gasped as he rolled over to get out of the way. "What are you doing? You slept in the hallway?"

He leaned on an elbow, rubbing his right eye as he looked up at her. "Yeah," he answered through a yawn. "I told you I'd be right here."

"You're kidding, right?"

"Does it look like I'm kidding?"

At least he'd found a sleeping bag. Avery stared down at him, not sure if she should laugh or cry. "Well, thanks," she said. "I mean, seriously ... that was really nice of you."

"Not a problem. You want some breakfast? I guess the guys are attempting to cook bacon this morning. We're lucky they didn't party last night so they're not all hung over. Honestly, I think they're finally getting tired of it."

She laughed. "Breakfast sounds great, but I've got to find your bathroom first. Sorry."

"Oh, right. It's around the corner."

"Thanks."

When she'd finished in the bathroom and made sure she didn't look too much like a zombie, she found the kitchen and realized Owen hadn't been exaggerating yesterday. The sink was piled high with dirty dishes and the floor was splattered with something resembling dried spaghetti sauce covered in toast crumbs. The table seemed clean enough.

Three guys, all in boxer shorts, looked up as she entered. They didn't seem to mind a girl wandering into their kitchen, but they seemed surprised to see *her*, the girl they'd heard crying all night long. Owen was at the table with a bowl of cereal, his spoon halfway to his mouth as he looked up at her.

"Hey," the guy at the stove said, nodding to her. "You want some bacon and eggs? I'm cooking for everybody."

"Yeah, thanks." She tried not to look at his naked chest and abs as she walked to the table and slid into the chair next to Owen. She was starting to wish she was back at home with Chloe.

"We don't have to stick around here all day," Owen said through a mouthful of cereal. "Tell me where you want to go and we'll go."

"Aren't you going to introduce us?" another guy asked as he poured himself a bowl of cereal and sat across from Owen.

"Oh, right." Owen smiled weakly. "Avery, this is Spencer, and over at the stove is our Master Chef, David, and next to him is Levi, who attempts to help him by cracking eggs into a bowl. Notice how much he has to concentrate."

"Shut up, man," Levi grumbled. "You're gonna be eating these eggs. Want me to spit in yours?"

Owen rolled his eyes and took another bite of cereal. "I already told them who you are," he explained to Avery, "so they know we're not together."

"Stay as long as you want," David said over his shoulder. He gave her an apologetic look. "I promise we don't bite ... unless you want us to."

"Thanks," she answered. A part of her wanted to say she wouldn't be spending another night, but she knew she probably would. Facing Chloe still sounded worse than hiding out in Owen's room again.

After she and Owen ate mediocre eggs and bacon, Avery changed her clothes and they rode the bus downtown to Pike Place.

"Jordan wanted to bring me here," she said as they walked through the crowded shops. Everything was colorful and loud, and she let herself absorb as much of it as possible, hoping it would sweep away other things inside her head.

"Do I get to meet this Jordan guy?" Owen asked as they stopped to watch a caricature artist draw a little girl.

"Of course," she answered. "How was your date last night?"

"It was great, actually. I have you to thank for that, by the way."

"Me?" She turned to look at him, stopping in the middle of the walkway as people brushed past them. "Why?"

He gave her a crooked smile. "You gave me the courage to start asking other girls out. You talked to me and didn't think I was some weird guy latching on to you. At least, I don't think you thought that."

"Of course not. I thought you were different, but I liked it." Her smile fell. "I'm sorry if I hurt you, Owen."

"Hurt me? No, you never hurt me." He nudged her to keep walking. "Sometimes things work out and sometimes they don't. I think it's how we react to it that matters most."

She wanted to turn to him right then and tell him what Kent had done, how he'd taken what he wanted even though he had no right, but she was too frightened to say anything. Maybe how she reacted was what mattered most, but what if fear kept her from doing what she knew she should do? What if her own memories betrayed her? She was a danger to herself, and she was glad Owen had found the courage to look for what he wanted elsewhere. For her, she would have to hold on to the one solid thing she still had, and that was Jordan. Tomorrow couldn't come fast enough. He'd texted her that his flight would land at two in the afternoon. He'd head straight home and she'd be there waiting for him, even though it meant missing work.

"Thanks," she said as they continued through the market.

He pushed his hands into his jacket pockets and looked at her out of the corner of his eye. "For what?"

"For being a real friend. I've had some bad experiences with friends lately, but you seem different. At least, I hope you are."

He tilted his head. "I'll never ask anything of you, Avery. Not unless you want me to."

She smiled and looked down at the boarded floor, smooth and shiny from wear. "That's why you're different," she said with a sigh.

# ❖23❖

Avery waited impatiently on Jordan's front steps, tuning her ears to any sound that might resemble the familiar rumble of his bike. She'd ridden the bus from campus thirty minutes earlier, hoping he'd be back by the time she arrived. No such luck.

When she heard the motorcycle, she stood on her tiptoes and spotted him down the road. Her heart pounded in her throat. If she'd had any doubt she was in love with him, it flew away in that moment. She'd never wanted to see someone so badly in her entire life. He parked his bike and took off his helmet, grinning as he walked across the lawn and she ran into his arms.

"I missed you," she gasped as he hugged her tightly, and he kissed her in response. He tasted so good. His presence seemed to wipe away the pain she'd felt in the past few days.

"Let's go inside," he finally said. "I'll get my bags later."

She glanced at his luggage tied to the back of his bike. "We can take them in now. What if it rains?"

"They'll be fine. Come on."

They wasted no time climbing the stairs to his room, but as she sat on his bed and watched him take off his jeans and T-shirt, a sick sort of dread crept into her heart. She pushed it away, blinking as he raised his eyebrows at her.

"Not in the mood all of a sudden?" he laughed, noticing she was still fully clothed.

She could do this. Nothing had changed between them. Slowly, she pulled off her shirt and started unbuttoning her jeans. Jordan watched every movement. The dread came back again, and suddenly she was sweating. A gasp left her throat as Jordan climbed onto the bed and helped her take off her pants. He rolled onto his back, pulling her on top of him, kissing her neck and shoulders as he skimmed his hands down the curves of her hips. She nearly choked on her own breaths, but he didn't seem to notice.

"I won a lot of money in the poker game I told you about," he said, reaching around to unclasp her bra. He fumbled with the hooks then gave up and slid his hands lower. "I thought we could go spend it tonight." He paused for a moment. "Wait, are you missing work to see me right now?"

She nodded, studying his face. He was clean-shaven, his features so square and crisp and clean. Something seemed different. Nothing about him had changed, but she felt as if she was looking at him through a new pair of eyes.

"It's not a big deal," she explained, pushing back the dread again. "I went to my classes, so I was still productive."

"Oh, good." He leaned up to kiss her again, burying his fingers in her hair. "It feels so good to touch you," he whispered, trying for her bra again. This time he managed to unclasp it and slip it off her body before moving on to her underwear.

Her breath caught in her throat as the memory of Kent came at her full force once again. The pain in her abdomen. The scratch on her thigh. "Jordan, there's something I ..."

"Hold on," he said through heavy breaths, and leaned around her to pull open a drawer on the table by his bed. He pulled out a little square wrapper. Black with white lettering. Not red and white. Avery squeezed her eyes shut, bile rising up her throat.

*Go away. Don't let it get it to you. Kent is nothing. It's over.*

Jordan ripped it open with his teeth. He looked into her eyes and grinned, completely oblivious. "I missed you so much." He raised the wrapper and wiggled his eyebrows. "Help me out with this?"

She stared at it, the bile in her throat stinging as tears sprang to her eyes. It all came back. Every single part of the memory all at the same time, and before she could stop it, she leaned over the side of the bed and threw up. So much for romance.

"Avery?" Jordan shifted out from under her and took her by the shoulders, forcing her to look at him as she wiped her mouth with the back of her hand. "Are you sick? What's the matter?"

He didn't even look at the mess she'd made, which was now soaking into the carpet. She couldn't tear her eyes away, knowing she had to tell Jordan everything. He cared about her more than anyone not part of her family had ever cared about her. He could help her.

"The party," she gasped. "Tam and I fought and the whole night was a disaster. I ended up drinking and I ..." Her voice wheezed as she tried to get out the rest of the story, as disjointed as it probably sounded, but her tears were too much. She broke down and buried her face in Jordan's shoulder.

"Tell me everything, Avery. It's okay. I'm here."

She took in a shuddering breath. "Someone hurt me," she whispered. "I didn't remember any of the details until later, but I think I was raped."

Jordan's arms tensed around her. Avery knew he was fighting back a stream of cuss words. "You're ... you're in shock," he said between carefully measured breaths. "Let's go over everything together. We'll call the police, maybe even take you to the hospital, okay?" He muttered something about not being there for her, and some other things she couldn't make out.

"I shouldn't have gotten drunk," she whispered. "I'm pretty sure that's why—"

"This is *not* your fault," Jordan snapped. "Don't even go there, Avery. Please tell me everything and we'll take it from there."

She focused on his arms around her, how safe she felt at that moment. Nothing could harm her as long as he was here. "Kent gave me a ride home," she began slowly. "I didn't expect him to be at the party, but when me and Tam got in our fight, I ran into him. He was the one buying my drinks, but maybe he put more than alcohol in them, because it was after he came into my aunt's house and I drank the cup of tea he made me that—"

"I've heard enough." Jordan pushed away from her and got dressed before she could even process what was happening.

"Are you mad at me?" she asked, pulling the blankets around her as goose bumps popped up across her body.

He grabbed his jacket from the closet and pushed his arms through the sleeves. "No, I'm not mad at you. It's Kent. I'm gonna kill him."

"But, Jordan ..."

His jaw tensed and his eyes blazed with anger. He pointed a finger at her. "*Nobody* hurts you like this, Avery. Nobody. I will take care of this. Go home to your aunt and I'll be back as soon as I can. Call me if you need me."

Before she could even respond, he yanked up the jacket zipper, grabbed his motorcycle helmet from his dresser, and left.

Avery stared at the open doorway, her mind reeling. When she turned to look at the fish tank, tears slid down her cheeks. The fish were in a world of their own, the light glittering off their shiny scales. She felt like that for a moment, as if she was surrounded by water and glass and she'd never escape.

⁓⁄⁊⁖⁓

After cleaning up Jordan's carpet, Avery paced his room. Now that he had left, she wondered if she'd done the right thing in telling him what had happened. What if he did something stupid? He'd been so angry when he'd left. She shut her eyes and tried not to imagine him beating the shit out of Kent just for her. Then again, Jordan had a point. If Kent had done this to her, he would do it to other women. Hell, he probably already had. It wasn't that she wanted to get back at him. All she really wanted was to make it all go away, forget it had happened. No matter what anyone said, she still felt responsible. She had made choices, after all, and she should accept where they'd led her.

No. Kent deserved to be punished for this. He didn't have to hurt her the way he did.

Squeezing the sides of her head, she collapsed on Jordan's bed and cried. She pressed her cheek against the sheets, balling her hands into fists. She had to blame someone, something. And she couldn't just stand around and wait for things to happen.

She sat up and wiped her face. She was such a mess. She had to get a hold of herself. Grabbing her phone, she dialed Jordan's number. He didn't answer. She tried three more times and then went down to the kitchen for a drink of water. She called Jordan's mobile again as she filled a glass at the sink. No answer. She left a short voice message and a text and then tried Kent. No luck. She stared at her phone, deciding more needed to happen.

"Hello?" Heaven answered when Avery dialed her number, not knowing what else to do.

"Hey, Heaven, it's Avery."

"Hey, where are you? Skipping out on work?"

"I was with Jordan."

"Ah, I see." A short snicker. "Ask him if he's seen my copy of *Jude the Obscure*. I think I left it there a few weeks ago. I've looked for it every time I—"

"He's not here," Avery said, trying very hard to keep the tremor out of her voice. "You know his friend Kent?"

"Yeah."

"Do you know where he might be? Jordan went to find him. I think there might be trouble. Jordan's pretty pissed off and I'm afraid he's going to do something stupid."

There was a pause. "Why is Jordan angry with Kent?"

"It's a long story, but can you see if you can get a hold of him, or even Kent if you have his number?"

"Yeah, of course. Are you all right?"

Avery stared at a picture of Jordan and Callie on the wall and ran her finger across the top of the frame. "I'm fine," she choked out. "What I really need is for you to help me get a hold of Jordan."

"Okay, I'll do that right now. I'll call you back."

Avery hung up, her hands trembling. She paced the kitchen, watching her blurred reflection slide across the stainless steel fridge over and over. She thought of Chloe next door, drinking tea by herself. Then she remembered Jordan telling her she should go home. He was right. She couldn't just hang around here, waiting.

With a heavy sigh, she tucked her phone in her back pocket and went through the house, turning off lights and snatching up her school bag. She'd left her other bag at Owen's place. She didn't have a key to Jordan's front door, so she went out the back door and left it unlocked, hoping he'd return soon. She needed him to come home soon or she might explode.

"Avery!" Chloe smiled as Avery walked in the front door, probably resembling a zombie more than anything else. Chloe stopped in the hallway. "You're home early. Are you okay?"

Avery shook her head and sniffed back a wave of tears. She had to get a freaking grip. When she looked into Chloe's eyes, she knew it was going to be impossible to tell her about Kent. It would be like trying to tell her mother about it. Too embarrassing. Too painful.

"Are you sick? Do you want a cup of tea? Or some soup?"

Avery could feel Chloe's desperation across the ten feet between them, but she had nothing left to give. She shook her head. "I'm just gonna sleep, if that's okay. If Jordan comes over, will you come get me?"

"Of course."

Once in her room, Avery looked around. Her bed was still a mess. When she looked at it, her stomach did a summersault. She couldn't sleep there, not with memories of Kent swimming in her head, the way he'd pinned her down, the way her head had spun, the smell of him, the feel of him forcing himself inside her.

With a shudder, she rushed to the bathroom and splashed water over her face. This wasn't going to work. She'd have to go back to Owen's place, but then she remembered him sleeping on the floor in the hallway. Both nights. She couldn't make him do that again.

She pulled out her phone again, dialing Jordan one more time. No answer. She tried Kent next, but he didn't answer either. Her hands shook so much she had to set the phone on the counter. It rang a second later.

"I can't get a hold of him," Heaven said, sounding worried. "It's normal for him not to pick up, but he usually answers his texts right away and I've been waiting fifteen minutes for him to answer mine."

Avery pushed back images of Jordan getting arrested for attempted murder, Kent beaten to a bloody pulp at his feet. She was overreacting, but she couldn't help it.

"Keep trying," she said after a long pause. "I will too."

"Okay, let me know if you hear from him."

"Yeah."

Avery hung up and looked at her phone. She wanted to call her mom and tell her everything, but what would she be able to do? Even if she dropped everything to come out here, Avery wasn't sure what it would solve. She needed Jordan. Backing up until she reached the wall, she slid down to the floor and hugged her knees to her chest. It was going to be a long night if she didn't hear from him soon.

—)ı(—

"Avery!"

She opened her eyes, vaguely aware of pounding on the door. Had she locked the door? Where was she?

The room came into focus and she realized she'd fallen asleep on the bathroom floor with her phone clutched in her hand. Scrambling to her feet, she caught a glimpse of herself in the mirror. The floor's tile had left a square imprint on her cheek.

"Avery, please open the door. Heaven's here."

Heaven.

Avery undid the lock and whipped the door open, her chest heaving as if she'd just finished a race. "Why is Heaven here? Where's Jordan?"

Chloe was dressed for bed. Avery rubbed her eyes, trying to get her mind to focus. "What time is it?"

"9:30. Come on."

Avery followed Chloe through the house, finally stopping in the entryway where Heaven stood wringing her hands. Her hair was a mess, her clothes oddly normal—a pair of ripped jeans and a button-down men's shirt.

314

"You didn't answer your phone," Heaven said in a clipped voice as Avery stopped in front of her.

"I fell asleep. I didn't mean to. I was waiting for Jordan to come back."

Heaven shook her head, and it was then that Avery noticed her bloodshot eyes.

"He's not coming," she said softly. "I got a call from my mom thirty minutes ago. He's been in an accident."

Avery blinked.

Then blinked again.

"On his bike?" she whispered. "He's okay, right? He always wears a helmet."

Heaven shook her head and sniffed. It was the first time Avery had ever seen her look so vulnerable. "My mom didn't tell me any more—just that I needed to come to the hospital. All she said was he's critical and I should get there soon."

"Critical?" Avery squeaked. She turned to Chloe for an explanation. After all, Chloe had dealt with this firsthand.

Chloe took a step backward as her face drained of color. "That could mean anything."

Avery turned back to Heaven. "What can I do? What do you need me to do?"

"You're coming with me, that's what." Heaven grabbed her arm. "Chloe, you can meet us there if you want, but Avery has to come with me. Jordan needs her."

With that, Avery was yanked out the door and led to Heaven's BMW. She kept her mouth shut as she got in the front seat and buckled her seatbelt, not sure what to say. Heaven was quiet too. The city lights slipped across the window, reminding Avery of the fish in Jordan's tank. Just the thought of those fish took her back to her moments in bed with him and made her choke up.

She had to sit on her hands to keep them from trembling. What if she lost him? What if everything good that happened between her and Jordan was yanked away because of one fatal accident? Her thoughts swirled inside her head, practically buzzing. She was going to be sick if she thought too much about what might happen. She had to hold on.

Karma was pacing in the waiting room. As soon as she saw them she let out a relieved sigh and wrapped Heaven in a tight hug. "I'm so glad you're here."

When Karma let go of Heaven, she looked at Avery and gave her a brief hug. "How nice of you to come," she said, her voice trembling as if she might start crying any second.

Avery gulped down what she really wanted to say: *I'm the reason your son could be dying. Please, please don't hate me.* Instead, she nodded and folded her arms. The waiting room was freezing.

Karma turned to Heaven and started talking a million miles an hour about the accident. Avery tried to follow along and piece together the story. It had happened on the I-5. An SUV was involved. Nobody else injured. Broken bones. Shattered bones. Fractured bones. A lot about bones and blood loss.

Avery swayed back and forth, unsure of what she should think or feel or trust. "Can we see him?" she asked.

"None of us can see him yet," Karma answered, and finally burst into tears. She turned in a circle and then crumpled into Heaven's embrace.

"Mom, calm down," she said, sounding almost as frail. Avery could see she was keeping herself together as best she could. "I know this is hard. It's hard for all of us. Here, sit down." She led her mother to a sofa and they both sat down. Avery watched them, unsure of what to do. She felt so out of place.

"We have to wait until he's stable," Karma whimpered. "They're doing what they can, of course, but they aren't telling me much of anything."

"That's normal," Heaven said, her bottom lip trembling as she looked up at Avery and motioned for her to sit down too. "We just have to be patient."

"Yes, yes, I know." Karma grabbed Heaven's hand and took a long, deep breath as her tears slowed. "We'll get through this. He'll be fine. He's been through so much already. He can't have gone through all of that just to have this kind of thing happen. Right?"

"Right," Heaven said, not sounding entirely sure of her answer. "He'll be okay."

Avery sat next to Heaven and shifted on the hard cushions. She buried her face in her hands. If she lost Jordan she wasn't sure how she'd be able to keep herself together.

# · 24 ·

Avery spent the rest of the night in a haze. Chloe arrived at some point, supplies in hand. She'd made tea and coffee in thermoses, and passed around a box of freshly baked muffins that nobody ate.

"Avery, honey, we can go home," Chloe said, sometime around three a.m.

Avery was lying on the sofa, her head resting in the crook of her arm. She peered at her cracked watch, her vision blurry. "I want to wait to hear if he's going to be okay," she mumbled. "Shouldn't they know by now?"

"Well, Heaven left a little bit ago to give some blood for him. I don't know if that's good or bad."

"She did?" Avery sat up. The waiting room was deserted and Heaven was indeed gone. Karma was dozing in a chair by the sofa. "I didn't realize they needed us to give blood."

"Heaven is the same blood type, so she volunteered. You don't need to worry about it."

Avery lay back down. "I'm going to worry until I know how he's doing," she said, eyeing the dark circles under Chloe's eyes. Her hair stuck out every which way. "You can go home if you want. I'll be fine."

"I'm not leaving you." She put a hand on Avery's arm and leaned closer. "I called your mother and explained everything to her. She's on her way out here."

"You *what?*" Avery sat up again. "What did you tell her? You mean about Jordan? You didn't tell her about me getting drunk, did you? I still need to talk to you about that. It's not what you think. It's not ..."

"Avery, Avery, calm down."

Chloe waited until Avery shut her mouth and rested her head back on her arm. At this point, everything felt like a hazy dream. She tried not to compare it to how she'd felt the other night with Kent, but snippets kept worming their way into her thoughts.

"Is there something you want to tell me?" Chloe asked as she knelt all the way down on the floor in front of the sofa. "You've been acting strange since you got drunk at that party. Something doesn't feel right about it. It was so unlike you."

"I wasn't just drunk," Avery cried into her arm. "Kent brought me home that night, and you weren't there, so he came inside and he ... he hurt me, and I don't ... I can't talk about it right now. I don't want Mom to know about it. I don't even want you to know about it. I didn't want Jordan to know about it, either, but I had to tell him and now look what happened. I hurt everyone in my life and there's nothing I can do to stop it."

Chloe sucked in a deep breath. "How did he hurt you, Avery?"

Sniffing, Avery shook her head. "I can't talk about it right now. I just ... I need *someone* to know besides Jordan. If I hadn't told him, we wouldn't be here. He'd be fine and I ..."

"Shhhh," Chloe whispered, and rubbed Avery's hand. "It's okay. When you're ready, I'm here, okay? But I'm worried. Please don't wait too long to tell me. If there's something we need to fix, you shouldn't wait."

Avery nodded. "I know."

Chloe kept rubbing Avery's arm, creating a warm path that made Avery close her eyes.

"I fell apart when I lost William," Chloe whispered, "but I promise you, Avery, you won't be alone in this. No matter what happens with Jordan, you won't be alone. Even if you tell me nothing, I'm a hand to hold. I wasn't there for your mother when she lost your dad, but I want to make up for that. I love you, Avery. Okay?"

Avery opened her eyes just enough to see Chloe's wild hair. Even though it took all the energy she had, she lifted herself up to give Chloe a tight hug.

—⟩⟨—

The waiting room was filled with people when Avery woke up, the atmosphere uncomfortably anxious. Chloe was gone. Karma, sitting on the edge of the sofa by Avery's feet, smiled weakly as Avery sat up. Her eyes were bloodshot, her clothes crumpled.

"Morning," Avery said softly. She hadn't wanted to fall asleep. She looked at her watch. 10:30. Yikes. She would normally be getting ready for Karma's biology class right now, which Karma had managed to switch her to last week.

"What about your class?" Avery asked.

Karma shook her head. "I've arranged a sub for the rest of the week."

"What's the news on Jordan?"

"He's stable. We should be able to see him in a few hours."

Avery hadn't realized she'd been holding her breath. She let it out in a long sigh. "Oh, that's good. Where's Heaven?"

"She went with Chloe to get us some breakfast." Karma tilted her head and smiled. "Your aunt is a

322

sweet person. Heaven told me about her before, but I had no idea how nice she really is. She brought you a bag earlier this morning. She's been running back and forth all night, bless her heart."

Avery looked down at the floor where Chloe had left an overnight bag and her school bag.

"Yeah, she's pretty great."

"Why don't you go change your clothes and get a little more comfortable?" Karma suggested. "I'll save your spot."

"Thanks."

Avery picked up the bag and found the bathroom. Chloe had packed her a few changes of clothes and underwear, plus some toiletries and her phone charger. When she stepped back into the waiting room, Chloe and Heaven were back. Avery had expected them to bring fast food, but it looked like Chloe had brought homemade pastries and coffee instead.

"Thanks for doing all this," Avery said as she sat down and accepted the thermos Chloe handed her. The coffee was just as she liked it, nutmeg and all.

"It's the least I can do. Your mom is at my place, by the way. She's pretty tired from driving all night, so she's sleeping right now. Do you want me to have her come here when she wakes up?"

Avery squirmed across her seat. "I don't know. She has no idea what's going on, does she?"

"I've told her as much as I know—about Jordan."

"I guess so, then. I do miss her."

"I know you do." Chloe patted Avery's knee.

The morning dragged on. Avery pulled out her homework, but it was difficult to concentrate on anything. All she could think about was Jordan lying in a hospital bed, his arms and legs in casts. How many bones had he broken? How long would it take him to heal? Did he want to see her or was he upset that all of this had happened because of her? The questions swirled around in her head, mixing with her biology and English homework in a twisted sort of cocktail.

She looked up when a nurse came into the waiting room and bent down to whisper something in Karma's ear. Karma grinned and stood up, holding her hand out for Heaven, who took it. They both looked over their shoulder at Avery, smiling with hope in their eyes. Avery watched them walk away, her heart pounding. Everything was going to be okay.

"I'm going to go pick up your mom and bring her here," Chloe said. "I'll bring some sandwiches too in case you get hungry. Do you need me to get you anything else?"

"That'll be great, thanks."

Chloe nodded and left the hospital. A few minutes later a man wearing an expensive suit rushed in through the doors. Avery blinked, realizing she knew him but unable to place him until he was long gone. Jordan's father, Tim. Now the whole family was here and she was camped out in the waiting room ... waiting ... for what? It was only a matter of time before everything came crashing down and they all found out Jordan had been hurt because of her.

Grumbling to herself, she tried to focus on her homework, her right leg jiggling nervously. There was no way out of this. She had to hang in there to see what happened. She needed to see Jordan just once to know he was okay, to know he didn't hate her for what had happened, to know things could go back to how they were before. She wanted to help him, but it seemed impossible at the moment.

"Avery?"

She looked up, surprised to see Heaven in front of her, crying.

Avery's biology book fell to the floor. "What's the matter?"

"Will you come see Jordan?" Heaven asked, wiping her cheeks. "My parents are talking with the doctor right now, so they're all distracted."

More tears. Avery studied Heaven's makeup-free face. Her dreadlocks were pulled back into a ponytail. They looked more unnaturally red than usual in the harsh hospital lighting. She still hadn't changed out of her jeans and button-down shirt. Avery wanted to wrap her in a hug, but Heaven wasn't the hugging type.

"Distracted?" Avery asked. "Why is that important?"

Heaven opened her red-rimmed eyes. "I *know* if he sees you it will all come back. If I can sneak you in there for just two seconds, it would be perfect."

Avery stuttered for a moment. Her stomach churned. "What do you mean 'it will all come back'?"

"He doesn't remember anything," Heaven said quietly enough so the other people in the waiting room couldn't hear her. "The doctor says the memories might come back to him in a few days, or never, but it's ... I think if he sees you it will help."

"What exactly has he forgotten?" This couldn't be happening. Nobody forgot things around here except her.

Silence. Heaven met Avery's eyes and shook her head. "You," she finally whispered. "He's forgotten you—everything that's happened in the past few months is just *gone*. He's going to slip right back into his mopey-Jordan phase when all this is over."

The entire idea of Jordan forgetting her seemed wrong somehow, like a shirt turned inside-out. Avery stuttered for a moment, unable to come up with anything.

"I think if he sees you it'll all come back," Heaven said, grabbing Avery's hand. "You're the last strong emotional tie he had before the accident. The doctor says he shouldn't see anyone outside of family this soon, but if I don't do this now, who the hell knows how long it'll be before they'll let you in to see him?

You're important to him, Avery. You've made him happier than I've seen him in the *longest* time. I'm not going to let that go to waste. Not now."

"This isn't a good idea," Avery gasped as Heaven tugged her into an elevator. She knew she wasn't ready for what awaited her. For the first time in her life she was about to find out what it was like for someone to forget her instead of the other way around.

Heaven was right. At the moment there seemed to be a lull around Jordan's room, but Avery doubted it would last long. She gathered up her courage and stepped into the room filled with monitors and lights and wires, all of it leading to the hospital bed where Jordan lay. She could see right away that he was in no state for visitors. He was still hooked up to an oxygen mask and an IV, his left leg and right arm in traction. His face wasn't scratched or torn, but his left arm was covered in bandages, as well as his collarbone. Along his shoulder, peeking out from underneath a bandage, was part of his tattoo. She wondered if it was permanently ruined now. She hated to imagine what the rest of him looked like beneath the blanket, his once perfect body now torn up.

For a long moment they looked at each other. His eyes were only slits, but the longer she stood there holding her breath, the wider they opened. She sensed Heaven behind her, waiting.

*Say something, Avery ...*

But she didn't know what to say or do, so she finally let out her breath and wrung her hands as all the memories of Jordan spilled over her in waves. Running into him on the stairs. The cactus. Making out with him on his couch. The chocolate torte. The benches in the park. Riding on his motorcycle. The rock candy sucker. The traffic lights on his skin through the coffee shop window. The amazing weekend at his house. The toothbrush he gave her.

She remembered all of it just as if it had happened that morning, just as she remembered everything about her father. She realized then it was the things that struck her straight to the core that she remembered best. Jordan was one of them, and now he didn't even know who she was. He studied her, his face wrinkling up with confusion.

"Do I know you?" he asked, his voice muffled by the oxygen mask.

Her eyes filling with tears, she nodded. She'd been right to worry about hurting him. Just as she'd predicted, she'd hurt him beyond repair.

"Heaven thought you'd remember me if you saw me," she answered as her tears spilled free, "but I guess not."

He made a weak attempt to raise his left hand. "Come here. Please?"

Heaven nudged her shoulder and she took a cautious step forward. If what they said was true, the Jordan in front of her was not the Jordan she knew. As she neared the bed, his eyes swept across her face. She studied him in return. Scruff had grown across his jaw since yesterday. Even his eyes, usually such bright points of blue, were now dull and cloudy. He was silent for a long time. The beep of the heart monitor seemed to go on forever.

"I don't know you," he said softly, each breath fogging up his oxygen mask. "They tell me I've forgotten things."

She nodded. "Do you remember how I told you I forget everything? I know how you feel." She wanted to laugh, but it suddenly wasn't funny anymore.

He shook his head, wincing. "I'm sorry I don't remember you ..." His eyes rolled back in his head and he tensed up as the heart monitor picked up speed. Avery looked at Heaven in alarm.

"Sorry," Jordan said and opened his eyes. "I'm sorry I don't remember you."

She gulped down a lump in her throat. "It's okay. Maybe you'll remember in a little while."

He nodded and repeated for the third time, "I'm sorry I don't remember you."

She held on to the tenderness in his voice, the way he shaped his words like he'd always shaped them, even though he was pumped full of pain meds. She hadn't even noticed the way he talked before. She hadn't noticed the little freckle under his right eye either. She'd thought there was so much time to get to know him, and now it was all slipping away. He might not ever remember her. Even if she stuck around, there was no guarantee he'd ever feel the same about her.

"Um, we gotta go," Heaven hissed, and grabbed Avery's hand to drag her out of the room. "Jordan, don't tell *anyone* we were here."

Turning to leave, Avery nearly tripped over her own feet.

"You seem really nice," Jordan softly called out just as she reached the door.

She looked over her shoulder and gave him a weak smile, the chasm in her heart so deep it nearly split her in two.

# · 25 ·

Avery's mother was in the waiting room when Avery returned. It didn't surprise Avery to see her chatting with some random stranger instead of Chloe.

"Avery!" Her mom jumped up and ran into Avery's arms. "Oh, honey, I've missed you."

Avery gave her a squeeze. "I missed you too, but it's only been six weeks, Mom."

"It feels like a lifetime. Talking on the phone isn't enough." She pulled away and cupped Avery's face in her hands. "Who is this boy? Did they let you see him? Is he okay?"

Avery glanced at Chloe, who shrugged. "Didn't Chloe tell you anything?"

"She told me he's your neighbor. She told me you spent a whole weekend with him and how important he is to you. Why didn't you tell me any of this, honey? It sounds like a big deal. My little baby is growing up."

Avery sniffed. Her mother and Chloe had no idea it was all over now. Jordan had forgotten her and nothing would ever be the same again. "I don't really want to talk about it." Her chin trembled as she stepped away from her mom's arms. "Nobody knows for sure if he'll remember me. We weren't even together for two weeks."

Her mother's mouth dropped open. "He doesn't remember you?"

"No, isn't that funny?"

"What are you talking about? That's not funny at all."

Avery muttered nonsense under her breath. She felt so tense and cold at the same time. She balled her hands into fists, shaking her head as she stomped toward the door. "I'm ready to leave," she said loudly enough for Chloe to hear.

The drive home was silent. Avery sat in the back seat, her arms folded. She rushed for her bedroom as soon as she was inside the house, and locked the door behind her. She glanced at her bed and cringed.

A knock on the door.

"Avery? It's Mom. I just wanted you to know Jordan's mother called. She said you're welcome to go back to the hospital anytime. She's not sure when you'll be able to see Jordan, but you can go just in case."

"Just in case?" Avery sighed. "I'm not sure I want to. I don't want him to remember what made him get in that accident in the first place. It's better if he doesn't remember it at all."

There was a long pause. Avery could hear her mom lean against the door. "You don't want him to remember you? Chloe told me you two were in love. Isn't that something you want back?"

"I don't know," Avery answered quietly. "I don't know what I want."

After another minute of silence, Avery realized her mom had walked away. She went to the bathroom and got in the shower, wishing she could wash everything down the drain. Kent, the accident, all of her mistakes, but most of all she wanted to wash away the ache in her chest, as if someone had carved out a huge hole and poured concrete into it. If going to the hospital every single day meant she could get rid of that feeling, she'd do it.

They moved Jordan out of the ICU after a week. Avery went to see him every day after classes were over. She stood in the doorway, watching Heaven and his parents fuss over him. When they saw her they waved her forward, but it was the same thing every time. Jordan would look at her, study her face, and then shake his head.

"You look familiar now, I guess," he said when it was just him and Heaven and Avery in the room, "but I don't know if it's because you've been coming for a few days or if I'm remembering you from before."

"But you don't remember anything that happened?" Heaven asked, squeezing her hands together. "Try, Jordan. Please?"

He squeezed his eyes shut. "Stop it, Heaven. Why do you always have to try to fix everything?"

"I'm not discussing this right now," Heaven muttered. "Avery's here and you should be trying to remember her, not arguing with me."

Jordan let out a long sigh and shifted his position as much as he could. That wasn't much, since his leg and arm were still in traction. "Maybe you should consider *me* for a bit, huh?" he snapped. "I don't know Avery, and I'm not going to magically remember her if it hasn't happened by now."

He spoke as if she wasn't there, and it was then she realized her earlier fears were completely founded. Jordan wasn't going to remember her, ever. He was stuck in the past, and everyone around him was stuck in the present. Every day he seemed to get angrier. He hated the hospital. He complained about the food and the room and the traction. Most of the time he looked at Avery as if she was one of the nurses, not someone who had fallen in love with him and then lost him.

"I think I'll head home now," she said softly as he and Heaven continued to bicker. "I guess I'll come back tomorrow."

But she didn't return the next day. On Tuesday, she stood in line at the hot dog truck, holding her umbrella close as a light drizzle fell from the sky.

"Already ordered for you," Owen said as he walked toward her from the front of the line. She hadn't realized he was ahead of her. Usually he met her at the back of the line. He held out her food.

"I'll pay you," she said, shifting her umbrella to the crook of her arm so she could reach into her bag.

"Won't even hear of it," he laughed. "Come on. Let's find someplace dry."

They walked to the gray building by the gardens and sat down to eat.

"How goes it at the hospital?" Owen asked. "Any progress?"

Avery shrugged. She had filled Owen in on the entire story, excluding what had happened with Kent. Chloe had been bugging her in private to tell her more, but a part of her refused to believe it had even happened. Another part of her couldn't let it go, couldn't let it stop gnawing away at her. Eventually it would consume her as soon as the bigger, more immediate, things going on were taken care of. Kent hadn't shown up for English class since it had happened. She was glad. If she saw him again she'd probably punch him in the face. Either that or run away. She honestly didn't know which.

"That good, huh?" Owen sighed. "I'm sorry. Is your mom still here?"

"Yeah, she won't leave. I thought I missed her, but now that we're living under the same roof again it's like I've gone backward. She and Chloe fight all the time about the dumbest things. Last night it was over how Mom washes the dishes. I just hide out in my room most of the time."

"Hey, I would too. You sure you don't want to stay at my place again?"

She looked up at him, searching for a hint of ulterior motive, but there didn't seem to be any. He was concerned and that was it. She reached up to push some hair away from his forehead, just to see if there was a spark between them when her fingers brushed his skin. Nothing. Maybe it really was possible to stay friends with a guy without it moving into the realm of awkward.

"I'll let you know," she answered. "I think Mom would flip if I just left. She's convinced she needs to be here in my time of need, so I don't want to slap her in the face or anything."

"Understandable. Well, the invitation is open—unless, of course, I start bringing my dates home for the night. I doubt that will happen anytime soon." He laughed as he dumped the last of his chips into his mouth. "But who knows."

"Still dating the same girls?" she asked, focusing on the uneaten food in her lap.

"Nah, I'm asking different ones out each time. Trying to find one that clicks." His laugh stopped halfway out his throat as he turned to look at her. His expression fell. "Sorry, I know you've lost Jordan now, so I—"

She waved her hand and looked out at the garden. "It was good while it lasted. I mean that, really. It was amazing. But like you said before, sometimes things work out and sometimes they don't. I'm trying to move on. I'll finish the quarter and decide what I want to do from there. Jordan is alive and he's going to be okay. That's all that matters, right?"

Owen nodded and inched a little closer so he could put an arm around her. She rested her head on his shoulder and took a deep breath. The rain pattered on the roof as she thought about Tam and Ryan and Jordan. She'd lost them all, like treasures she'd put away in a place she couldn't remember. But Owen was still here, even if it didn't go beyond friendship. He meant the world to her now.

"Do you think it's bad of me to give up on him so soon?" she asked. "Because I don't think I can keep going there to see him. It feels wrong, like I'm trying to force something on him. Heaven keeps telling me it'll come back to him. I think she's terrified of dealing with his grief all over again. She puts too much on herself ... and on me, too. I don't think I can do it. I don't ..." Her voice faded as she bit her bottom lip to keep her tears away.

Owen squeezed her shoulder.

⊸〉〈⊷

"You can't just stop coming to see him," Heaven said when Avery walked into work that afternoon. Heaven hadn't been there for over a week, so Avery was surprised to see her.

"We're moving him to his house in a week," Heaven continued. "Mom and me are going to stay there until he's healed enough to move around on his own. It'll be easy for you to come see him since he's right next door."

Avery dropped her bag on the floor and sat down. Her ivy plant was looking awful. She reached out to touch the leaves and one fell off. "No use in keeping the light on," she said, and switched it off. "I'll take the poor thing home tonight. Maybe Chloe can revive it."

Heaven wheeled back in her chair and folded her arms. "Don't do this, Avery. You can't do this to him."

Avery turned on her. "Do *what*? It's pointless. He's not going to remember me."

"How do you know that?"

"He's not going to remember me! I know all about forgetting things, okay? It's never the same when it comes back. It's disjointed and backward half the time, and the same emotions don't just come attached to the memories. It's always tied to the present and what's happening at the moment. I've seen the way he looks at me now. Even if he remembers me, I'm not the same Avery as before. You're a psychology major. You should know this shit."

"You're wrong," Heaven snapped. "He fell in love with you once. He'll do it again, but you have to make the effort."

Avery shook her head and got up to grab a book from the shelves. She found one with a torn cover and slammed it down on the table. "You don't get it. You just want to fix things. Haven't you ever tried to fix a broken teacup before? You can't just glue it back together and expect it to be the same. There will be missing pieces and it's more likely to break again. He's that teacup, Heaven, and I could break him even worse than before. It's over, okay?"

She started working on the cover, her movements brisk and efficient. She was right and Heaven knew it. There was no going back once the cup was broken.

—⟩⟨—

The next morning Avery woke up on her bedroom floor. It was where she slept now since her bed triggered the most horrible memories. Worst of all was that she was pretty sure the entire incident with Kent had happened on top of her dad's quilt. It was in the laundry now, but she knew the washing machine could only do so much. She'd found different sheets and blankets in the linen closet and was sure to keep her door shut at all times so her mother and Chloe couldn't see her new sleeping arrangements and start asking questions.

She shoved the bedding under her bed and then stepped into the shower, determined to go on with her day-to-day routine. She couldn't let her memory issues rule her life anymore. But as she stood under the stream of hot water, she closed her eyes and thought about Jordan and how he'd lost everything connected to her. Heaven had been right. He was a wreck now— not remotely the person he'd been before. Was it possible Avery had changed him that much? So much of what she admired most about him, his confidence and control, was gone now. She wanted to believe it was still there, that he would somehow dredge it up again, but after seeing him in the hospital she wondered how deeply buried it really was. He was so angry now, so hurt, so lost, and there was nothing she could do. He hadn't given her any indication that he wanted her in his life now, so the only thing she could do was stand back, move on, take a shower, go to class.

Her hair still wet, she dressed and grabbed her school bag, stopping in her tracks when she opened her door and heard the familiar bickering between Chloe and her mom in the kitchen. Avery's shoulders slumped as she leaned against her doorframe and waited for it to blow over.

"I never ordered you to come here, Susan," Chloe's voice tumbled through the house. "Don't blame me if it's interfering with your work schedule. I had no idea you were so married to it in the first place."

"I'm not *married* to anything. Avery has always been my first priority."

"Oh? Then why have you barely spoken to her since you arrived?"

"Because she doesn't want me to. She needs space, can't you see that? I'm here for her when she needs me ... *if* she needs me."

"She's been just fine without you. I've taken good care of her."

Avery could hear the edge in Chloe's voice, even if her mom couldn't. It felt wrong to have told Chloe something had happened with Kent but keep it from her mom.

"Is there a reason she's such a mess?" her mom asked. "It can't just be about Jordan. She won't tell me anything, Chloe. We used to be so close and it's just … it's gone now."

The silence that followed was heavier than any Avery had felt in a long time.

Avery's mom's voice finally broke the silence. "It hurts that she's not talking to me, but I keep asking myself if this is more about you than Avery. I've let Avery go to figure out things on her own, but now I'm afraid you want to hold on to her for yourself. If you wanted your own child you should have found someone after William died. But your heart is *still* broken, isn't it? I'm afraid you still blame me for rubbing salt in your wounds by marrying John and having Avery. How dare I be happy when you were so miserable! After all these years, can you please forgive me?"

"Why do you think I haven't forgiven you?" Chloe shrieked.

Avery felt a hot tear roll down her cheek and swiped it away with a jerk of her hand. She'd heard enough. Gritting her teeth, she stomped down the hallway and out the front door, letting the door bang on her way out. She was nothing but a pawn in their war. Everything they had said was true. Her mom had let her go, but her influence still hung over Avery's head, and Chloe wanted to hold on to her because it helped assuage her own pain. Well, let them battle it out. Avery wouldn't be there for them to throw around.

She kicked some pebbles off the sidewalk, ripped some leaves off a bush, and muttered under her breath about how much she wished things were simpler.

*You sure you don't want to stay at my place again?*

Owen really was the only person she had left whom she could talk to about anything going on. She could stay there and get away from her mom and Chloe for a while. She would insist on sleeping on the couch instead of taking his room, at least, and her packed bag was still there anyway.

Instead of continuing on to campus, she paused at the bus stop and looked at the schedule. A bus was due to arrive in fifteen minutes going in the direction of Owen's house. He didn't have class until eleven. It was nine now, and she didn't have class until 11:45. Perfect. Her breath caught in her throat as she realized how much she'd remembered without even looking it up.

Once on the bus, she stared at her hands. She hadn't realized she'd been biting her fingernails lately, but there they were, chewed down to the nubs. They looked awful. She tucked her hands under her thighs and stared out the window. She would tell Owen everything, she decided. She wasn't afraid to tell him about her forgetfulness because he'd been the one person least affected by it. He was happy now, dating other girls, and she was pretty certain even if she had dated him they would have ended up exactly as they were now—just friends.

She got off the bus and walked the block and a half to his house. It looked quiet. She hoped he wasn't asleep. Walking up the steps, she rang the bell and waited. He said he didn't like his housemates, but she got the feeling he liked them a lot more than he let on. It made her wonder if she should try to find a house to rent too. Maybe it was exactly what she needed.

The door opened and Avery looked up, hoping she'd see Owen instead of one of his half-dressed housemates. Instead, it was a half-dressed woman. Avery blinked a few times, not sure she was seeing what she was seeing.

"Tam?" she said, remembering the last time she'd seen her, all dolled up in costume. Now she was wearing a pair of boxers and a camisole riding up her midriff. Her hair tumbled around her face in a mess of matted curls.

Tam looked just as surprised, her eyes widening. All that stood between them was the screen door.

"Who ... what ... who ...?" Avery couldn't get her complete question out. Maybe Tam was with one of Owen's housemates. *Please let it be one of them.*

"Hey, who's at the door?"

Owen appeared from around the corner, shirtless, wearing boxers with the same design as Tam's. Avery just stared at both of them, her mouth hanging open.

"Ave?" Owen came closer, glancing at Tam with a worried expression.

"Tam is one of the girls you've been dating?" Avery finally managed to spit out. "I mean, I told you about Tam, right?" At that moment she couldn't recall anything she'd told him.

Owen rushed forward, stepping in front of Tam. He pushed open the screen door and looked Avery in the eyes. "I thought I told you Tam was in my economics class. I just asked her out a few days ago, and last night ..." He glanced back at Tam, who folded her arms and smirked.

Avery gritted her teeth and counted to ten. "You should know Tam doesn't play nice. She knows you're friends with me, and she probably thinks I'm interested in you. I'll bet you a million bucks she slept with you to get back at me for kissing her boyfriend last year in high school."

Owen swallowed and the screen door shut a little between them. "I know you mentioned Tam that first day we had lunch, but I—"

"I'm just warning you about her," Avery interrupted. "See you around, Owen."

She turned and walked back down the steps.

"Wait, Avery!"

She didn't turn around.

"Avery, why did you come here? What's the matter?"

Stopping in her tracks, she sniffed and stared down at the sidewalk. She felt Owen slipping away from her, just like everyone else. She had been a fool to think he would be any different, but with Tam in the picture there was no way her friendship with him could stay the same now.

"I just needed a place to stay ... and a ... a friend to talk to," she finally answered, glancing over her shoulder. "But I'll be fine. Bye."

"Do you want your bag? You left it here."

She ignored him and kept walking. By the time she reached the bus stop, she was seething even more than before. Had Tam planned all this or was it just a nasty coincidence? Either way, it stung. Just a few weeks ago three guys were interested in her, and now she was right back where she'd started. She had predicted it, but she hadn't wanted it to come true. Perhaps she had done it to herself just by expecting it to happen.

"Avery!"

She turned to see Owen, now dressed, running barefoot down the sidewalk with her bag in his hand.

She glanced at her watch. The bus had twenty minutes. Great. No escape.

"I don't really feel like talking right now," she muttered once Owen reached her. He held out her bag, waiting for her to take it.

"Why are you so upset?" he gasped. "You're the one who said you didn't want things to go anywhere with us. I thought you were happy for me."

"I was, but that was before Tam."

"What's so wrong about Tam? She's not out to get you, Avery. She told me what happened with you two in high school. She just wants to move on."

"Yeah, right." Avery folded her arms and stared across the street.

Owen dropped her bag on the sidewalk and let out a heavy sigh. "I don't understand you. You reach out to people in the strangest ways, almost desperately, and then you resent them if they reach back."

She turned to him, her fingers twitching at her sides. "That's not how I am."

"Isn't it?" He glared at her. His hair was a mess and his goatee was a bit scraggly. "I'm really sorry about Jordan," he said, looking down at his bare feet. "I'm really sorry you've lost something that meant so much to you, but maybe you shouldn't give up so fast. People have a lot more to offer than you're willing to give them credit for, you know."

"No they don't."

She turned back to the street and shook her head. She thought about Kent and how sure he had been that she would forget what he'd done to her. He'd probably listened to her desperate message and realized she was going to remember a lot more than he thought, and then panicked. Even though he probably knew as well as she did that it would be difficult for her to prove anything now, she doubted she'd see him again anytime soon.

Owen narrowed his eyes. "You're really jaded, aren't you?"

"I have a right to be jaded," she growled. "When I trusted a friend to take me home and he drugged me and took advantage of me, I have every damn right to be jaded."

Her entire body shook as she realized what she'd just revealed.

Owen stood stone still. "Who did that to you?" he whispered.

She shook her head again and wrapped her arms around herself, trying to keep her tears inside. "It doesn't matter."

"Yes, it does. Avery, tell me who did that to you." He touched her arm, and she remembered resting her head on his shoulder as they'd watched the rain.

"One of Jordan's friends. His name's Kent," she answered. "I can't remember his last name, but it's in my phone. I can't remember so many things. I never told you I mixed you up with Kent and Jordan. I thought you were all the same guy." A slightly hysterical laugh rose up her throat.

Instead of telling her not to laugh like she thought he might, he laughed with her. "That's pretty funny."

"Yeah ..."

"Do you want to come back to my place?"

She took a breath and calmed herself enough to stop trembling. "Why?"

He shrugged. "You seem pretty upset. Do you want something to eat? Tam and I were starting some pancakes."

Pancakes with Tam. Ugh. She knew he was only trying to get her to stay longer so he could try to help her. But she needed to be alone ... far, far away from Tam. She looked down at her bag. "Not today, but thank you ... for listening. For everything."

He slid his hands into his pockets and gave her a longing look. "I'm here when you need, okay? This thing with Kent—"

"Thanks, Owen," she interrupted. "I'll deal with it my own way. I'm sorry I even mentioned it."

He let out a sigh. "Avery, please let me help you. It sounds like something you shouldn't be handling on your own. Please?"

"I'll see you around," she snapped, rudely enough that he took a step backward.

"Sure," he said, his voice cracking.

As he turned and walked back to his house, Avery knew things would never be the same. Studying with him would be too awkward now. Even meeting him at the hot dog truck would be awkward. No, if Tam was involved, the friendship was over.

# ·26·

Avery knew she had no choice but to go home after work. She spent two hours repairing books at the library and clocked out early. The room was too quiet without Heaven, who had left a note asking her to visit Jordan at the hospital that evening. Staring at the note, Avery felt the hole in her chest grow bigger. Seeing him would only widen it even more.

When she got home she hurried up Chloe's front steps. She practically ran through the entryway, intent on reaching her room without seeing anyone.

"Avery!" her mother called out.

Squeezing her eyes shut and plugging her ears, Avery turned around. "I don't want to hear it, Mom," she snapped, her voice extra loud in her head as she kept her hands over her ears. "I don't want to hear you two fighting anymore. I can't stand being in the middle of it. Sometimes I wish you would go back home."

Silence. Avery cracked one eyelid, peeking at her mother standing in front of her. Slowly, she lowered her hands from her ears and opened her eyes all the way. Her mom was at the far end of the entryway, and she looked horrified. Her mouth dropped open as she glanced behind her shoulder at the dining table filled with people. "We didn't expect you home for another hour," she said in a hushed voice. "We were going to surprise you."

Avery stared at the people at the dining table. They looked familiar—an older man, big like a teddy bear but strong and muscular, and a beautiful woman with dark blonde hair. Avery blinked. The Royals. Victor and ... she couldn't remember his wife's name. She couldn't see Ryan or Chloe, but it was possible they were in her blind spot.

"What are they doing here?" Avery whispered. "Don't we usually have them for dinner earlier in the month? You know, the week of Dad's—"

"We missed it this year because you were here. I thought I'd call them while I'm here and see if they could visit." Her mom's shoulders slumped, her expression filling with disappointment. "I thought you'd be happy to see them and talk about your dad."

"I ... it's just after this morning ... after you and Chloe ..."

"You heard all that? I'm so sorry." Her mom rushed forward and folded Avery into a tight hug. Avery peeked at the table again, blushing when she realized Victor and his wife had turned around to watch. She pulled away and took a step back into the hallway.

"I'll be in my room," she said softly, and rushed to her bedroom as fast as she could.

Her mom knocked on the door a second later. Avery muttered under her breath, pulling the door open. "What, Mom?"

"Dinner's almost ready. We were planning to eat as soon as you got home. Don't you want to join us?"

"Not really."

Her mother's lips tightened. "Chloe and I fight because we're sisters, honey. It's nothing personal against you."

"Sure doesn't feel that way."

"Well, it's true. We both love you, okay? I just want you to be happy. I'm sorry about what happened with Jordan, but we don't even have to talk about that if you don't want to. I'm here to be with you, that's all."

Avery opened the door a little wider, her heart sinking as she watched her mom's hopeful expression crumble. She gripped the door handle. "I'm sorry I said I want you to go back home."

Her mom nodded. "I miss us as a family. I've been lonely, and I thought coming here and trying to patch things up with Chloe might help."

"Is that why you keep fighting with each other?"

"It's our way of sorting through it, yes."

Avery folded her arms. "Is Ryan here?"

Her mom's cheeks reddened. "Yes, I'm sorry. He's living with his mom and Victor now. I couldn't exclude him from the invitation."

"It's okay."

Avery wasn't sure if it really was okay, but she didn't know what else to say. Seeing him would be incredibly awkward, to say the least, but what did she have to lose? She'd already lost everything except her family. She thought about Tam's pouty face at the party, about her dad's grave covered with fall leaves as the flags flapped in a cold breeze, about Owen walking away from her that morning, about Kent disappearing from every part of her life except her nightmares, about Jordan in the hospital, probably complaining about his casts and not thinking of her for one single second. She opened the bedroom door all the way and hugged her mom as tightly as she could. If this was all she had left, it was okay. Her mom had always been the only one who understood and forgave her for everything.

"I love you, Mom," she whispered. "What's Chloe making for dinner?"

—⁌ ⁍—

Ryan seemed uncomfortable the whole way through dinner. He poked at his green beans and sipped his drink, and when everyone else was finished his plate was still mostly full.

"Not hungry?" Victor asked after he finished up a story about her dad, one Avery was sure he had told twenty times and she'd forgotten.

"Nah." Ryan looked up, sweeping his gaze past Avery. He'd avoided looking directly at her all through dinner. "I was wondering if you guys would mind if I took a walk outside? My stomach's not feeling the best tonight."

Avery watched him walk out the front door. She felt her entire body relax once he was gone. The last time she'd seen him had been when they'd kissed. She looked down at her hands, surprised to see them trembling. For the next hour she listened to the others talk about her dad. Chloe even had a few stories Avery was surprised to hear. She smiled, listening as best she could as her mind kept wandering outside with Ryan. Finally, Chloe served dessert and Avery ate half of hers before standing up to excuse herself.

"Got some homework to do?" her mom asked, smiling as she reached for Avery's hand.

Avery squeezed her mom's fingers and smiled at Mr. and Mrs. Royal. "Yeah, a bit. Thanks for coming, you guys. Me and Mom appreciate it a lot."

Victor nodded. "Always worth it. Good luck in school."

Avery headed for her bedroom but stopped when she reached the entryway. Maybe Ryan was close by. Something inside her desperately wanted to see him. She still felt shaky, as if her body hadn't used up all the adrenalin from seeing him again. She quietly opened the front door, grabbing a cardigan off the coat rack before slipping outside.

It was dark and the streetlights shone like little moonbeams down the street. The smell of cigarette smoke drifted to her nose and she looked over to the hedges dividing Chloe's yard from Jordan's. On a flat boulder near a tree sat Ryan, smoking.

Avery walked down the steps, shoving her hands in the cardigan's pockets in an attempt to control her anxiety. It wasn't as if Ryan had ever hurt her. She had no reason to be nervous.

"Smoking help your stomach?" she asked, smirking.

He shifted a few inches across the boulder to give her room to sit down. She took the invitation and sat next to him. She shivered a little. The cold of the boulder seeped through her jeans.

"Want some?" Ryan held out his half-finished cigarette.

"I don't smoke," she laughed. "I didn't know you did."

"Habit I picked up a few months ago," he said, shrugging. "Try it."

She took the cigarette and put it between her lips, inhaling as lightly as she could. The smoke filled her mouth and she swallowed a bit and coughed deep in her throat. Opening her mouth, she watched the rest of the smoke float away. Ryan watched her, and for some reason she couldn't explain, she took another drag, and another. Her body started to relax as she got the hang of it.

"Like it?" he asked as she returned the cigarette.

"Not really, but it was worth a try." She leaned forward and ran her hand through the cold grass. "So, what happened to your lofty goals of photojournalism? What about the Marines?"

"Haven't decided on anything yet," he said after a long drag on the cigarette. "I've just been living with my mom and Victor in California. It's nice there and I've been able to get by without doing much."

For the first time that evening she really looked at him. His hair was shaggier now. The scruff on his jaw looked untidy. It made his crooked nose even more apparent. She opened her mouth, a million questions on her tongue. She couldn't choose just one to ask as she remembered the unapologetic way he'd kissed her. It was clear to her now why he'd let her throw herself at him like that. He'd thought maybe he could get away with stealing a piece of her and Tam. He couldn't make up his mind, just like he couldn't make up his mind about his life now. He seemed completely lost, and in that moment she finally realized kissing him hadn't entirely been her fault. She wanted to hate him for that, but now that so much time had passed, she only felt sorry for him.

"Are you okay?" she asked, turning to face him as he finished his cigarette and stubbed it out on the rock. "I mean, after that whole Tam thing?"

He reached into his back pocket and pulled out a lighter and a pack of cigarettes. "Shouldn't I be asking if you're okay? I heard about what she did to you."

She watched him light a new cigarette. The flame flickered through the darkness and lit up his face. He looked so sad. "Yeah, it was pretty bad, but I hope you don't blame yourself. It was really all my fault."

"Yeah, I heard about that too."

She stiffened. "You did?"

"Tam sent me an email about how you forget everything. She told me your side of the story." He looked at her out of the corner of his eye. "Why didn't you tell me? I would have understood."

Avery stared at the glowing end of his cigarette. "You mean she didn't blame it all on me?"

He shook his head. "She told me about how you forgot our kissing deal, how it made you look like you were trying to steal me away from her. She told me she wanted to forgive you. She said she missed you and she was sorry, but I think she had too much pride to let go. I tried to get back together with her after all of that, but it didn't work out. There was always the memory of you between us and she couldn't handle it."

Avery's mind reeled. "If she wanted to forgive me, then why did she bully me the *whole* year? She could have stopped it."

Ryan blew out a long stream of smoke. "Like I said, it was her pride. Sometimes it's easier to hold on to what hurts you."

Avery looked up at the sky as she let that thought sink in. There were no clouds, and some stars twinkled through the city haze. A soft breeze blew through the leaves, whispering like hushed voices. She turned to glance behind her shoulder at Jordan's house. His bedroom light was off. She imagined what it would be like for him when he could come home, immobilized, reading a magazine or watching his fish or flipping through television stations. She turned away. Even though she was refusing to see him anymore, her heart was still gripped tightly by the memory of him.

"You didn't answer my question," Ryan said as he finished the second cigarette and put it out on the rock. "Are you doing okay?"

"I asked you the same thing."

For the first time, his lips cracked into a smile. "I guess you did, huh?" He leaned a little closer to her, searching her face. "You don't need to worry about me. I'll be fine."

"I'll be fine too," she answered, dropping her gaze to his mouth. She didn't really want to kiss him, but for some reason it was an appealing thought. Then she remembered Kent and she backed away and cleared her throat. "Thanks for asking, though."

"Anytime."

He lit up another cigarette and she pulled her cardigan closer as he started talking about photography and the things he was looking forward to doing someday. It seemed he knew what he wanted. He just hadn't grabbed it yet, just like she couldn't grab what she wanted.

Glancing up at Jordan's window again, she swallowed a lump in her throat. It was hard to grab what you wanted—especially if it was the same thing hurting you.

─╱╲─

Another week went by in a blur. Avery kept on top of her homework, made it to her classes on time, and clocked in for her full shift at work every day. Heaven was there sometimes, but more often than not she left a note inviting Avery over to the hospital, and then to the house once Jordan was discharged. It was relentless and pointless. Mrs. Meadows, or Professor Meadows, as Avery called her in public now, cornered her every day after class.

"Jordan is improving," she told Avery on Friday. "I think he's accepted how long it will take to heal. He's not as angry."

"That's good," Avery said, forcing a smile.

Karma smiled back. "Do you think you'd like to come over? It should help him, especially now that he's improving."

Avery shook her head and hugged her biology book to her chest. "I don't think so. Not yet ... but thanks."

Karma's lips twitched and Avery knew she was fighting back a plea. "Only if you want to, of course," she said softly. "I'll see you in class on Monday."

Avery nodded and turned to leave.

"Avery?"

"Yeah?"

Karma gave her a desperate look. "Jordan is planning to move once his casts come off and the doctor okays it. I just thought I'd warn you."

Avery blinked. "Move? Where?"

"Chicago. I've tried to talk him out of it, but I think it's probably the best thing for him at this point, considering ..." She left the rest unsaid, but Avery knew it was along the lines of, "considering the fact that you won't even make an effort."

"Thanks for letting me know," Avery replied. She breathed a sigh of relief once she was outside. Granted, it was raining, but at least it was fresh air. Digging in her bag, she found her umbrella.

With the rain pattering her umbrella, she passed the hot dog truck and tried to ignore the rumbling in her stomach. She had about an hour and a half before her last class of the day, but she was afraid to stop, especially since she'd been avoiding the food trucks for over a week now. Seeing Owen again would just be too weird.

She kept walking. For a long time, she stared at the ground as her mind rolled over her conversation with Ryan. It was good to have closure with him now. It was good to know Tam had told the truth when she said she was sorry for what she'd done, but Avery still didn't know what Tam was doing with Owen or if she was going to break his heart. If that happened, Avery was sure she'd never be able to forgive her. As for Jordan moving, she couldn't even let her mind go there. Maybe it was for the best that he was going to leave her life completely. She bit her bottom lip to keep her tears from falling. She couldn't cry on campus.

*Keep it together, Avery.*

When she looked up she was at the medicinal gardens. She entered the little gray building and shook the rain off her umbrella. There were a few students waiting for buses, but none of them noticed Avery as she stared out at the gardens dripping in the rain.

"No hot dog today?"

She jumped at the sound of Owen's voice.

"Nah," she said, waving her hand. "Just trying to get my thoughts together before my next class."

He had on a weatherproof parka. He pushed the hood off his head as he entered the building and sat next to her.

"You're avoiding me, aren't you?"

She nodded. There was no use lying to him.

"Just so you know, Tam isn't trying to get back at you. When she found out you're a friend of mine, she was surprised."

"I find that hard to believe, but I trust you, so ... okay."

He laughed and leaned forward to look at her. Finally, she stopped staring at the garden to meet his eyes.

"I'm sorry if I hurt you," he apologized.

She wrinkled her brow. "You didn't hurt me. I just thought I'd lost you."

He shrugged. "There's a lot of history between you and Tam, and I respect that." He leaned back on his hands and looked up at the ceiling. "But before we decide to call off our whole friendship because of Tam, there's something I need you to see." There was an almost gleeful bounce in his voice. "Do you think you could skip your next class?"

She looked at him closely, wondering what he could be talking about. "I suppose I could. I haven't missed much of that one."

"Good, then let's go." He stood and held out his hand. "We can hop on the next bus up to my neighborhood."

"O-okay." She took his hand and rainwater from his parka dripped onto her sleeves as she stood up. "What is it you're going to show me?"

He grinned and pushed back some of his wet hair. "Something I'll bet you've waited a long time to see."

# ·27·

Avery couldn't stop jiggling her knee on the bus ride. Owen, sitting next to her, clapped a hand on her thigh and squeezed. She stared down at his hand and stopped.

"Calm down," he laughed. "You'd think I was taking you to your execution." He lifted his hand and she let out a nervous giggle.

"Would you *please* tell me what's going on? Does this have anything to do with Jordan?"

Fiddling with the zipper on his parka, he looked out the window. "In a way, I guess."

"Oh, great. You do realize there's no way to make him remember me, right?"

Owen turned back to her, his eyes filled with worry. "That's not what this is about. This is something you've pushed aside that needs to be fixed."

"Just tell me, please," she whispered.

"Too late. We're here."

The bus pulled to a stop and Avery followed Owen down the aisle and out the doors. Her heart pounded in her throat, harder and harder as they reached his house and she forced herself up the front steps. This had something to do with Tam, she was sure of it. But if Owen thought he was going to force them to forgive each other, he was dead wrong.

"Owen, if this is about Tam," she began as he opened the door and stood aside for her to enter, "I think you should know ..."

She stepped inside and her thudding heart screeched to a halt. It took her a full thirty seconds to take in the scene in front of her. Her knees nearly buckled. This really wasn't about Tam. Or Jordan.

A dining chair sat in the middle of the cleared living room. Sitting in it was Kent, his mouth gagged, his hands tied behind the chair. His face was purpled with bruises and cuts, some of them still bleeding. His bottom lip was split, oozing red. He looked up at her through the swollen, puffy flesh around his eyes.

"Owen, what is this?" her voice cracked. "What have you done?"

Surrounding Kent were Owen's three housemates.

"Spencer, David, and Levi," Owen said, pointing out each one. "I know how you forget names."

She nodded, almost in a trance as she looked at their balled fists. Their knuckles were red. They all looked at her with triumphant expressions.

"We decided to give Kent some payback," Owen said softly. "And if you want to give him some of your own payback, please be our guest. Kent Russell, correct? I hope we got the right guy."

Avery nodded, even though she couldn't remember if Russell was his last name or not. "How did you find him? I never told you his last name."

"I tracked him down for you."

Avery spun around to see Tam standing in the hallway, her arms folded as she leaned her hip against the wall. She stifled a yawn.

"How?" Avery asked. She wasn't sure how to feel facing Tam at such a vulnerable moment. If she'd tracked Kent down, then she knew what had happened. *All* of them knew what had happened. Her face reddened.

"It wasn't too hard," Tam explained, unruffled. "You told Owen it was a friend of Jordan's named Kent, so I talked to Professor Meadows after class. She told me his last name and his parents' names. It wasn't too hard to find him after that."

Avery's face reddened even more. "You didn't tell her about ..."

Tam shook her head. "Of course not. Your secret's safe with us, Ave ... until, of course, you press charges against the bastard." She slid her eyes to Kent and contorted her face into a menacing glare.

"I-I don't know," Avery stuttered as she turned back to Kent. "I want to talk to him."

"Sure thing," Levi said. He grabbed the gag tied around Kent's head and yanked it out of his mouth. Kent groaned as it rubbed against his split lip.

"Want us to leave you two alone?" Owen asked, touching her shoulder. "We'll just be in the next room."

"Yeah," she replied as she stepped forward. "Yeah, that would be good."

When they had all cleared the room, Avery stepped around the couch and stood in front of Kent. She saw that his feet were tied too. He wasn't going anywhere.

"So," she said in a trembling voice, "I really want to kill you right now." She tried to look him confidently in the eyes, but she couldn't do it. The memory of him on top of her, pushing her down on the bed, spun around her in circles. But she *had* to look in his eyes. He'd hurt her in so many ways and she needed to do something about it. If it hadn't been for what he'd done, Jordan would be fine. If it hadn't been for what he'd done, she wouldn't feel so violated, so broken.

Finally, she met his eyes. He blinked. "I'm sorry, Avery," he muttered. His voice was raspy, as if he'd gone hoarse from yelling.

"That's all you have to say? That you're sorry? Why did you do it, Kent? I trusted you. You were my friend."

His eyes turned glassy with tears and he looked away, his expression filling with disgust. "When I took you home and your aunt wasn't there and you kept talking about Jordan and I realized you were in love with him, I couldn't ... I ... this guy at the party gave me something. He told me the drug messes with your memory. I guess I didn't give you enough to make you forget. I'm sorry."

She balled her fists at her sides. "You're apologizing for not drugging me *enough*? Are you joking?"

He finally looked her in the eyes again. "No, that's not what I meant."

"Then what the hell did you mean? You're just upset you got caught!" She gritted her teeth as she looked down at him. She didn't know how long it would take her to get over what he'd done to her, but she was certain that it was possible now. No more pushing it aside. She nudged his foot with her toe, and he looked up at her again.

Without a second thought, she smashed a fist into his already bruised cheek. A short cry escaped her throat as pain flooded through her hand and up her arm.

Kent spit out some blood and looked up at her with a wounded expression as she rubbed her knuckles and took a step back.

"You're going to turn yourself in," she said in a gritty voice. "Say it."

He choked on his words, and she kicked him in the shin, making him wince.

"Yes, I am," he gasped. "I'm going to turn myself in."

"I'll make sure of it. In the meantime, I don't think it will hurt you to sit here for a bit longer with my friends. I don't think they're quite finished." She turned and walked out of the room, rushing into Owen's open arms in the kitchen. He patted her on the back.

"Good job, Avery."

"We'll let him squirm for a while," David said, chuckling as he shoved a fist into his palm. "Then we'll finish up and take him to the police as soon as you're ready."

Avery nodded as Levi and Spencer followed David out.

"Sorry, Tam," Avery muttered, stepping away from Owen. "Don't mean to be hugging your boyfriend."

Tam smiled. "Friends hug each other," she said softly. "Don't they?"

"I guess so."

"Listen, Avery," she said, stepping closer. "I'm really sorry about everything. If you don't want to forgive me, I'm okay with that. You don't have to. I've forgiven you and that's what matters."

Avery blinked. Her hand was throbbing and she wished someone would get her a bag of ice. Tam seemed different somehow. It wasn't just that she was dressed in a pair of Owen's sweats and one of his T-shirts that didn't match, with her hair a mess and no makeup on. It was something else. Was it possible Avery hadn't lost all her friends? She glanced at Owen, who was smiling at her, and then Tam who was waiting for a response. She looked so nervous, so worried. Her eyes were filled with tears, and as one rolled down her cheek Avery realized it was the first time she'd ever seen her cry.

"I forgive you," Avery said. "I appreciate what you've done about Kent. You wouldn't have done that if you didn't care about me. And for what it's worth, I'm really sorry I kissed Ryan and betrayed you."

Tam nodded. "I don't want you to lose your friendship with Owen, either. Can we start over? No judging, no remembering the past?"

Avery shook her head. "No, it's good to remember. It's what helps us get to where we're going."

Tam thought about that for a minute. "Yeah, you're right. So, maybe you should get a certain someone to remember *you*, then."

Avery turned away. "No."

"Why not? Owen told me what happened. Are you really going to give up so fast?"

Avery looked at Tam, realizing how far they'd come. Was it possible to repair something so utterly broken? She'd never thought Tam would change, yet here she was. Then again, Avery realized as she looked down at her red knuckles, Tam wasn't the only one who had changed.

⚊⁊\⁚

Avery stirred ganache in one of Chloe's pans on the stove. It smelled so good, just like Jordan's house that time he'd baked the torte.

"That should be good enough," Chloe said as she wiped her hands on her apron and opened the refrigerator. "The torte should be cooled enough by now. Oh, and don't turn the sauce down yet. Let it burn just a little bit."

Avery wasn't sure why Chloe wanted it to burn, but after a moment she noticed the sauce thickening.

"Look at it closely," Chloe ordered. "Does it have the consistency of caramel yet?"

"Yeah, it's getting there." The smell was rich and dark and sinful. Avery closed her eyes for a moment, remembering the taste of ganache on her finger, the feel of Jordan, the warmth of his mouth and hands.

Chloe finished removing the springform pan from the torte. "All right, stir in the cream," she said.

Chloe hadn't done much at all in the torte preparation. She'd really only given Avery directions and overseen everything. This was Avery's project. She stirred in the cream until the ganache was perfect, then they both spooned it over the cooled torte.

"I don't know if it's the same as what he made," Avery said as they both stood back to study the beautiful dessert, "but it should be good anyway."

Chloe smiled at her. Avery smiled back, glancing at the framed picture of her and her mom and Chloe. She was glad her mom had come and they'd fought for hours on end. By the time it was all over, Avery realized it was exactly what they'd both needed. Her mom had left a few days ago, giving Chloe the longest hug in history, crying as she said goodbye. Things were different now. A good kind of different.

"This probably won't make him magically remember you," Chloe said.

Her smile fell. "I know, but he's probably leaving in a few months, maybe earlier. That'll be enough time."

"For what?"

Avery took a deep breath. "To say goodbye."

Avery stood on Jordan's front steps and rang the bell. Heaven answered, her eyes growing wide and round as she spotted Avery. Heaven was dressed in jeans and a ratty T-shirt, which was all she wore to work nowadays. Avery wanted to ask her why she'd changed her wardrobe so drastically, but she didn't dare breathe a word about it since it obviously had to do with Jordan.

"Can you give this to him?" Avery asked, holding out the torte on a metal serving tray. "And this?" She pulled out an envelope from her back pocket.

Heaven took the torte and the note. "Why don't you give it to him yourself?" she asked, the usual twitch of her lips giving away her frustration. "Seriously, Avery, he's remembering so much. If you'll just see him again ..."

Avery let out a heavy sigh. "Fine, I'll give it to him."

It had been three weeks since she'd seen him last, when he was still in the hospital and angry. She hoped he wasn't angry now.

Entering the house, she held her breath. It all looked the same, but it felt different, as if she didn't belong anymore. All the pictures of Callie were gone. That was odd. Avery followed Heaven into the living room where Jordan sat on the same sofa where he'd kissed her all those weeks ago. She pushed away the memory of his warm skin, his shirt hanging open as he described his tattoo and said he loved it because it reminded him of life. She knew now that he'd meant it reminded him of how precious life could be since he'd lost Callie. She still wondered if the accident had ruined the tattoo.

"Hey, Jordan, someone's here to see you," Heaven said as Avery stopped behind her.

Jordan twisted around to look at both of them. When his gaze landed on Avery, nothing crossed his face. No emotion, no recognition, nothing. She would be surprised if he even remembered her from the hospital.

"Hi," he said flatly, and turned back around. He had only one free arm since the other was in a cast all the way up to his armpit. His leg, also still in a cast, was propped up on the coffee table. He paused the show he'd been watching, and Heaven motioned for Avery to follow her over.

"Avery's here to see you," Heaven said as she leaned down to set the torte on the coffee table. "She made you this amazing dessert."

Jordan looked at the torte for a long minute, but if Avery was hoping to see any spark of recognition, she was deluding herself.

"It looks good," he said, smiling as he looked up at Avery. "Thanks." His brow furrowed. "Wait, you're that girl from the hospital, right? The one they kept telling me I've forgotten?"

Avery nodded. "I wrote something for you. It's ..."

Heaven handed the envelope to Jordan, who only stared at it until she finally dropped it onto his lap. "It's what?" he asked, bitterness edging his voice.

"It's just ... it's my memory of when you made me a chocolate torte like this one." She swallowed and pushed her hands in her pockets. "You don't have to read it, but if you're curious, it's all there ... well, what I can remember, anyway. See, I have trouble remembering things too, but writing it down helps. I know you might not ever remember me since everything that happened with us was so close to your accident, but I'm ... I ... this is my way to say goodbye to you."

His eyes snapped up to her. "Goodbye?"

"Yeah, since you'll be moving when your casts come off, right?"

He blinked. "Yeah, going to Chicago."

She nodded and gathered her courage. It was so weird to face him like this, knowing she wasn't important to him in the slightest. It hurt to see that he wasn't even making an effort to remember her.

"I was hoping," she said boldly after glancing at the torte, "that you'd be okay with me coming over every week to give you a new memory of mine. It would help me out a lot, even if you never remember me."

Jordan looked at Heaven, who kicked his one good foot on the floor. "Yeah, sure," he said, shrugging. "I guess that would be fine."

"Great. So, I'll see you around."

"Yeah, see ya." He turned back to the TV and unpaused his show without another glance at her.

"I'm so sorry," Heaven whispered as she opened the front door to let Avery out. "This is normal for him now. He's not as nice as he used to be. Even before the accident—before you—he wasn't this irritable. He's getting a little better, but it's slow."

Avery saw the disappointment in Heaven's eyes, and leaned forward to give her a tight hug. "It's okay," she sighed. "I think it's okay to let people change."

Heaven pulled away and took in a long breath. "I guess you're right. When I decided to go all dreadlocked and Goth, Jordan never judged me. My parents didn't try to stop me either."

Avery smiled. "So don't try to change him back to what he was?"

"Yeah."

Avery waved goodbye as she walked down the steps, her heart a little lighter. She had to figure out what to write next for Jordan, whether he read it or not.

—⁄|＼—

Avery visited Jordan every week on Saturday afternoons. She spent the morning writing down her memories of him, scrawling the words across her creamy yellow stationery. With every drop of ink, she felt her heart healing just a little more. It felt so good to let the memories drain out onto the paper, like bleeding herself free of him.

The second visit she took him a cactus, and after that a rock candy sucker and a bag of sour jellybeans. She took a picture of the benches overlooking Lake Union and painted a picture of the fish tank in his room. It was a childish watercolor, but when he looked at it he seemed to know exactly what it was.

"How do you know about my fish tank?" he asked.

"I spent a whole weekend in your bedroom," she answered, blushing. "Just read the memory." It was probably the most intimate one she'd written so far, but she knew it had to be done.

The week after that she gave him a new toothbrush, and after that a stuffed flounder—only, this one was a stuffed animal, not a dish from a fancy restaurant. By the time she was finished, his arm cast had been removed. His leg still had two more weeks to go, according to his doctor. She sat next to him on the sofa as he set the stuffed flounder on his lap and ran his thumb across the plush.

"I've been reading everything you've written," he said softly as Heaven left the room. "I still don't remember you, though. I'm sorry."

He lifted his eyes to hers. They were so blue, and she felt like they were stabbing right through her. Somewhere, deep down in her gut, she'd hoped by this point he would have recalled just the tiniest piece of her, but it was pointless. And while he was kinder to her now than he had been when she'd first come over, he wasn't giving off any signals that he wanted to know her any better. Whatever had formed between them now hardly felt like friendship—more like a mutual understanding of something she couldn't even pinpoint.

"Like I told you," she said after tearing her eyes away from his. "I'm not doing this to make you remember. I appreciate you sticking with me on it, though. This is the last one."

"Not a problem."

She waited for him to say something else. When he didn't, she forced herself to look into those blue eyes again. Damn it, *why*? Why did it have to be this way?

She was doing okay now. School was going great, her friendship with Tam was fixed, and her mom and Chloe got along now. Even her memory seemed to be improving a little. But, as Jordan had told her, people would always leave gaps in your life when they left, and even though he was right in front of her, she couldn't ignore the gap she felt from his absence.

"I wish you the best," he said. "I really do."

Her chin trembled as she looked down at his outstretched hand. There was a scar along his forearm now, still a bit pink. She took his hand and let him squeeze her fingers. There was no spark there, no shock or fireworks as there had been before all of this had happened.

"Bye," she said as he let go.

"Goodbye, Avery."

As she left the room, she let her tears spill down her cheeks. They were soon lost in the rain as she walked back home.

# ·28·

If anyone had told Avery she would eventually work as a waitress, she would have laughed her head off. Now, as she bustled around the tables in the fancy restaurant filled with live trees, she smiled to herself. She loved the feel of this place, as if she'd stepped into an arboretum. It was one of the reasons she'd decided to apply here. Also, it turned out that with a pad of paper in her hand she had no problem remembering things people told her. She loved the handy seating charts that told her exactly what parties were where. Most of all, she loved the large tips. She made a lot more here than she had repairing books.

Avery smiled as she imagined some poor freshman in that basement room. Heaven wasn't there to train anyone anymore since she'd graduated last year, so it was up to Chloe now. Poor Chloe. But she had understood when Avery told her she wanted a job that kept her on her feet and paid a bit more. And she also understood Avery couldn't keep going to that job where the smells and the feel of books and broken spines and torn paper in her hands reminded her so much of Heaven and her brother. It was her sophomore year now, and he had long since moved to Chicago. His father had even sold the house. Chloe had been happy about that, at least. No more loud parties since the couple who moved in were in their sixties.

"Bad news," Sam, the head waiter, told Avery as she entered her station to put in the newest orders. "Amanda is in the bathroom throwing up and I have to attend to table fifteen. Is there any way you can take table five their wine? It's right here." He handed her Amanda's leather-bound order book. You know what to do, don't you?"

Avery took the book, her hands trembling a tiny bit. Amanda was the sommelier.

"I'll do my best," she said, smiling confidently at Sam. In the hectic atmosphere of the restaurant's behind-the-scenes there was nothing to do but say yes and carry on. She preferred it this way. It was easier to get through each day, easier to deal with the haunting memories of Kent one tiny step at a time, easier to forget about Jordan.

She found the correct bottle of wine and folded up a crisp cloth napkin on which to display it. On her way to the table, she concentrated on mustering up every ounce of professionalism she could. She was carrying a three-hundred dollar bottle of wine, which meant whoever was sitting at table five was pretty damn rich.

She spotted an older man in a nice suit and walked to his side of the table. He was tall and thin and vaguely familiar. She blinked, caught off guard as she searched her brain for a name or a snippet of memory.

"I'm Avery," she introduced herself with a short bow. "I'll be your sommelier for the rest of the evening."

The man grinned up at her as she held out the wine for him to inspect the label. Finally looking down at it, he nodded. "Looks great."

"Wonderful, sir." She pulled out Amanda's corkscrew and proceeded to uncork the bottle. As she twisted the corkscrew around and around, she glanced at the rest of the table and nearly choked when her gaze landed on Heaven, of all people. Her dreadlocks were no longer fire-engine red, but a conservative auburn. She smiled at Avery and gave her a little wave.

*Stay calm, Avery.*

As discreetly as she could, she shifted her gaze to the one person on earth she had no desire to see at the moment. Jordan, completely healed now and as handsome as ever, sat at the other end of the table next to his mother. He looked amazing in a gray silk shirt, his hair styled a different way than she'd seen before, his square jaw shaved smooth, his blue eyes twinkling as he laughed at something his mother had said. Luckily, he hadn't even noticed Avery. She pulled out the cork from the wine bottle and placed it on a little plate.

Tim, whose name she suddenly remembered out of nowhere, lifted the cork to inspect it. He smiled and nodded for her to pour him a taste of the wine.

"It's wonderful to see you, Avery," he said as he mindlessly swirled the dark red liquid and then smelled it. He didn't stop looking at her until he'd tasted the wine and nodded his approval. "Perfect, thank you. We'd all like a glass and then please leave the bottle."

She smiled as she poured his glass and moved on to Heaven.

"I hear you left the book repair business," Heaven said. "How are you doing? Overwhelmed this semester yet?"

Avery smiled at her. "I'm sure I'll get overwhelmed at some point."

Heaven laughed. "It's inevitable."

Avery moved on to Karma's glass and then Jordan's. He didn't pay her any attention, but why should he?

"Avery!" Karma said loudly as Avery set the wine bottle on the table. "How are you? I haven't seen you on campus this quarter. Are you taking any biology classes?"

"Not this quarter, but I'll be taking another of yours next quarter."

"Oh, that's wonderful. I've missed seeing you."

Avery glanced at Jordan, who was finally looking up at her. Recognition filled his eyes, but she was sure it was only from the times she'd visited him after the accident.

"I've missed seeing you too," she said, smiling warmly.

"Is this your job for the year?" Karma asked, looking around the restaurant. There was no hint of disgust in her voice, even though Avery suddenly felt very low on the social ladder.

"Yes," she answered. "It's been a lot of fun so far."

"It's a wonderful place. We'll let you get back to work." Karma smiled at her ex-husband, who nodded to Avery.

She left in a hurry, not looking back to see Jordan. It was best if she didn't go back to that table ever again. Seeing Karma at school was one thing, but seeing Jordan and his entire family again was quite another.

"What's the matter with you?" one of the other waitresses asked as Avery leaned against the wall out of sight of the dining room. "You look like you've seen a ghost."

Avery clutched her chest, her breaths quick and hard to catch. "I did," she whispered.

With an hour left in her shift, she waited tables and tried to avoid number five as best she could. As she refilled drinks and took orders, she couldn't stop thinking about Jordan. It had been a year. She'd thought she was over it by now, but seeing him brought it all back, all those memories she wished she could forget. She had healed, but her heart still yearned for what she'd had with him. The problem was *her* Jordan didn't exist anymore.

When her shift was over, she stopped in the bathroom and looked at herself in the mirror as she washed her hands. She was a different person than she'd been, and she could admit that she was happy. Lonely, perhaps, but happy with who she was. It really was possible to be both, at least for a while.

"Thanks for covering for me," Amanda said as she emerged from one of the stalls, ashen-faced.

Avery spun around. "You're still here? I thought you would have gone home by now."

"I'm leaving now," Amanda answered as she stumbled to the sinks. She was in her forties and very beautiful, with a heart-shaped face and tiny nose. Her dress suit was rumpled now, and her dark hair had mostly fallen out of its French twist. "I feel like shit. I've just barely been able to drag myself off the floor."

Avery rushed to put an arm around her. She felt her forehead. "You're as cold as ice. You can't drive home like this."

"I think I caught my husband's flu bug," she moaned.

"I'll drive you home. Just show me to your car."

"All right, but how will you get home?" Amanda slumped a little as Avery helped her out of the bathroom.

"I'll just call a cab from your place. Don't worry about it."

Avery looked up just as a figure rounded the corner, nearly bumping into them.

"Oh, excuse me," he said.

It was Jordan, probably coming out of the men's restroom around the corner. She looked up at him, determined to play this as casually as possible.

"Not a problem," she said. "I'm sorry we were in your way."

"Looks like you might need some help?" he asked, nodding at Amanda. "Is she okay?"

Avery shifted her weight as Amanda leaned heavily on her shoulder. "Not really. I'm going to drive her home."

"Let me help you out to the car," he said. "Please? I need some fresh air anyway."

She tried to hide her smile. "All right."

Taking Amanda gently by the arm, he propped her against him and helped her out to the employee parking lot, Avery on his heels.

"It's the black Ford over there," Amanda said as she clutched her stomach. "I'm going to puke again." She ripped away from Jordan's grasp and retched onto the pavement.

"Poor thing," Jordan said, waiting until she turned back to him to take his arm again. He led her to the Ford, where she fished out her keys and unlocked the passenger door.

"Thanks," she said, looking up at Jordan.

He helped her into the seat and closed the door. "You'll be all right?" he asked, handing Avery the keys.

She took them, trying to avoid his eyes. Even under the parking lot security lights they were beautiful. Why was she such a sucker for those eyes? They were one thing that definitely hadn't changed about him.

"Yeah, thanks for your help." She nodded to him and started around to the other side of the car.

"Wait, Avery."

Stopping in her tracks, she turned to face him again. It didn't surprise her that he remembered her name, but something in his voice sounded so desperate. It was unlike anything she'd heard from him before.

"Yeah?"

"Thanks again for all those things you gave me, and for the memories you wrote down. I've read them about twenty times now."

She felt her lips rise at the corners. "Really?"

"Yeah." He looked down at the pavement and kicked at some loose gravel. "I've tried so hard to remember you, but it just won't come back. We must have had something pretty great for you to write all that for me, huh?"

She nodded. "I'll never forget it."

Continuing to kick at the gravel, he focused on her. "I feel like a different person now, but when I saw you tonight at our table I realized how much you must have meant to my family."

"They were pretty desperate for me to stick around," she said as a wave of nostalgia washed over her.

He nodded. "The truth is I've felt something missing in my life since the accident. For the longest time I thought it was Callie, but now I'm starting to realize it's something else."

She almost took a step forward, but held herself back.

"I think it's you I've missed," he said. "Isn't that crazy? I don't even remember you."

She smiled. "You once told me we can't replace the people in our lives. Everyone leaves a gap and it can't be filled once they're gone. I guess even if you forget someone, that gap they left is still there."

Putting a hand to his forehead, he tightened his jaw and nodded. "It sure feels like that," he said, sounding almost angry.

She cleared her throat. "Do you remember everything else?"

"For the most part," he answered, lowering his hand. "It was just those few weeks before the accident that are gone. Go figure."

She laughed and then felt her shoulders fall. "Yeah, but maybe it wasn't meant to be."

One of the lights above them flickered on and off and then back on. Jordan looked up at it, blinking. Silence stretched between them. Avery knew she should get into the car and drive away, but she couldn't seem to move.

"So, are you okay?" he asked, breaking the silence. "All that stuff with Kent? You didn't have to tell me about that, but I'm glad you did. It's better that I know the truth about him." He reached out as if to touch her, then lowered his hand. "How are you doing ... with that?"

She looked down at her feet, her cheeks growing hot. She shouldn't feel nervous, but she did. "It's going okay," she sighed. "I pressed charges against him, and

390

I've seen a counselor on campus about it. That has helped."

"Oh, good."

More silence. Avery didn't know what to say or how to react. Everything seemed to hinge on what might happen in the future. Would they continue this strange relationship or go their separate ways again?

"I'm leaving for Chicago in the morning with my dad," Jordan announced after clearing his throat.

"Oh." She blinked a few times. "I hope you have a safe flight."

"Is your shift over?" he asked, taking a step forward.

"Yeah, that's why I'm free to drive her home." She waved a hand at Amanda, now falling asleep in the front seat.

"Ah, gotcha."

Avery's heart felt like it might charge right out of her body. Finally, she took a step forward and raised her chin. "I may forget a lot of things," she said as she looked straight into his eyes, "but I will never forget a true friend. You got in that accident because you were helping me. I've learned how to forgive myself for a lot of things, but that has been the hardest one."

He grimaced just as the faulty light above flickered off for good. His face bathed in dark shadow, he said, "I hope you don't blame yourself for the accident. The reports said it was raining and I was speeding. It was my own fault, trust me."

391

She nodded and took another step closer. "I've also learned not to rush into things when it can hurt other people." She thought of racing across her lawn to kiss Ryan. "But I was wondering if you'd let me kiss you just one last time?"

A grin broke out across his face. His teeth were bright in the moonlight. "You think a kiss will break the spell of my forgetfulness?"

She grinned in response. "Hey, you never know. Are you willing to give it a try?"

He looked around the parking lot and then at the sleeping Amanda.

"You know," he finally said, "I think I might be." He took another step forward, bringing himself close enough to touch her. He tentatively wrapped an arm around her, trembling. "This will be like my first kiss with you," he said, "and you say it will be your last?"

She glanced down at his arm around her. Being this close to him again felt right.

"Will it be my last?" she asked, trying not to wince. She would be okay with whatever happened. She had to be. She'd been okay up to this point. It was seeing him that had made her slip into wanting him all over again. She hadn't realized just how lonely she'd been the past year, how big the gap he'd left really was.

Sadness filled his eyes, but she caught a glimmer of hope too.

"I guess we'll see," he whispered as he bent closer to her mouth and drew her into a kiss that sent sparks all the way down her spine. She felt him smile against her lips, his arms pulling her closer just as the broken light above winked on.

# ⁖ acknowledgments ⁖

No story is ever written alone. Many friends have made this story possible on many levels. Like Avery, I've lost friends because of mistakes I've made—some of which are not things easily fixed nor blamed on any one person. Avery's story has been a way for me to explore all the emotions that come with such experiences. It has been easier to find a resting place for these experiences by writing this novel.

Thank you to every person who has laughed and understood my forgetfulness, even if it creates problems. Mom and Dad, you've put up with it longer than anyone, so thank you.

To current and future friends and acquaintances, if I look at you all squinty-eyed and confused, know that I realize I'm supposed to remember something about you—probably your name or where I saw you last. But don't worry. The most important things will always stick. I hope.

# about the author

Michelle lives and writes in Utah, surrounded by the Rocky Mountains. She adores cheese, chocolate, sushi, and lots of ethnic food, and loves to read and write books in the time she grabs between her sword-wielding husband and energetic daughter. She believes a simple life is the best life.

www.ingramcontent.com/pod-product-compliance
Lightning Source LLC
Chambersburg PA
CBHW051315250626
47155CB00007B/2337